PENGUI

FERRY (

Manohar Shetty has publish
work has appeared in impor
literary journals in India and abroad. He edited a monthly
magazine for eight years in Goa, where he lives with his wife
and two children.

Ferry Crossing

Short Stories from Goa

Edited by

Manohar Shetty

PENGUIN BOOKS

Penguin Books India (P) Ltd., 11 Community Centre, Panchsheel Park, New Delhi 110 017, India
Penguin Books Ltd., 27 Wrights Lane, London W8 5TZ, UK
Penguin Books USA Inc., 375 Hudson Street, New York, New York 10014, USA
Penguin Books Australia Ltd., Ringwood, Victoria, Australia
Penguin Books Canada Ltd., 10 Alcorn Avenue, Suite 300, Toronto, Ontario, MAV 3B2, Canada
Penguin Books (NZ) Ltd., 182-190 Wairau Road, Auckland, 10, New Zealand

First published by Penguin Books India (P) Ltd. 1998

Copyright © Penguin Books India (P) Ltd. 1998

10 9 8 7 6 5 4 3 2

Typeset in *PalmSprings* by SÜRYA, New Delhi
Printed at Chaman Enterprises, Delhi

'Innocence' by Chandrakant Keni first appeared in English in *Visions, Revisions,* Katha, 1995; the extract from Orlando Da Costa's *O Signo da Ira* (The Sign of Ire) was first published in English in a special issue of the *Journal of South Asian Studies,* Michigan State University, 1983; Hubert Ribeiro's 'At the Shrine of Mary of the Angels' first appeared in *The Illustrated Weekly of India,* 7 January 1973; an earlier version of 'The Sacristan and the Miser' by Lambert Mascarenhas appeared in *In the Womb of Saudade,* Rupa & Co, 1996.

Grateful acknowledgement is made to the authors for permission to translate and include their stories; also to Manoharrai Sardessai for 'The Africa Boat' and 'The Hour's End' by Laxmanrao Sardessai, Celina M. Zuzarte for Leslie de Noronha's 'Uncle Peregrine', and Milkweed, USA for the two extracts from Victor Rangel-Ribeiro's *Tivolem.*

While every effort has been made to trace copyright holders and obtain permission, this has not been possible in all the cases; any omissions brought to our notice will be remedied in future editions.

To Vicki

Contents

Acknowledgements

I am indebted to several people who have been of help to me in compiling this anthology. Thanks are due to the Homi Bhabha Fellowships Council for their generous support; to all the translators, particularly Vidya Pai in Calcutta and Heta Pandit in Goa; to Kiran Budkuley and Gurunandan Bhat of Goa University, who at various stages translated and sifted through reams of material from Konkani and Marathi; to Somnath Komarpant of the Department of Marathi, Goa University, for his valuable suggestions; to Isabel Santa Rita Vaz and Oscar Noronha, who helped with the Portuguese section; to Damodar Mauzo who located out-of-print books and stories for me; and, finally, to Joel D'Souza for typesetting the manuscript and for his incursions into the world of popular fiction in Roman script Konkani.

Introduction

O ne of the main aims of this anthology is to correct the distorted picture of Goa among most people outside the state. A Portuguese colony for well over four centuries, Goa was liberated in 1961 by a well-meaning but amorphous nation which had itself ceased to be a colony barely fourteen years earlier, and in less than a decade, it had become the focal point of a facile concept of Indian spiritualism and flower-power rebellion. This dramatic and swift transition only served to disfigure the realities of a people trying to find their feet. Added to this was the trivialization of Goa by the demands of tourism and the advertising industry, abetted by the popular media and cinema, which, over the years, created a caricatured perception of the state. It came to be seen as a place peopled by a feckless, bohemian race tippling away their lives in cosy tavernas, on balmy beaches and in the shadow of hoary mansions and whitewashed churches.

Such distortions, perhaps inevitable in any place which, quite literally, sells itself for mass tourism, have gone beyond popular stereotypes and can be found even in such publications as the *Encyclopaedia Britannica*, which says: 'The Christians generally speak Portuguese . . . Many Goanese are partly of Portuguese descent and bear Portuguese names as a result of intermarriages between early Portuguese settlers and local inhabitants.' Most historians in fact agree that inter-racial marriages were rare and that miscegenation was looked down upon, by both sides. The Portuguese names came by during mass conversions when the presiding Portuguese civil or military officer left the legacy of his own name on those baptized. The word 'Goanese' is seen as pejorative because of its association with jobs like those of valets, stewards, butlers and cooks which at one time many Goans undertook on foreign ships.

One can dismiss with an irritated shrug the frivolous thrillers set in Goa and the fits of nostalgia and precious recollection indulged in by absentee landlords in Bombay and elsewhere. And it would be a waste of space to recount the number of gaffes about Goa and the extravagant ornamentation of the place by gossip writers and other columnists. But when writers of the stature of Anita Desai and John Irving present readers with outright howlers, one is compelled into taking remedial action. Anita Desai in *Baumgartner's Bombay* writes of a 'poison called feni' being brewed from cashewnuts, unwittingly turning this humble liquor into some exorbitantly expensive nectar. In the admirable *A Son of the Circus*, John Irving writes: 'In the village—or perhaps the source of the smell was as far away as Panjim—they were distilling coconuts for the local brew called feni. The heavy sickly fumes of the liquor drifted over the few tourists and families on holiday at Baga Beach.' A whiff of feni travelling all the way from Panjim to Baga? An olfactory miracle, surely; even the 'perhaps' is no defence. And coconut feni is not distilled from coconuts but from the sap of the coconut tree. The 'sickly-sweet fumes' is more accurately descriptive of cashew feni made from cashew fruit pulp. Irving's engaging characters might also find it interesting to note that the imposing churches of Old Goa were built by the Portuguese with Italian architects during the artistically fruitful period when Spain ruled over Portugal, between 1580 and 1640.

These observations might on the surface seem like pettifogging, but this kind of carelessness by such eminent writers underlines how deeply ingrained the flippant attitude towards Goa is. A recent Governor of Goa, sunning himself silly at the private beach of the Cabo Raj Bhavan, reflected on his tenure in Goa as a thirteen-month-long 'super-deluxe holiday at the cost of the President of India'. Such facetious and supercilious comments are proof not only of the sheer laziness of the particular Governor but also of the sense of forbearance and tolerance of the local community.

Such has been the gilded smokescreen created by tourism and its avaricious auxiliary industries. It becomes necessary, therefore, to clear the air and place the facts as they are. Few in the rest of the country even realize that the Catholic community in Goa is very much a minority; that the most widely spoken language in Goa, Konkani, is an official language under the Eighth Schedule of the Constitution; that the caste system (the word is derived from the Portuguese 'casta') remains deeply rooted in the Catholic community too; or that the tiresome eulogizing of vapid, risibly moralistic pop stars has been at the expense of some of the finest Goan exponents of Indian classical music. The fact of the matter is that the business of living is as serious and humdrum in Goa as it is anywhere else in the country, and literary and other artistic endeavours are pursued in a most unholiday-like manner. The stories presented here will, hopefully, alter a few ingrained perceptions about Goa, not the least by showing that a rural Goa with strong traditions does exist alongside the five-star ersatz of the coastline.

The credible fictional literature of the region is very young and has only recently begun to grow. The stories have a freshness and are lucidly and simply told. While they may not teem with complexity and hidden meanings, they are also not coyly ambiguous or clouded by wilful obscurity. Many of the stories in the four main languages—Konkani, Marathi, Portuguese and English—used in the region are also marked by a sense of humour, a contagious light-heartedness. Serious avant-gardism and credible experimentation have still not entered the making of fiction in Goa. There are reasons for this nascent state. Konkani, now spoken by five million people, has had a troubled past. Historically both Konkani and Marathi were studied and the grammar well documented by the Portuguese, but only as a tool towards proselytism. The advent of the Order of the Inquisition (1560-1812) ripped the heart out of Konkani. The Inquisition, more severe and repressive in Goa than anywhere in Europe, banned the use of the language and the local community was compelled to study Portuguese. Fleeing from their razed temples and the excesses of the Inquisition, many Hindu families settled in neighbouring areas, taking with them their family deities and their native language. Konkani was thus fragmented into four scripts: Devnagiri, Kannada, Malayalam and Roman.

The stories in Konkani in this collection have all been translated from the Devnagiri. Stories from the Kannada and Malayalam scripts have little or no affinity with Goa. Roman script Konkani is, however, a different kettle of fish. It is widely used by the Catholic community both in its prayer books and in the manifestation of popular culture such as the tiatr and in titillating novels and novellas. One exponent of this genre of pulp fiction has alone written over fifty novels and novellas. However, despite repeated forays into this branch of Konkani, not a single noteworthy piece could be salvaged for this anthology.

While Konkani was laid low for centuries by the Inquisition, Marathi was kept alive as the language of the princely courts. It was also the language in which the Hindu scriptures were preserved during the height of Portuguese religious repression. Some northern parts of Goa, with their close proximity to Maharashtra, were only annexed by the Portuguese almost 300 years after the subjugation of the south. By that time, evangelical fervour had subsided, and the compulsions of commerce led the Portuguese to soften their stand on the regional languages. Marathi thrived especially in these New Conquest areas. From the latter half of the last century, the Portuguese rulers regularly printed bilingual editions of newspapers, in Marathi and Portuguese. Marathi was also widely used in the official administration of Goa.

For several years the politics of language further divided and sidetracked many Konkani and Marathi writers of the region, and whatever the tall claims about the quality of the fiction (almost all of it dreary, prolix and preachy) produced by the old and blindly venerated stalwarts, both the literatures can be said to have progressed only during the past few decades. The fictional literature of the area is thus written on a virtual tabula rasa; the responsibility of creating a tradition, at least in the area of fiction, rests on the current crop of writers.

The output and quality of fiction in Portuguese relating to Goa and Portugal is surprisingly thin. But there are mitigating circumstances. During the colonial era, the Portuguese Lyceum (pre-university) concentrated mainly on the sciences. The humanities were largely restricted to the teaching of French—which was the second language—Portuguese history and literature and classical Latin. History was a compulsory subject, while Greek and Sanskrit were optional. The Portuguese educational system did not offer graduation or post-graduation courses in literature or in any other subject in the humanities, and indeed not in most science categories either. Opportunities for higher education were available only in the fields of medicine and pharmacology and for indoctrination into the Catholic priesthood in the seminaries (though Portuguese universities, particularly Coimbra, do have a great tradition in the teaching of humanities and law). A degree in the arts and literature doesn't, of course, automatically produce writers, but the aridity in this area of education only served to worsen the drought.

Historically, the Portuguese empire reached its peak in the sixteenth century. For a period the arts related to the colonies flourished in the era known as the Classic Epoch (1498-1580). Then followed a slow but painful decline of Portuguese colonial power. Goa, once the El Dorado, the prized possession of the Portuguese, was reduced to an outpost, as its rulers turned their attention increasingly to Brazil. The soldiery and others sent to Goa were invariably reluctant young draftees and conscripts, and never more than a few thousand at any given time. From such men, often desolate, several thousand miles and an arduous sea journey away from their homeland, one would normally expect outbursts of frustrated creativity. Unfortunately, apart from some gallant serenades to Portuguese beauties, there is no evidence of them seeking solace in the healing powers of fiction or even poetry. In more recent times, the oppressive Salazar regime imposed such severe censorship that writers in Portugal and its colonies would have had to resort to a magician's wizardry to escape its noose. Fiction relating to Goa, either by Goan or Portuguese writers, barely entered the picture. Portuguese is now a dying language in Goa, spoken by a waning class, saddled with a legacy of a few turgid, unwieldy novels and some vacuous quasi-mythological poetry.

Given the levels of higher education on offer, many Goans migrated to Bombay and Portugal and to British- and Portuguese-ruled colonies in Africa. But when Goans leave their homes, they do so reluctantly, their bags lined with the red earth of their villages. Three of the stories in this selection, set in Uganda and Kenya and dealing with the lives of immigrant Goans, bring in this interesting offshoot.

It is not the intention in this anthology to showcase

a great and neglected literature. This volume does not claim to put Goa on the literary map of India. It is merely an effort to erase some of the misleading graffiti on Goa. It asks the reader to take a simple but refreshing ferry crossing into the heart of India's youngest state.

MANOHAR SHETTY

Innocence

Chandrakant Keni

Squatting in the shade of the cashew tree, Jayyu held the cashew fruit steady with the big toe of her right foot and began to peel it.

Devu came and sat before her, his loincloth full of fruit and nuts.

'Move away. The sap might get into your eyes,' Jayyu warned him.

'Jayyu,' Devu whispered, making no effort to get out of the way.

'What are you staring at? Didn't you hear what I just said?'

Devu paid no attention to her. 'Jayyu, how is it that your thighs are so fair?'

Jayyu's dress had crept up when she sat, exposing her thighs, but she was not aware of it till Devu asked her this question.

She laughed. 'You roam about all day wearing nothing but a small piece of cloth. That's why your thighs are burnt and dark.'

'Then the rest of your body also must be so fair! Is it?'

Now Jayyu was embarrassed. She dropped the cashew and tugged at her dress, her face red.

'Will you let me touch your thigh, Jayyu?'

'Your hands are covered with sap.'

'No, they aren't. I swear they're not. But I'll wash them in the spring if you like.'

'But why do you want to touch my thigh?'

'Please, Jayyu. Once. Only once. Don't say no.'

Without waiting for an answer, Devu placed his hand lightly on her left thigh and let it wander. Both of them felt a shiver run through their bodies. Jayyu shut her eyes. She felt a pleasant sensation, as though someone was gently stroking her body with a peacock feather. Devu felt like he had touched the sky.

Jayyu was about fourteen years old and Devu a couple of years younger. They had, for many years now, been coming to this hillock with their cattle. They would run around, play all sorts of games, pick wild fruit . . . Today Devu had come up with this new game.

'That's enough,' Jayyu declared after a few moments. 'Let's peel some more cashews.'

'Let me touch the other thigh too. Please . . .'

'No.'

'Didn't you like it?'

'What?'

'Didn't you feel nice when I touched you?'

'No. And what did you get out of it?'

'I liked it.'

'You've gone mad,' Jayyu spluttered. 'Come on. Let's finish peeling the fruit. God knows where the cattle have strayed . . .'

Devu withdrew his hand. Emptying his load of cashews, he too set about peeling them. Neither of them spoke as they worked.

From time to time Jayyu would dart a quick glance at him.

Suddenly, a jet of sap squirted into Devu's eye. He rubbed it furiously with the little finger of his left hand.

'Aaah! It's burning. I hope I don't go blind!' Devu whimpered as he stood up, still rubbing his eye.

Jayyu got up. 'Oh, my hands are covered with sap. But wait,' she said. Bunching the end of her dress, she blew hard on it. Then she pressed his eye with the warm cloth.

'It's still burning, Jayyu. What shall I do?' wailed Devu.

'Let's see if I can remove it . . . Don't move,' she said, standing close to him. Jayyu ran the tip of her tongue lightly over and around Devu's eye.

The burning stopped. 'Ah,' Devu sighed in relief, closing his eyes.

All of a sudden, Jayyu pulled Devu close and pressed her lips tightly against his. For a moment their warm breaths mingled. Then she quickly pushed him aside.

'Cattle also show affection like this, don't they?'

Jayyu turned red. 'Because cattle don't have hands!'

'Shall we put our tongues into each other's mouths?'

'Our mouths! Won't they . . .'

'We can wash them at the spring afterwards.'

'No, baba. I'm scared.'

'Scared of what?'

'All the women say be careful of men. If you go too close to them, you'll become pregnant.'

'How can you be pregnant if you're not married?'

'You can! Don't you know Shevanthu, the beggar's daughter? She is not married, but she is pregnant. It seems she went too close to that fellow who drives the truck at the mines.'

'How do you know all this?'

'I heard the women talking about it at the well yesterday.'

'Let's get married.'

'Married? But you're so small. A husband must be old. He must be working. The women are looking for a bridegroom for me.'

'Who is he?'

'How do I know?'

'Will you go to your husband's house then?'

'I'll have to . . .'

'And I'll be left all alone here?'

'You too will get married one day.'

'But can I get a bride like you?'

'What do you mean like me?'

'With fair thighs.'

'All women have fair thighs.'

'Really?'

'Of course.'

'Jayyu, will you really leave me here and go to your husband's house?'

'All girls have to go.'

'Let's run away.'

'Run away and go where?'

'I don't know. I am confused. My head's spinning.'

'Your head's spinning because you're scared. Get up now. See how late it is. Let's go home.'

Reluctantly, Devu walked down the slope with Jayyu. His mind was in a whirl. Jayyu spoke to him twice but he did not answer. When they reached the foot of the hillock, she stopped.

'Are you angry with me, Devu?'

'No, I am not. I swear.'

'Why are you so quiet then?'

'Will you really go to your husband's house, Jayyu?'

'Look, Devu, you wanted to put your tongue into my mouth, didn't you? Come, let's go under that banyan tree . . .'

'No. I don't want it anymore.'

'But why?'

'You'll be someone else's wife.'

'So?'

'Jayyu, don't go. Don't go to your husband's house.'

'We'll see about that when the time comes. Why make yourself miserable now?'

Jayyu took his hand in hers. At that moment, like a dam that had burst, Devu began to cry. Drawing him close, Jayyu wiped his tears with the end of her dress and patted him comfortingly. Resting his head against her, he cried for a while. Gradually he calmed down. Waves of contentment washed over him.

The moment was shattered by a piercing whistle.

'Very passionate you two are getting!' taunted Santan, the toddy tapper, from his perch atop a palm tree.

Devu cringed. Jayyu ran away.

Translated from the Konkani by Vidya Pai

That Blank Space

Chandrakant Keni

Ramesh lives on the ground floor of a chawl. The staircase leading to the upper floor passes right in front of his door, so he can see whoever comes to the chawl or goes out from it. Ramesh can recognize most of those who frequent the place, though many of the people who trudge up the stairs or rush down them as though chased by a tiger pretend not to have noticed the young man sitting on his threshold.

Savita, who lives on the second floor, is a teacher in some school. She catches the first bus in the morning. Ramesh knows this because this is the time when he sits outside his door, reading the newspaper. He hears her footfalls on the stairs, then her perfume wafts back to his nostrils and lingers long after she has disappeared from view.

How does she manage to wear fresh saris every day? What must she be earning, Ramesh wonders, not taking his eyes off the newspaper in his hands. She probably has four or five saris which she shuffles around judiciously, that's why each one looks fresh and new, he tells himself. Actually, he doesn't know very much about Savita, except her name, of course. He doesn't even know what she looks like. He's never home when she returns in the afternoons, and on holidays she's never to be seen.

All the womenfolk in the chawl know each other, but how can he ask one of them about her? It'll set them gossiping all over the place. Nevertheless he manages to corner a little boy who lives on the second floor to ask him the name of the school where Savita teaches. But the youngster just stares at him blankly and a disappointed Ramesh waves him away.

The whole problem seems to stem from the location of that staircase. Seated as he is, Ramesh can see the face of anyone climbing up the stairs but he can only see the back of anyone who descends. If someone were to ask him to identify Savita in a group of two or more girls, he'd have to go and look at them from the rear, Ramesh laughs out aloud. But he'll recognize her back at once, with her hair held loosely in a clip and the end of her sari fluttering in the breeze . . . and, of course, he'll recognize that perfume.

This is his final year in college and he must concentrate on passing with good grades so that he can start looking for a job. This is no time to daydream about girls, Ramesh chides himself, brushing off all thoughts of Savita as he would specks of dust. He resolves not to raise his head when he hears her footsteps on the stairs.

Actually, there's no other place where he can sit and study in peace. With seven members of his family crammed into two tiny rooms, Ramesh has always had to sleep in the veranda outside the door. Awakened at the crack of dawn by the milkwoman, he washes himself at the community tap in the courtyard and, drawing up a chair, immerses himself in his books till the newspaper arrives. By the time he gets back home from college and the library, it is late in the evening and the chawl is at its noisiest, making it impossible for him to concentrate on any serious work.

We must leave this place and go somewhere where we can live like human beings, he tells himself disgustedly. But in a moment reality dawns. This can only be possible if they have a lot of money, if he gets a good job, if he clears the examination which looms ahead. It was only yesterday that his mother had brought up the topic of his responsibilities.

'Your father will be retiring soon, and then everyone will be looking to you for support,' she said.

'How long can he look after all of us? Two years, may be four . . . after that he'll have to worry about his own wife and children,' someone else remarked.

Ramesh had remained silent. His thoughts have begun increasingly to take on an entirely different colour in recent times, as a picture of the family he will have in the future floats up before his eyes.

Whenever he indulges in reveries of this sort, a shadowy, insubstantial figure looms before him as the wife he will have some day. Ramesh loses all sense of time as he lovingly fills in details of her face and form. The woman in his dreams takes on the appearance of a favourite movie star on one day, or looks just like someone he has passed on the road on another.

One day someone remarks that Ramesh ought to take a working woman as his wife. Her salary will help him to support his parents and his brothers and sisters.

From that moment on, the figure in Ramesh's dreams has an added qualification . . . she is a doctor one day, a teacher on another, a clerk in a bank on a third.

How about fitting Savita into that blank slot in the dream, Ramesh thinks to himself. But how can he do that? He has never even seen her face. Like the sticky sap from the jackfruit which cannot be easily wiped away, the idea continues to nag him, allowing him no peace. Only a drop of oil will clean the messy sap. Only a good look at Savita will restore his peace, he knows, so he sets about concentrating all his energies towards that end.

Waking up earlier than normal, Ramesh is bathed and dressed and stands combing his hair before the mirror when his mother enquires whether he has to go to college earlier than usual that day.

'No. But I have to go to a friend's house to borrow a book,' he says, marvelling at the ease with which the falsehood comes to him.

'Haven't you gone yet?' his mother asks, exasperated, quite some time later, on seeing him seated outside the door.

'I'll go after some time. Who knows if my friend is up as yet,' he mutters, getting increasingly restless as the wait lengthens. Could it be a holiday today? What could possibly keep Savita so long, he wonders, his mind in turmoil as he clutches at the newspaper and the minutes tick away.

Suddenly footsteps ring out on the stairs. Tossing the newspaper aside, Ramesh rushes to the staircase and begins climbing the steps. His heart beats rapidly, his eyes are fixed to the ground. Savita descends slowly and soon she passes him by. The very air that touched her body seems to caress his face, but Ramesh cannot raise his eyes from the floor. Hearing her footsteps recede, he sighs deeply and turns around for one last look. At that very moment Savita pauses at the foot of the stairs and glances over her shoulder. The camera in Ramesh's eyes captures that blissful moment as a ghost of a smile flickers over her face . . . . Could that possibly mean anything, he asks himself.

Translated from the Konkani by Vidya Pai

When an Ass Mounts a Cow . . .

Pundalik Naik

Antulya had a couple of hours to while away, but there was no one around to gossip with him. So, like a crow that's always on the lookout for any foul scraps, he was the first to notice the scene. An ass, a mere bundle of bones, was trying to mount a sleek, well-fed cow. The cow was rushing here and there in desperation while the ass, mad with desire, scampered at her heels.

Antulya stood there enjoying the sight. For a moment he thought he was the ass himself, rushing in pursuit of the cow. Then, realizing that others had noticed the scene, he picked up a stout stick and rushed to the cow's defence. The ass was hell-bent on achieving its heart's desire and it was only after Antulya had rained a series of blows on its bony back that the animal's lust evaporated and it loped away, braying and kicking up its heels. The cow meanwhile stood a little distance away, surveying the action.

Antulya returned to his place, smiling widely and breathing hard. What he had seen was enough for him to talk about for the rest of that day. Like flies which are drawn by the smell of cattle, the people who had little or no work to do swarmed to Antulya's side to hear what had happened. The stonecutter's ass had chased Sakhya's cow, this much was certain. But, like a holy man who tailors the scriptures to suit whoever is sitting before him, Antulya changed his story according to his listeners' demands. If the listeners were as young as him, the story was laced with colourful details; if they were elderly people, Antulya dwelt at length on the pitiful state of the cow; and if his listeners were children, he lost no time in emphasizing how brave and strong he had been.

The hours passed and the story began to swell with repetition. The initial giggles and good-humoured wisecracks about the ass died down, and as the heat of the sun became intense, the incident took on some unpleasant overtones.

'If this is true, it is sacrilege indeed!' Pachi spat out a stream of betel juice and turned to Sakhya. 'Imagine . . . if Antulya had not intervened, what a terrible thing would have happened! An ass on a cow? Tomorrow it might be on your . . .' He spat out the dire prophecies left unsaid along with the betel juice.

'This isn't a laughing matter,' Pachi rebuked the gigglers in the crowd and the titters stopped completely. Everyone assumed an air of grave concern just like Pachi and the atmosphere was charged with tension, as though disaster had already struck.

'We're Hindus, we revere the cow!'

'Yes, we even drink its urine.'

'Don't refer to it as mere urine. It's gomutra. Whom do we serve before all others at any feast? The holy cow, right?'

The discussion gained momentum. Everyone strove to fish out details they had read or heard about to illustrate the venerability of the cow. Sakhya was the only one who was silent in all that tumult. Strange, because his opinion was necessary; it was his cow that had been wronged. Normally, the slightest pretext was enough to set him fuming, to make him demand an inquiry and a community meeting to set things right. Today he sat there silently, waiting for an opportune moment to let fly his feelings.

'Are we just going to wag our jaws and go home? Or is this wrong to be set right? Will something be done?' Pachi spat out a final stream of juice.

'Let the community meet and decide,' Sakhya said gravely and everyone accepted his suggestion as the final word.

Kesav was entrusted with the task of informing everyone in the village. 'Come to the temple this evening,' he said. Normally he'd elaborate on the topics that would be discussed, but this time he did nothing of the sort. 'Come to the meeting. You'll know soon enough . . .' he said.

It was only when he was pressed repeatedly that he blurted out, 'Disaster . . . an ass mounts a cow . . .' swallowing the rest of the words.

As twilight deepened, the news of the meeting spread throughout the village. The village elders perked up. Their responsibility towards the village weighed heavily on them now. There was not another man as poor and as wretched as the stonecutter, yet there were some who wouldn't hesitate to pull him down. This was a momentous event and everyone wanted to be part of it.

Even before the community gathered in the temple, a select band of village elders met on Dadi's veranda. Any important matter was always thrashed out here first of all, as everyone placed their views before Dadi. Then, in the temple, Dadi would speak out on behalf of everyone and all those present would nod sagely as if to indicate that the words emerging from Dadi's mouth were indeed their very own thoughts.

Tossing the end of his towel on to one shoulder, Dadi leaned against the balcony and ran his fingers through his greying hair. Then everyone began to speak at once.

'It's sacrilege!'

'A sin!'

'There will be no morality left.'

'A shame!'

'Why should an ass be kept in the village?'

'Yes, that's right.'

Dadi listened carefully to everyone's opinion. He said, 'Let's decide what must be done when we meet at the temple. But let me say one thing right now . . . the one responsible for this unnatural event must be made to suffer and the community must see that this is done.'

Everyone accepted Dadi's decision as the final word.

Word about what had happened finally reached the stonecutter's ears. It was late in the evening when he got back home and his daughter came running, dragging her lame leg, to give him the news. The man had never expected something like this even in his wildest nightmares, and all of a sudden his strength drained out of him and he sank to the ground.

He didn't have any trouble with the ass these days. If some food was available, he'd toss it before the animal. If it wasn't, the ass would find enough to keep itself going by foraging through the village. He didn't keep it tethered in one place either. It was a pitiful creature, and the mischievous children in the village loved nothing better than to tie an empty tin to its tail and set it scampering in a frenzy. The stonecutter's daughter would then abuse the children and limp painfully after the animal, trying to quieten it and the children would dissolve in laughter. The stonecutter had thought of getting rid of the wretched animal, but it was for his daughter's sake that he had bought it in the first place.

It was about five years ago that he had landed a contract to cut stone in the quarry by the lake. The stone had to be carried to the dam that was being constructed on the river and a family of labourers had come down from the Ghats for the job. They had brought a pack of ten asses which were to be loaded with the stone slabs. To speed things up and earn more money, the stonecutter had enlisted his twelve-year-old daughter to help load the animals, but the very next day the child dropped a stone slab on her foot, injuring herself. Almost half of what the stonecutter earned from that job was spent on tending to his daughter. Though the wound healed soon enough, the girl was left with a permanent limp.

It was around that time that he had bought one of the asses in that pack, hoping that it might help him transport the stone slabs. The ass had remained in the village, roaming around freely, like the hens did around the priest's house.

'The village elders want to see you in the temple tonight.' Kesav brought the summons to the stonecutter eventually, and without waiting for a reply, moved off hastily.

'What has this animal brought upon us,' the stonecutter thought fearfully as his eyes fell on the scrawny creature standing in the courtyard. Then he called out to his daughter, 'Jani . . .'

The temple was filled to overflowing with more people crowding in than at any festival. The latecomers pushed their way into the temple and, having paid their respects to the deity, looked around for a place to sit. Each person who jostled his way in seemed bent on proving how important his presence was on this occasion.

The priest, Govardhan Bhatt, winked broadly and smiled at everyone but his heart was being eaten up with regret. Had he heard about this matter earlier, he would have brushed up on some of those religious tomes and fished out some sparkling sayings about how venerable the cow was and how totally depraved the ass. Or maybe a few mantras to illustrate the point. But no matter how deeply he pondered the point and how hard he scratched his head, the only mantras that came to mind were the ones he repeated unthinkingly every day. So he satisfied himself by declaring that it was a transgression of everything moral as he wiped his hands on his silk dhoti that looked like it had not been washed for years.

As befitting his rank in the village society, Dadi was the last to enter the temple. Everyone's eyes were trained on him. Many rose respectfully to let him pass and take his seat. Glancing around, Dadi realized that everyone was watching him, so he rose and went to the temple square. Tossing the end of his towel on to his right shoulder, he passed a hand through his greying hair.

He began, 'There is no need for me to tell you what we have gathered here for . . .' The only sound that could be heard was of people letting out their breath. 'But it is only right that everyone be informed yet again.'

Dadi pointed to Antulya and called him to stand before God and declare what had actually happened. Antulya embarked on a little speech as it were. He'd never had an opportunity to do so before, and he seized the chance, much to the chagrin of the other youth in the assembly. Antulya went over the incident in vivid detail. Then Sakhya got to say a few words and he too saw to it that no sympathy remained for the poor stonecutter. Then there was a bit of a discussion and the same words that had been whetted and polished with repeated use throughout the day were spouted yet again.

The stonecutter was then invited to present his defence. The man tried to say something but words failed him and he was on the verge of tears.

'Why pretend to cry now?'

'Didn't you know this when you set out to rear an ass?'

'Do you think we are fools, is that why we don't rear asses?'

'Do you plan to ruin the village?'

'Throw him out of the village!'

The whispers began to be heard from different parts of the temple and the stonecutter was reduced to a pitiable state. 'I accept that it was my fault, punish me if you will. Only, don't cast my daughter and me out onto the road. The child needs to be sheltered,' he wept. His daughter Jani stood inconspicuously beside a pillar. Yet in all that crowd Dadi did not fail to notice her. The stonecutter began to plead for mercy but no one seemed inclined to take pity on him. He had never taken anything from anyone in the village, he implored. But he had never given them anything either, the villagers retorted. At last it was time for the final verdict to be announced. All eyes turned to Dadi, who became even more grave as the village elders vested in him the authority to speak on their behalf and returned to their seats as though their work was done.

'Brothers and sisters . . .' Dadi launched into a speech. 'It's a big responsibility that you have given me. The responsibility of declaring the verdict. But I shall not do so blindly. All of you know that I have often created such upheavals in court that the finest of families have been forced into the dust. But today, standing in front of God, I must put my hand on my heart and only then must I arrive at a decision.

'We all know how we Hindus revere the Cow. I'm sure Govardhan Bhatt will testify to that. But do you know that even in our society some people slaughter the Cow and eat its flesh? If we are not moved when people slaughter the Cow, why do we make such a fuss when an ass is caught trying to mount one?

'And anyway, from what Antulya has said, the ass was only chasing the cow. Nothing further happened. Besides, is it really the ass' fault? This is the only ass in this village. Does it not need a mate? After all, why do we get married? As for punishment . . . God has made that creature an ass, isn't that punishment enough? What further punishment can we give it? Coming to the stonecutter—he bought that ass to help him earn a living. How can we deprive him of that? All we can do is to tell him to take care in the future, to ensure that nothing of the sort happens ever again. I feel we should consider the plight of his daughter and be lenient. This is the only verdict we can arrive at. Anything else will be an insult to the community's power of judgement.'

Dadi returned to his seat and for some time no one spoke. In any case, it was inconceivable that anyone would dispute what he had said. After a while everyone nodded as though to indicate that this was exactly what they had all decided after a whole day of discussions, and then everyone got up to go home.

The stonecutter was a relieved man. He'd heard all sorts of stories about Dadi, of how he was always ready to set other people's houses on fire, of how he sought to give only a little and gain a lot, like exchanging berries for gourds, so to say. But today he had seen Dadi in his true colours. It was as though the deity in the temple had appeared before him in the form of Dadi. The crowd began to thin and the stonecutter, followed by the lame girl, threw himself at Dadi's feet.

'It's all because of your mercy,' he cried.

'All right, all right. Now, what's her name?'

'Jani,' the stonecutter replied.

It was past midnight when the stonecutter and his daughter got to their little hut and Jani went in to get a light. The stonecutter picked up a rope and, looping it round the ass' neck, tied it to a stake. Suddenly there was the sound of footsteps and Dadi came into view. 'Where's Jani?' he said. Without waiting for a reply, he pushed himself into the hut and bolted the door. The lamp went off. Jani screamed.

The stonecutter stood transfixed, his frantic eyes darting from side to side. He noticed a stick lying on the ground. Grabbing it, he began to rain blows on the ass' back, cursing it in a frenzy. 'You wretch! None of this would have happened but for you!' he shrieked as the ass brayed in pain, as though its poor little heart would break.

Translated from the Konkani by Vidya Pai

The Turtle

Pundalik Naik

A s soon as Vasu stepped into the village the children crowded round him, yelling, 'Turtle! He's brought a turtle! Vasukaka has brought a turtle!' Normally no one paid much attention to the children. But this time the word 'turtle' caught everyone's ears. Godmausi, who was snipping off the heads of dried shrimps, leaned over to get a better look. Shantabai's new daughter-in-law paused with her foot on the pedal of the sewing machine and poked her head out of the window. They stared from doors and windows, then out they came from every house to mill around Vasu, to goggle at the object in his arms. 'It's ages since anyone brought a turtle to the Kharvadda,' they breathed.

Vasu pushed his way into the house and gently lowered his burden to the floor. The turtle drew in its flippers at once, and like an insect retreating into its hole, its head withdrew into its shell. Everyone crowded round the creature, gazing at it in wonder. Shantabai's daughter-in-law pushed her way through the awestruck children, straining to get a better look. Most of them had never seen a turtle before and those who expected to see a little creature, like a tortoise perhaps, were quite taken aback by its size. For the children especially it was as exciting as the first time they had set eyes on an elephant. A few people prodded the shell gingerly to see if it was hard or soft. Through all this the earth-coloured creature lay motionless on the ground.

Vasu leant against the wall, nursing his aching arm. He'd set out in his canoe early that morning, and as he let out the line for the first time he hadn't forgotten to say a prayer to his family deity. He'd baited the hook and dropped the line overboard, waiting patiently in the drifting canoe, but though morning passed and the afternoon sun began to scorch his back, not a single fish nibbled at the line. He had grown tired of the wait and was about to dismantle the line when he felt a sudden tug. Vasu tried to pull the line in and to hoist the fish on to the boat but he had to strain every muscle and use all his skill to remain in control. As one of the best fishermen of Kharvaddo and a descendant of generations of fisherfolk, Vasu was well acquainted with the behaviour of different types of fish. But what sort of fish was this, he said to himself, as he struggled to pull it in. Finally, after a hard struggle, he managed to heave the catch on to the canoe, which tilted dangerously to one side. Vasu stared in amazement at the turtle that lay in the boat. He inspected his bleeding hand, bitten deep by the fishing line, and wiped his sweating brow. He'd seen bigger specimens than this one, he reflected, but he couldn't remember anyone having caught such a large turtle on a line ever before. His father had netted a turtle once and he'd brought it home, much to the delight of everyone in Kharvaddo. People had streamed in to take a look at the creature much as they did to see the Ganesh idols on Chavathi. The house was decorated as though for a great puja as the turtle was worshipped and then taken out in a procession before it was released into the sea.

Vasu could barely remember all this, but his father had never tired of repeating the whole story, of how he had begun to prosper after that event, even winning the fishing rights to the village pond. The catch was always plentiful and money seemed to flow in. It was around this time that Vasu's father had arranged Vasu's marriage with a lot of pomp and show, but he hadn't lived very long after that. Things were very different now. It was an impoverished existence for Vasu, his wife and their two-year-old son.

His wife beckoned him into the house and he followed her, not quite sure what he ought to say.

'What shall I cook now?' she asked.

'I caught that turtle. Nothing else. If I'd caught anything else I'd have got some money. In fact, I'd told Dambaab I'd get some fish for him.'

'And you brought that turtle.'

'I had to. I caught it on the line, didn't I?'

'You could have sold it. Surely someone would have paid four or five rupees for it. At least we wouldn't have to worry about food for a couple of days.'

'What's wrong with you?' Vasu was aghast. 'A turtle is sacred to us fisherfolk. Have you ever heard of any self-respecting fisherman selling a turtle?'

But she was more concerned about the empty

vessel on the hearth and nothing he could possibly say would affect her. All his explanations were like streams of water flowing from an upturned pot. Quite beside himself with rage, Vasu began to rain blows on the hapless woman.

'What sort of a woman is this!' he cursed. 'She has no respect for tradition. How many years is it since anyone caught a turtle, a sure sign of good fortune. How many people must be envying me today! Who knows, things may change like they did for my father. Money might flow in again. Maybe we can get new clothes and enough food to eat. Can one tell what lies ahead? Perhaps that is why I caught this turtle today, perhaps it is an indication of good fortune . . . and this wife of mine! She's not fit to be the wife of a self-respecting fisherman! Sell the turtle for four or five rupees, she says!'

Suddenly he remembered those woodcutters sawing planks from the jackfruit tree in Dambaab's field. They'd stopped their work as he passed by with the turtle in his arms.

'Will you sell that?' they'd asked.

'It's a turtle!' he had retorted scathingly. He had wanted to say much more: Does a fisherman ever sell a turtle? Would you ever sell the gods that you worship? But he had managed to hold his tongue.

'Look, we'll give you four or five rupees for that,' they'd offered, drooling at the sight of the meat. But Vasu had walked on without a backward glance. His irritation had mounted with the heat of the noonday sun, his feet burned in the hot red dust and the voices of the woodcutters grated on his nerves as they asked him again and again to sell the turtle.

'Has the puja been done?'

Vasu came back to his senses. There were two elderly men from the village standing before him.

They placed the turtle ceremoniously on a platform and decorated it in a manner fit for worship. The children were dispatched to fetch flowers. Meanwhile Vasu had a bath at the well, and as he dried himself he told his wife that he was going to worship the turtle, half expecting her to provoke another lengthy argument. But his wife merely indicated that everything he needed for the rituals was laid out already.

'What about the prasad?' she asked quietly.

'Prepare something from that coconut left over from yesterday,' he said. He then performed an elaborate puja, worshipping the turtle with all the rituals normally reserved for the deity, in the inner sanctum of the house. Prasad was distributed to the children and everyone dispersed, only to reassemble at twilight to gape at the turtle all over again.

In the neighbouring houses fireplaces were lit to prepare the evening meal. But in Vasu's kitchen no fire had been lit since morning. His wife sat leaning against the wall, silently immersed in mending a fishing net. The child sat beside the turtle as it had done all day. Vasu squatted on his haunches with his head in his hands, hoping that his wife would break the silence. But ever since the quarrel in the morning she had withdrawn totally into herself. Vasu stared at the hearth, at the cold ashes which seemed to taunt him and laugh at his helplessness. The container on the shelf, empty of rice, seemed to float down and pin him to the ground. The pot on the hearth seemed as empty as his fortunes, the black stand that supported it waiting for his flesh to be roasted on it.

Abruptly, Vasu sprang from his hunched position, and tucking the loincloth tightly about his waist, pushed his way through the crowd of children gathered around the turtle. Grasping the rope tied around the creature, he hoisted it up into his arms.

'Where are you taking it?' people around asked in consternation.

'To the sea . . . to release it there . . .'

He strode away purposefully, the turtle no longer weighing him down. Striding through the darkness, he reached the camp where the woodcutters were sitting, puffing on beedies. He flung the turtle down beside them and stood there silently with his right hand outstretched. The woodcutters whispered to each other, their white teeth gleaming against their dark skins as they smiled broadly. One of them got up, and drawing out a single two-rupee note from the pocket of his shirt that hung from a branch, placed it silently on Vasu's palm.

Vasu set off, his cheeks burning as though someone had slapped him. His ears seemed to reverberate with the buzzing of the woodcutter's saws even though the sawing had stopped long ago. Clutching the money tightly in his fist, Vasu made his way to the shop to buy rice.

Translated from the Konkani by Vidya Pai

Bhiku's Diary

Meena Kakodkar

Bhiku's shop lay across the road from Velingkar's chawl. The 'shop' was actually an outer room of Bhiku's house. This house, built by Bhiku's grandfather, was quite modest. (Bhiku himself could not have built a house even if he had wanted to.) It had two bedrooms, a living room, a kitchen with an attached wash area, a porch in the front. There was also a pig-toilet in the backyard. So what if it did not have plumbing; it was still his private toilet. At least he did not have to suffer the indignity of getting up very early and trekking down to the stream to answer nature's call. All the residents of Velingkar's chawl did that. So what if it was only a pig-toilet; at least you didn't have to worry about who would pass by and see you. The only creatures around were the pigs, and they didn't care.

The residents had, however, erected a toilet for the women at the rear of the chawl about fifteen to twenty years ago. Bhiku found it difficult to keep track of time now, but he could still remember Gharudada's daughter, Nalu, who was then of marriageable age,

going round to the rear early in the morning with a
tumbler in hand. Bhiku himself was an eligible bachelor
then. Now Nalu's *daughter* was on the verge of
matrimony and Bhiku was still as eligible as ever.
Anyway, the question is not about Bhiku's
bachelorhood. The question is about the time the
residents of Velingkar's chawl built a toilet for the
women.

Bhiku and his old mother led a more carefree and
comfortable life than most of the chawl's residents.
With the earnings from the shop, Bhiku could have
taken care of a wife and children had he married. But
even though he was nearly forty-five years old, he had
not married. He felt, however, that he had not yet
crossed the limits of eligibility: these days, when the
brides were forty-plus, what was wrong with the
bridegroom being fifty years old?

From his shop Bhiku could see all the houses of the
chawl but was interested only in Gharudada's house.
Gharudada had one son and five daughters. The eldest
daughter was Nalu and the youngest Leelu. Bhiku had
been smitten by Nalu, who was like a doll when she
was young. He still felt that Gharudada should have
approached him for Nalu's hand in marriage, but
perhaps he had been too familiar a person. Just as you
cannot spot a chameleon in the foliage of its hiding
place, so had Gharudada not thought of Bhiku as a
suitor for Nalu. After Nalu's marriage, Bhiku set his
heart on the next daughter, Shilu. After her marriage,
he set his heart on the next and then the next, until
only Leelu remained. Having thus set his heart on
becoming Gharudada's son-in-law, Bhiku spent most
of the day with his eyes trained on his house.

It is not that Bhiku did not receive any marriage proposals. But his expectations were so high that he did not bother to consider any of them. Maybe if the girl had been like Nalu he would have given it a thought, but that never happened.

Here it would be appropriate to tell you about Bhiku's appearance. He was about five feet tall and his breath was something unmentionable. Taking into account all the muscles in the body and the hair on his head, he weighed about thirty-seven kilos. But this did not stop him from expecting a tall, fair and well-built wife. Now all his expectations were on the verge of being buried.

Nalu and Leelu were worlds apart. Leelu was not as beautiful as Nalu, she was tall, flat as a board, and dark. Gharudada had tired of looking for a suitable husband for Leelu, but he still did not consider Bhiku. This hurt Bhiku. He felt that Gharudada should marry Leelu off to him rather than make a spinster of her. Keeping this in mind, he would always give a discount to Leelu and Gharudada on anything they bought from his shop.

Being a loner, Bhiku found it difficult to talk to people. He did not smoke and kept himself busy with his work. He tended some vegetable plants in the garden patch behind his house. The Velingkar chawl residents did not have even an inch of space to plant anything. Bhiku would regularly send gourds, ladies' fingers and brinjals from his patch to Gharudada's house. He was trying to prove to Gharudada that even if he was not very presentable, he led a comfortable life; he had a separate toilet and tended a flourishing vegetable patch. What galled Bhiku was the studied ignorance that Gharudada maintained about all these virtues.

Besides his vegetable patch, Bhiku had another interesting hobby. He maintained a diary. He had begun writing one the previous year when someone presented him with a diary and a calendar. Bhiku could never throw away anything without having used it fully, and so he began writing in the diary. Once he started, he would religiously set aside some time each day to record at least the transactions he had made during that day. Bhiku was smart when it came to running his shop, as these few samples from his diary illustrate:

> 22 February: There was an unexpected demand for potatoes today. I managed to palm off some rotten potatoes along with the good ones.
> 23 February: Two customers returned with some rotten potatoes. Customers these days do not have the slightest qualms and return goods if they find them even slightly bad. I must find a way to tackle this problem.
> 24 February: Put up this sign today: 'Goods once sold shall not be taken back.' Now let them come back with rotten potatoes.

Apart from the daily proceedings in his shop, he would jot down his observations on Gharudada's house. He would occasionally vent his anger and frustration in his diary:

> 5 May: Saw Gharudada sitting in the balcony with his head in his hands.

Leelu's proposal must have been rejected. Naturally . . .

6 May: When Gharudada cannot see suitors sitting right in front of him, where in blazes is he going to find them? He married off that Nalu to someone in Pernem who does not have a house, not even a bicycle.

12 May: Leelu's pride is as bloated as her body. She won't even make polite talk with me. I gave her such a large discount on everything she bought today, but the shrew has eyes only for that Tukaram Mechanic.

There was nothing else in Bhiku's life worthy of being entered in his diary. His world was made up of himself, his shop and the few people around him. He found it difficult even to confide in his mother. She had given up asking, 'Bhiku, when are you going to marry?' a long time ago. 'In time, Mother, in time . . .' had been Bhiku's stock response before he too stopped. It was past the hour of bringing a bride to the house, and Bhiku spent much time thinking about this.

He had his business, his house, no vices, no missing limbs; in fact, he was sure, he would make an ideal husband. He did not think appearance was as important as family background and character. Height was not a problem either—didn't his uncle have a happy family even though he was shorter than his wife by almost half a foot? . . . Yet Bhiku was so worried that he might never get married that he had shown his palm to all the astrologers he could find, from the famous ones from Belgaum to the footpath variety with their parrots.

They all agreed on one fact: 'A late marriage is indicated.' Nobody had elaborated on how late 'late' was, and Bhiku still clung to the hope of getting married.

Anthony's garage was visible from Bhiku's shop. Bhiku had seen one of the mechanics, Tukaram, smile slyly at Leelu, and he'd seen Leelu giving him one of those looks. Bhiku had concluded that if this continued, it would not be long before Gharudada was disgraced. He knew that Tukaram, tall and fair, was a lady's man and was seen with a different girl every day. He was also known to drink occasionally. What galled Bhiku was that Leelu was attracted to such a man. He thought of talking to Leelu, or warning Gharudada about the impending disaster, but could not summon up the courage to do so.

Whatever the position of Gharudada's family today, it was a well-known and upper-caste one. Bhiku thought that Leelu should not even speak to Tukaram, who was not of her caste. He felt that it would be better if Leelu was married off to him before she created an embarrassing situation for Gharudada. When he could no longer stand the looks that passed between the two, he took the opportunity one day, when Gharudada came to purchase some beedis, to broach the topic of Leelu's marriage.

'You see, Gharudada, everything should happen at the proper time . . .'

'I know that, Bhiku, but these things are not in our hands, now are they?'

'Even though it is not in our hands, before things get out of hand . . .'

'But we can't find a suitable suitor for Leelu. You very well know how she is—flat and broad as a plank. To get someone suitable . . .'

Bhiku could not muster the courage to tell Gharudada about his uncle who had married a taller woman but had still managed to lead a fulfilling life.

'I have visited Mumbai and Karwar, but to no avail.'

'Why visit Mumbai, Karwar, when all you have to do is ask the shopkeeper right across the road,' Bhiku thought bitterly, but he didn't dare utter a word.

Life went on as usual. And then it happened, just as Bhiku had prophesied. Leelu ran away with Tukaram.

There was pandemonium in the neighbourhood. Everyone talked about how Leelu had tarnished the family name. Gharudada collapsed helplessly. All four daughters, Nalu, Gulu, Shilu and Pommi rushed back home with husbands in tow. There was a frantic search all over. The family was in a quandary on how much they could reveal and what they should keep to themselves. After all, it was a question of family honour. They were sure that a wayward lout like Tukaram would have fun with Leelu for a couple of days and then leave her helpless. Gharudada and his wife shed tears at the thought of what Leelu's fate would be.

At this hour of misfortune, Bhiku closed shop and walked over to Gharudada's house, who promptly burst into tears at the sight of Bhiku.

'Bhiku, things did get out of hand as you had said. The girl has ruined me.'

With some difficulty, Bhiku said, 'Do not give up hope, you will definitely find her.'

'And what after we find her? Who will marry her now?'

And Bhiku took the plunge, 'Someone would . . .'

'Of course not. We could not get anyone before, and now I won't have the nerve to approach anyone.'

'We are humans after all . . . we make mistakes.'

'You sow what you reap . . .' and Gharudada sat down with his head in his hands.

When Gharudada's wife heard Bhiku's words, she called Nalu inside. Then Nalu called all her sisters and they were followed by their husbands. Finally Gharudada was summoned inside. And there followed excited whispering, some of which filtered out to Bhiku.

'Why don't you ask him?'

'Ask him what?'

'Whether he would marry Leelu, of course!'

'No, Leelu is so . . . and he is so . . .'

'This is no time to think of all that.'

'I did not mean age, I meant in size.'

'Oh, I know, Bhiku will reach her waist . . . but who will have her now?'

'Nobody will marry her now, the fool.'

'If that is the case, then ask Bhiku if he would . . . he's not so bad, is he?'

'Let's wait till we find Leelu. What's the point in asking before she is found? And what if we never find her?'

'How can we not find her when even the police are looking for her?'

Bhiku, sitting outside, felt pleased by all the whispering going on inside. He was sure that when the astrologers had said 'A late marriage is indicated', they had meant this. So when Gharudada brought the matter up with him, Bhiku immediately gave his assent.

No one thought of asking Leelu her opinion and nobody considered the possibility of Tukaram marrying Leelu. They had all concluded that a good-for-nothing like Tukaram would cheat Leelu.

On returning home, Bhiku, in high spirits, spoke to his mother and even discussed repainting the house.

When Leelu did not return at sundown, Bhiku felt very restless.

Two more restless days went by. On the third day, a taxi pulled up outside Velingkar's chawl. Hoping that Leelu would get off, Bhiku fixed his gaze on the taxi.

Leelu got off the taxi and she was not crying. She had green bangles on her wrists and a mangalsutra around her neck. On seeing Tukaram follow her out of the taxi, Bhiku forgot to tie up the parcel he had in his hands.

Hoping to see Gharudada kick Tukaram out of the house, Bhiku looked on, along with the rest of the residents of the chawl. No one could see or hear anything that went on inside.

About an hour or so later, Leelu came out with Tukaram and sat in the taxi. Bhiku noticed that even though no one had come to see them off, no one had prevented them from leaving either. The taxi drove away. Bhiku felt his hopes of marriage being squashed under the wheels of the taxi.

Bhiku had not expected Tukaram to marry Leelu, nor had he expected Gharudada to mutely allow Leelu to walk away with Tukaram. He was not in any frame of mind to understand that Gharudada had no alternative but to do what he did. After all, Leelu had married Tukaram and stayed with him for a couple of days. Bhiku felt a black cloud of hate rise in his heart. And that night he recorded in his diary:

> 1 December: From today, no discounts
> for Gharudada.

Translated from the Konkani by Sacheen Pai Raiker

Transgression

Mahableshwar Sail

As soon as I caught a glimpse of Meeravaini watering the tulsi plant in her courtyard, I tugged at my shirt, straightened my collar and grasped the pile of books I had tucked carelessly under my arm. She was almost inside the house when she saw me. She paused at the threshold, smiling quietly. Her calm, clear face always lifted my mood.

'Back from school, Vasant? It's so hot out there in the sun, why don't you put a towel over your head?' she asked solicitously.

I stood there smiling.

'How are your studies progressing?'

'All right.'

'Just "all right" won't do. You have to pass, that too with good marks. The ninth standard is only a step away from the school-leaving certificate exams.' She came close to me and ran a hand affectionately through my hair. 'You must be hungry. Come, I'll get you something to eat.'

'Don't bother. Mother will serve some rice as soon

as I get home,' I said.

'As if your mother will be back from the fields so soon.' Dismissing my protests, she lead me in. I sat on a bench in the hall and watched her as she went about completing her puja. Tossing aside the withered flowers that adorned her husband's photograph, she placed a fresh garland in their place and stood for a moment, eyes closed, in silent meditation.

I surveyed the scene as though I had never seen it before. The lush growth of the tulsi on its pedestal which shone smooth and glossy, smeared with cowdung paste. Parijat flowers scattered all over the courtyard and a few silent buds dangling from the branches overhead. The sewing machine on the veranda laden with partly sewn clothes, and on the floor scraps of colourful cloth strewn about. I picked up a few scraps as Meeravaini approached.

'May I?'

'What will you do with those?'

'Teacher has taught us how to make dolls with scraps of cloth.'

Meeravaini made a face. 'Old enough to grow a moustache and he wants to make a doll, he says,' she snorted. 'But don't forget to show me the doll,' she added as she placed a dish full of food and a glass of lime juice before me.

'Vaini, did you make all this now?'

'No, it's left over from breakfast. Who is there to eat in this house? I can barely swallow anything, sitting here all by myself.'

I was feeling very hungry and in a matter of moments all the food was gone.

'Greedy fellow! And he said he wasn't hungry!'

I laughed.

'Vaini, who took this big photograph of Anna?'

'Do you remember seeing him?'

'Only a little.'

'What do you remember?'

'I remember him striding along, carrying a whole bunch of coconuts in his hands. And once he was dressed in a yellow dhoti, he was carrying a tray full of things for a puja. I remember he was going towards the river.'

'Do you remember seeing me walking behind him?' she asked.

'No, vaini,' I said as I got up to leave.

Following me to the door, she enquired anxiously, 'You'll do your lessons well, won't you? Get up at five in the morning and sit down to study. Want me to come and wake you up?'

'No, vaini, I'll manage,' I assured her as I set off home.

Actually, I can't find words to express all that Meeravaini had done for me. When I'd passed the seventh standard, my parents felt that I had studied enough. But Meeravaini took them to task for that. Do you want him to wallow in the muddy fields just like you do, she demanded. You toil in the fields twelve months a year, yet you can't earn enough to fill your bellies, do you want your son to suffer the same fate? And then she had come with me to the local school to fetch my certificate, and taken me to the high school for admission, paying the fees herself. She was a good human being, always ready to help anyone in need, as though she had been sent by the gods themselves. No wonder everyone respected her.

It was just a couple of years after their marriage that her husband had passed away. For eight or ten years now she had been leading the lonely life of a widow, hermit-like in her renunciation. All the exuberance of youth was stifled by the white garments she wore, but she was always careful to keep them unblemished and clean. A large part of her day was spent at the sewing machine, sewing clothes for people. She also got a steady income from the fields she owned and her days passed comfortably enough.

That year I did well in the ninth standard exams and Meeravaini was delighted to hear about it. She distributed a fistful of sugar to everyone present there. But when she heard that Vishwas, who also lived in the neighbourhood and studied in my class, had failed the exam, she sent for him and tried to encourage and console him as much as she could.

I was now preparing for the SSLC exams and Meeravaini's house lay on my way to school. The sight of that freshly swept courtyard with the bushy tulsi plant never failed to fill me with reverence. Three or four little palms laden with coconuts adjacent to her place cast a cooling, refreshing shade all over the house and courtyard. The mere thought that this delightful house was the place where Meeravaini, large-hearted and ever willing to help, spent all her time was enough to bring me solace.

It was time for the fields to be ploughed. One day mother returned from the fields only to collapse onto her bed. Her teeth were clenched tight as she shivered with a chill. After a while she began to feel feverish, her forehead burned and she moaned deliriously as though in great pain. I do not know how Meeravaini came to know about her state but she was soon at mother's bedside with a flask of hot coffee and a couple of tablets in her hand. Mother gulped down the medicine and the coffee, her whole body bathed in sweat, and soon the fever began to subside. She sat up gratefully, praising Meeravaini's healing touch.

'It's the powerful touch of a pure and chaste woman,' Aunt Dulu, who was sitting beside her, said and giggled.

Since I had to attend extra classes that year, I was almost always late in getting back home. One day, as I waited at the bus-stop in front of our school, I saw Sukanti, who lived in our neighbourhood and studied in the ninth class, waiting there as well. She was late, she said, because of the extra classes they had for their plays.

'We should get home soon, before it begins to rain,' I said.

'Yes, this wretched unseasonal rain,' she said. 'Haven't even brought my umbrella.'

The bus drove up and we climbed in. We hadn't covered even half the distance when raindrops began to patter on the bus. When we reached the stop closest to our village, it was raining very hard indeed. There was no shelter anywhere around and our village was half a mile away. We stood under a tree for a while but the streams of water pouring through the leaves only drenched us further.

'Come on, Sukanti. Let's go,' I said, grasping my books firmly under my arm and heading into the rain. Sukanti was soaked through her nylon dress which stuck to her body so that her rounded breasts, hips and thighs were clearly outlined. I had always regarded her as no more than a child, but the sight of her that day filled my mind with a strange sense of unease. I felt nervous, strange; forbidden thoughts came to my mind and my stomach began to feel funny. I quickened my stride, leaving her behind.

'Don't rush like that, I'm coming too,' she gasped, running up to avoid being left behind.

Glancing over my shoulder, I noticed a shadowy figure approaching us through the driving rain. Tall, fair, bespectacled, the man was dressed in immaculately pressed clothes.

'Hey, girl, want to share my umbrella?' he called out as he drew abreast. Sukanti cowered beside me and for a moment I thought he'd just pick her up and walk away. But the stranger merely lengthened his strides and was soon far ahead.

'Who's that? Not someone we know,' Sukanti said hesitantly.

'Must be someone's guest,' I said.

'Look at him inviting me under his umbrella. Didn't even bother to ask you!' Sukanti spluttered while I merely smiled. By this time we had reached the village and Sukanti ran off home. I paused for a moment beside Meeravaini's gate, noticing that a branch of a tree had crashed onto the tulsi, damaging the pedestal as well as part of the plant.

'Why don't you take an umbrella when you go to school?' Meeravaini snapped when she caught sight of me. She didn't ask me in, nor did she offer me a towel, I noted sadly. I was just turning away when I noticed a stranger seated in her house. Meeravaini was standing close to him, towel in hand.

My mind was in turmoil that evening. Who could

that man be? Why was Meeravaini so brusque? None of the words in my books made any sense that day. I seemed to be haunted by the awesome shapes which the stranger's spectacles assumed before my transfixed eyes.

The next morning, as I was getting ready for school, old Shivram stopped by our courtyard.

'Do you know, Anusuya, Meera is looking for a house. One of her relatives has been transferred to this area as the village accountant it seems.'

'Has she found a house?' Mother asked.

'A house for rent! And in this village! Someone will have to put him up as a guest,' Shivram said.

'Where is he staying now?'

'In Meera's house.'

'Then why doesn't she put him up herself?'

'Who, Meera? Is she the sort to do that? She doesn't have a choice, that's why he's staying there now.'

Mother didn't say another word and soon old Shivram moved off.

I didn't see much of Meeravaini after that even though I looked carefully every time I passed by her courtyard. The sewing machine was silent and there was no one on the veranda. I kept thinking something terrible must have happened, that bespectacled stranger must have kept her locked up in some inner room . . .

A fortnight passed in this fashion, though sometimes I glimpsed shadows moving in the hall. Sometimes I heard the murmur of voices or echoing footsteps within the house. Then one day I saw Meeravaini herself standing at the door, engrossed in conversation with a fisherwoman who had some bright red flowers in her hair. She glanced at me and then turned back to the fisherwoman as I stole away.

One evening as I was taking the cows back to the cowshed I passed a group of men and overheard a strange conversation.

'What movie are they showing at Karwar these days?'

'Sex and Sheer Bliss,' someone said.

'Who is the heroine?'

'Meera!'

'And the hero?'

'That bespectacled accountant.'

'So, she's kept him in her house?' one of them exclaimed.

'Not just in her house, in her skirts!' And the whole group roared with laughter.

I was terribly upset. What had happened to everyone in this village? Imagine talking like that about Meeravaini! A thorny weight seemed to press against my heart.

When I got back home, it was time for the lamp to be lit before the gods. Sakharam was beating the gong and Mother busied herself with the lamp. Aunt Dulu was seated on the stairs, muttering something. Mother kept responding from time to time.

'Who is he, really, Dulu?'

'Who else? Meera's lover, that's who.'

'But when I asked her she said he was her cousin.'

'What is this wretched world coming to! The mouth will rot if it utters such falsehood. All that nonsense about his being her cousin has just been made up to hide her sin! Yesterday, it seems, the two of them went off to Karwar to see a movie. And all the way in the bus they sat leaning against each other. Suresh told me this. He works in Karwar, you see. Now why would such an educated boy lie about something like this?'

I waited nervously to hear what Mother would say to this but she chose to hold her tongue. Aunt Dulu opened Mother's little paan box and took out a betel leaf. Adding a smear of lime and a sliver of betelnut, she popped it into her mouth and, chewing furiously, spat a stream of juice out of the doorway before setting off home.

I went in and picked up my books, but my brain was in a whirl as I stared at the pages.

'I don't want to eat,' I said when Mother called me for dinner.

'What's wrong with you? Come here at once,' she snapped, so I went quietly and began to eat. I hadn't quite realized how hungry I actually was; the meal was over in a very short time.

That night I had a strange dream. All the tiled roofs of the houses in the village seemed to be crashing to the ground and heaps of broken tiles could be seen all over the village. I could look into each house from above but the doors were always tightly shut. Before one such door stood Meeravaini with the upper end of her sari trailing on the ground. Her blouse had blown off in the breeze and the fair expanse of her stomach, breasts and neck lay open to everyone's gaze. A stream of crimson blood gushed out of a vein in her neck. The stranger, who seemed even taller and bigger in my dream, was clutching his belt as though it were a whip and chasing all the men in the village. So many men, some of whom I knew, others who were absolute strangers—all seemed to be running from his clutches and I, too, was one of them.

Next morning on the way to school I asked my friend Maruti, 'What are people saying about Meeravaini and that man?'

'It seems they take off all their clothes and lie down together.'

'How do you know?'

'Everyone in the village says so.'

I turned quite cold.

One day that old good-for-nothing Durga made a snide remark about Meeravaini. I couldn't control my irritation, and snapped, 'You old creature, you're almost at death's door. Not one tooth in its place and yet you talk like this!'

Durga's indignation knew no bounds. Heaping abuses on me he shrieked, 'You little scoundrel, go! Go hang around her like all the others, maybe you'll get a piece of her too!'

Everyone who was standing there laughed at me. I was deeply hurt. I wanted to go straight to Meeravaini and tell her, 'What is this you are up to? Aren't you aware of what people are saying about you? They are mocking you openly . . . why don't you do something, where are you?'

Mother and I were busy in the courtyard, winnowing the freshly threshed rice. There was some sort of a commotion near Meeravaini's house. I tossed the winnowing fan away and rushed in that direction. Mitra, who lived some distance away, was standing by Meeravaini's door.

Brandishing a newly stitched dress, Mitra screeched, 'It's more than one-and-a-half months since I gave you the cloth. And I've made so many trips to see if it was done! And now that you've finished, it's so short and poorly stitched! You've stolen part of the cloth!'

Meeravaini screamed from within, 'Don't talk rubbish, Mitra. You bring a tiny scrap of cloth that isn't enough to even hide your modesty and you expect to get a big dress out of it! A wretched piece of cloth no better than a rag and you say I've stolen it!'

'You've grown too full of yourself! What a nice piece of cloth that was and you call it a rag! But things will look like that to you now . . . you've got yourself a lover, haven't you?' And Mitra stomped down the steps.

Meeravaini sprang up from her stool at the sewing machine and lurched to the door. Her eyes spat fire, her face was flushed as she screamed, 'Yes, I've got myself a lover! Not just one, I'll get seventeen lovers if I choose! I'm not scared of anyone! I don't have to worry about escaping from my husband's wrath, nor do I have to creep away to meet my lover the way you do!'

Mitra was nowhere to be seen. I was aghast at her words. This was a side of Meeravaini I had never seen before. She stood at the threshold in a fit of rage, totally unmindful of the fact that her sari had slipped from her shoulder and was trailing on the ground, just the way it had that night in my dream. I noticed, to my consternation, that her breasts were remarkably firm and suddenly I wanted to meet her alone, to gaze at her from close quarters, talk to her to my heart's content.

The next afternoon when I got back from school, I dropped in at Meeravaini's place. She was busy at the sewing machine and asked me to sit down.

'What brings you here?'

'Nothing in particular, vaini, I just wanted to tell you that I have passed the second term exams.'

'Good,' she said, somewhat brusquely.

'There's a new conductor in the bus. He picks up a quarrel with people every day. He insists on a full ticket . . . even for the children who go to school.'

'Is that so?' she said absently, refusing to even look in my direction. She seemed to be totally absorbed in her sewing and as the machine whirred and stopped and whirred again, I became aware of someone snoring loudly within the house.

She didn't look towards me but I could see a fair bit of her leg where her sari had ridden up to one knee. I watched her chest heave rhythmically with the movement of the machine, and the sight of her stomach with its smooth, fair folds added to my pleasure. This woman takes off all her clothes and lies in bed with that stranger . . . the very idea threw my mind into turmoil.

What was happening to me! How could such dreadful thoughts about Meeravaini ever enter my mind! I was terrified to think that the only thoughts about Meeravaini that I had now were about her body. Till just the other day, I hadn't even been aware of her body. What was wrong with me now? I got up in confusion and said good-bye.

'Is there anything in particular that you wanted?' she asked.

'No. I just dropped in,' I said as I hastily descended the steps. The loud snores that echoed from the inner room seemed to dog my footsteps as I left her house.

Translated from the Konkani by Vidya Pai

Ekolyo

Vasant Bhagwant Sawant

It was at the height of noon that Ekolyo the wild boar gored Babuli. After milking his buffalo in the morning Babuli had set it out to graze, and he was on his way to the rumada grove to fetch it in time for the afternoon milking. Descending the hillock that stood by Isheti's fields, he had just turned towards the little stream where the buffaloes wallowed in the water when the little puppy that was scampering before him rushed, sniffing and barking, into the bushes that stood by the path. Startled, Ekolyo erupted from the undergrowth and sped straight towards Babuli who stood in his path. The man saw the massive creature hurtling towards him, but even before he could jump aside the animal had plunged his sharp tusk into Babuli's thigh and was dragging him along. After ten or twelve bounds, the boar shook his tusk free of the mass of flesh and vanished into the undergrowth.

'Oh, Mother! . . .' Babuli's screams of agony reached the workers in Isheti's fields who were washing their lunch boxes in the stream. Calling out to the labourers resting under the palms, the men rushed towards the sound to find Babuli lying in a pool of blood. A chunk of flesh hung loose out of his thigh; he was bathed in sweat and his face was drawn in agony. He moaned in pain as he tried to draw himself up.

One of the labourers sprinkled water from his lunch box on Babuli's face and eyes and offered him a little to drink. Then, bandaging the deep wound roughly with a towel, two of the labourers pulled his arms around their shoulders and helped him to hobble out of the forest and on to the little path that wound its way past the edge of the village. The news had been carried there by one of Babuli's neighbours and soon the entire neighbourhood had gathered at the edge of the forest.

Babuli was helped onto the carrier of someone's bicycle and taken to the government hospital where the doctor cleaned the wound, applied some ointment and bandaged it after putting in sixteen stitches. Babuli nearly fainted with the pain.

After spending an uneventful morning at the river, Mhaddo was polishing off the pickled mango left over from breakfast before getting down to the serious business of drinking at Juje's wine shop.

Filling up a second glass of feni, Juje said, 'Arrey Mhaddo, our Babuli has been gored by that Ekolyo, the wild boar . . . he's in hospital . . . Did you know?'

Mhaddo froze. Then, gulping down his drink and biting fiercely on the sliver of raw mango, he climbed onto his bicycle and pedalled furiously to the hospital. When he got there, Babuli's wife was wiping her husband's face after feeding him a meal. Seeing

Mhaddo, the woman quickly retreated to the far end of the bed. As Babuli launched into his story, a picture of Ekolyo floated up before Mhaddo's eyes.

It was only the day before yesterday, as he was carrying a load of mud away from the stream at twilight, that he had seen Ekolyo quenching his thirst. He was massive in size, a true heavyweight, and the two tusks on his snout stood out prominently, Mhaddo remembered. The mud and slime that caked his body gave out an unmistakeable odour. Sensing Mhaddo's presence the animal had stopped drinking midway, and raising his head, had melted into the surroundings.

That wild boar must he tracked down and killed, his flesh must be cooked on every hearth in the village, Mhaddo said to himself. On his way back from the hospital, he stopped at a shop in the marketplace and bought some rounds of ammunition—gunpowder and lead pellets for his gun. Then, sitting in the courtyard, he pressed the gunpowder with a wad of coconut husk. Topping this with a layer of lead pellets, he pressed the whole mixture and sealed it tight into his gun before laying it aside.

By this time the whole village knew that Mhaddo was going out on a hunt that night.

A hunter by caste, Mhaddo took after his father, people said, but he had killed much bigger game than his father ever had. He was never known to have missed a target. So when Mhaddo set off on a hunt, all the womenfolk in the village set about grinding chillies and other condiments in preparation for the feast that lay ahead. Whatever game he brought back was always distributed in all the houses of the village, though Mhaddo himself received a welcome in only two houses.

Mhaddo was only a child when his father, in a sudden fit of anger, killed his mother and, fearing the wrath of the soldiers, fled from the scene. He had never been heard of since, but Mhaddo grew up with the tag 'son of a murderer' fixed to his name. His aged grandmother brought him up, and though he grew tall and broad and strong as a tree trunk, he remained a loner. If he lifted a hand to strike someone it was certain that he would not draw back. His wild and reckless ways drove his grandmother to her death, but even this did not change him in any way. Accompanying the other cowherds to the forest, he once grabbed hold of the milkwoman's little daughter and dragged her behind a bush. The resultant furore was enough for all the villagers to decide that henceforth no girls would be sent to the forest to tend the cows.

Mhaddo grew up like a wild pony on the hillock. His huge frame and ragged look ensured that no father ever offered him a daughter's hand in marriage, so though he was thirty-four or thirty-five years old, he was still a bachelor. There was a rumour in the village that Mhaddo became wild and excited whenever he saw a woman, so all the womenfolk took care to stay away from his path. This man who ate the portion kept aside for two labourers, who could single-handedly do more work than three fully grown men, presented an awesome sight indeed as he roamed about with his gun slung on his shoulder. He'd while away his time in the forest or by the river, hunting when the nights were dark enough, drinking till he was ready to drop. Nobody wanted to associate with him because of his savage ways, yet everyone wanted a part of what he brought back from the hunt. So whenever he set out to hunt, accompanied by Juje's son Andrew or sometimes by Babuli, everyone thought of him as one of their own.

Clad in short trousers and a khakhi coat, Mhaddo had a gun slung on one shoulder and a bag containing ammunition on the other. Then, at sundown, he set off with Andrew in the direction of the forest. The workers in Isheti's fields had told him that Ekolyo came every day to feed on the carcass of a bull that was buried just off their fields. Mhaddo decided to lie in wait for Ekolyo there.

The two men were busy clearing a little patch of ground beneath a cashew tree on one side of the pit where the buffalo's remains lay, when they heard a sudden tumult in the distance. Both men froze as Ekolyo appeared, hard in pursuit of a wild sow who was trying her best to escape his advances. The young ones in the herd scattered, squealing in fright, and another wild boar jumped aside in alarm as Ekolyo charged after the sow, mad with desire. The terrified sow plunged into a thicket of prickly bushes, burrowing deeper and deeper, trying desperately to get away. Realizing that he would not get at the sow, Ekolyo grunted in anger, and pawed the earth, throwing up a thick shower of mud. Then, turning his bottled-up rage and frustration on the wild boar that stood watching the scene, he thrust his tusk into its back, again and again, drawing blood as he chased it into the forest. It was only then that the sow dared to emerge from the thicket as Mhaddo and Andrew stood there transfixed.

Mhaddo slid his hand into his bag and drew out a

bottle of liquor, but remembering that Ekolyo was somewhere near by and might get a whiff, he quickly put it away again. Ekolyo's frenzy seemed to have cast some sort of a spell over the man.

'Mhaddo, Ekolyo must be weighing many tonnes, mustn't he? He must have been cast out of the herd when he was young . . . See how massive he's grown feeding on carcasses.' Andrew's words fell on Mhaddo's ears, but he was lost in his own thoughts. 'The poor wretch,' Andrew continued. 'He's not used to the sight of a female, see how maddened he is with lust.'

Mhaddo signalled to him to be quiet as the sound of footfalls came from somewhere beyond the pit. In a minute they heard the crunching of bones as Ekolyo began his repast. Mhaddo set his headlight in place and picked up his gun. Resting the butt lightly against his chin, he pressed the switch on the hunting lamp with one finger and immediately the whole pit was awash with light. Ekolyo, crunching through the bullock's bones, turned his head from side to side, scanning the surroundings with his bloodshot eyes.

Mhaddo stared at Ekolyo as though the animal in the pit was not a wild boar but he, Mhaddo himself. This is Ekolyo, a loner since childhood just like me. He eats whatever he gets, just like I do. He craves for a female, the same way as I do. Mhaddo's finger remained on the trigger, these thoughts swarming confusedly in his mind.

'Come on . . . Shoot him . . . Quick!' Andrew's scream broke through his thoughts and almost reflexively Mhaddo pressed the trigger. The explosion echoed through the forest. Ekolyo was mortally wounded, yet summoning up the last reserves of strength, he thrashed about, squealing wildly, till he finally keeled over into the rushing waters of the stream, as hot tears rolled unchecked out of Mhaddo's eyes.

Translated from the Konkani by Vidya Pai

Theresa's Man

Damodar Mauzo

Sleep has vanished from his eyes, but the lassitude refuses to go away. The cold morning breeze sends shivers down Peter's spine but he is too lazy to pull the bedsheet over himself. He knows Theresa is in the bathroom; the sound of water splashing reaches his ears. The sound irritates him. 'I have to fill up the vat with water and all she does is empty it.' He does not dare voice his thoughts though, since he knows what Theresa's acidic retort would be.

Theresa enters the room having washed her hands and feet, Peter looks at her with languid eyes. Theresa has just a camisole on her wet body. Water has splashed over certain parts of her body and the camisole clings to her. She takes a stick and removes a towel from the rope strung high up. As she raises her arms, the sleeves drop and . . . Peter shuts his eyes for a moment, then looks again. Her camisole has ridden up her legs. Her fair thighs seem like young, robust banana tree trunks to Peter. Unwittingly, his eyes have now come wide awake with the spectacle of his wife's thighs.

Theresa wipes her face and neck with the towel. The rough texture of the cloth leaves red marks over her fair skin. Her mother-in-law is preparing tea in the kitchen. She uses the cheap aluminium vessels roughly, invariably denting them, but no one admonishes her. Theresa has concluded that she can't afford steel utensils, not in this life anyway. Peter has decided that since he does not earn money, he has no right to say anything in the matter.

Most wives would refer to their husbands fondly, like 'Tony' for 'Antonio' and 'Vitor' for 'Victor'. Theresa insists on calling poor Peter 'Pedro'. Though he does not like it, he knows she doesn't care.

'It's almost eight o'clock, Pedro.'

Peter thinks, 'It's easy for her to get up so early, she is used to it.'

'Get up, Pedro. It's time for the train. Drop me to the station. Quick!' Theresa shouts, and with a purposeful stride she walks over to him and pulls his hand. 'Get up quickly, you lazy bum! If I miss the train the boss will scream at *me*, not you.'

Peter gets up in a stupor, and walks to the bathroom. He splashes cold water on his eyes to cool his flaring temper. He walks back after having washed his face and pulls up his trousers. Putting on his shirt, he mumbles to himself, 'This has become a habit. I cannot sleep in peace anymore. The lazy woman cannot get up earlier to dress up!'

Theresa seems to have heard all this. She walks up to Peter and screams, 'Look how shamelessly he talks! Shameless idler! All he does is sit at home and eat away. What is wrong in dropping me to the station on your bicycle when I'm late? Does your back hurt? I work all day to feed you and you complain! I am fed up with you! Marrying you has ruined my life!'

'You wanted a love-marriage, didn't you? Now suffer!' Her mother-in-law slyly pours fuel into the fire. Theresa, burning with rage, lets out a low moan and bursts into tears when she hears her mother-in-law's words.

Peter has already calmed down by then. He wears his slippers, walks over to the kitchen, and pours himself a cup of hot tea and gulps it down. His gaze is rivetted by the bright red blouse Theresa has on. Her earlobes are red and her red skirt is wrapped tightly around her waist. The sight draws furrows across Peter's forehead as he makes his way to his bicycle.

One foot on the threshold, he waits for Theresa to appear. This was how he waited for Theresa at the station, two years ago . . . but then he was in love with her.

'What is the delay now? Come quickly,' shouts Peter.

Theresa comes out wearing high-heeled shoes that go clackety-clack as she walks and sits on the bicycle.

She thinks of days gone by as the cycle moves. How Peter would wait unfailingly early in the morning outside her house to give her a lift to the station. He would turn up at the station in the evening, ignoring her protests. One day, as usual, Peter was pacing up and down outside Theresa's house early in the morning. He had waited for an hour and was getting worried. When he saw Theresa returning from morning mass he had rushed up to her and asked, 'Aren't you attending office today?' Trying to control her laughter, Theresa had said, 'Isn't today a Sunday?' You should have seen the expression on his face! Theresa laughs at the memory and this annoys Peter. 'Isn't this the same person who was crying at home? Now she is laughing at some private joke. Maybe she's thinking of someone in the office. Was all the crying at home just an act, then?' Peter thinks.

As the station comes into view, they see the train at the platform. Peter pedals furiously and brings the cycle to a halt near the platform. The guard waves the green flag, the whistle blows. Theresa starts running, clutching her purse tightly. As the train leaves the platform, she grabs the handle at the entrance of the compartment. Peter sees that she cannot raise her foot onto the train because of her tight skirt. Her sleeves are askew as she holds the handle. The train moves and she is pulled along. She is alarmed. Suddenly, a man from the compartment grabs her arm and pulls her into the train. Theresa does not turn to see her husband once she is on the train. Peter sees her thank the young man and smile.

'Brave man to pull her like that.'

'Lucky fellow. He took the opportunity . . .'

'Well, the girl enjoyed that too. Why else do they work?'

'That's right. Once you're working, you can have fun and no one can question you.'

Peter goes wild with anger when he hears this conversation on the platform. He wants to slap them all but decides against it as there are four of them.

He pushes off on his cycle, madder than ever with his wife. 'Why can't she leave a bit earlier . . . and that tight skirt! Why does she insist on wearing that? I have to face all the embarrassment here. The fellow pulled

Theresa with both his arms around her waist . . . must have been thrilled—and those chaps called him a lucky man. "The girls enjoy that. Why else do they work?" That is what they'd said. That's it! From now on, I'm going to tell Theresa, no more office, no more tight skirts!'

After their marriage Peter had told Theresa several times to give up wearing those tight skirts but Theresa maintained that as a receptionist she was compelled to wear such clothes. But she studiously avoids wearing tight skirts and sleeveless blouses when at home. That's why Peter resents it even more. Secretly, he wants her to wear tight, short skirts and sleeveless, deep-necked blouses when at home. Theresa is under the impression that Peter does not like her wearing such clothes, and avoids doing so at home. Poor Peter, he doesn't have the guts to tell her what he wants.

'Peter,' Guilhermina calls. Peter has no intention of stopping at Guilhermina's house, but he has heard that her father has returned from Africa. Curious about what he has brought from Africa, Peter turns his cycle around to Guilhermina's house. Her father is lounging on an easychair in the veranda.

'Peter, isn't it? How are you? And what do you do now?' He speaks with a pronounced accent.

'Business,' Peter hesitates to reply, eventually mumbling the word. He usually has no problem with this answer.

'What business is that?'

Peter has a fitting reply to this: 'Is there ever a limit to business? Any limit to trading? I trade coconuts in the coconut season, watermelons when those are in season, and if neither is in season, I trade in fish!'

In fact, Peter has never done any business. Ever since he passed the SSC examinations narrowly, he has held just two jobs. The first one he took was in a pharmacy. His daily routine was to get up early in the morning and cycle to Margao. There was no time for a nap after lunch and he could return home only after eight in the night. This routine did not appeal to Peter and one day, having suffered the boss's ire, he slipped away. He did not even bother to claim his salary for the thirteen days he had attended work. He decided that he would tell his mother and whoever bothered to ask that he was going into business. He had told Theresa the same story, and being deeply in love then, she had felt quite proud of him.

Once they married, Peter had taken the next job because of Theresa. She had forced him relentlessly and begged a favour from her boss to get him a job in the same office, but in a different department. So Peter had to get up early, take the train to the office, and then grab a pen and set to writing. There was no time to catch some sleep in the afternoon. All those English words, 'freight', 'filing', 'checking slip', 'statement', 'consignment', gave him a fever. Using the fever as an excuse, he did not return to work.

'You're doing nothing at all. Take up a job . . .' Guilhermina's father's words are like bitter medicine down Peter's throat. 'How will you manage without working?'

'His wife works,' Guilhermina says, rubbing it in.

'What? You send your wife to work? What kind of a man are you?' exclaims the father. 'You should never give freedom to your wife. She'll get too big for her boots, you know. A man should . . .' He bites down on his words as Guilhermina's mother appears on the scene.

Peter is impatient to leave. He knows that Guilhermina's father's luggage is on its way in a transport company's truck and he might be asked to help unload it. He goes to the village square, buys some fish and goes home.

'Thank God, you've come. I was waiting for you.' Peter's mother is happy to see him. Peter knows why he is being welcomed and quietly picks up the pot and goes to the well. He fills a barrel and other utensils with water from the well. He sees no sense in avoiding these chores as his mother cannot manage them. Should he refuse, then would come his mother's retort: 'Why can't you help since you're not doing anything anyway?' To this he has no reply.

He lies down in the veranda. He cannot sleep with all the little suspicions crowding his mind. What is Theresa doing right now? She must be giggling in the office. Is she with the boss? Or the chap who lifted her into the train? Wonder who he is. She must know him . . . how well, I wonder. Theresa's sleeveless blouse, her open arms, her tight skirts; the way he lifted her, holding her arms, the taunts from the bystanders . . . These thoughts swarm around him like honeybees.

'Will you be eating today, Peter?' his mother asks sarcastically.

Peter eats to his heart's content and sleeps soundly till five o'clock.

'Oh, so you've woken up. Now where will you go to waste your time?' Peter's mother welcomes him into the real world. 'He cannot go out and get a job, and he's married! He cannot take care of his wife, nor can he control her. She is too stylish—her clothes, her hair, worse than a whore's. She's wrapped her husband around her little finger and now dances around the place. Just watch her when she returns in the evening! Her husband is an empty coconut and her mother-in-law is the husk!'

'Just shut your mouth now, will you?' Peter screams.

'You can tell me to shut up, but you dare not tell her that, you coward! If you had the guts you would have slapped her and put her in her place. But you . . . If the Good Lord calls me up soon, I shall be free from all this!'

Peter does not wait to listen to the rest. He pedals his bicycle furiously till he reaches Caitano's bar, where a game of dice is going on. Amidst the shouting and swearing, everybody is highly excited. Peter helps himself to a tipple and sits down to watch the game.

'Eight!'

'Twelve!'

'Tablan!'

'Great, congrats.' And they start to move out.

In this genial noisy atmosphere Peter feels a bit relaxed. But just then, Agnel claps his hands and asks everybody to be quiet.

'Listen, who was there at the Vasco-bound train this morning?'

'I was,' Martin calls out.

'No. You keep quiet. Who else?' Peter is wary of Agnel's caustic tongue.

'Now, listen. Our dear baab Peter's wife, bai Theresa, would have fallen under the train this morning . . .'

'What . . .' everybody exclaims.

'But she was lucky. Bai Theresa's friend was

travelling in the same compartment, maybe just waiting for her. Just like a hero in the movies, he put his hands under her arms and pulled her up like this into the train.' Agnel plays it all out for his audience with actions that infuriate Peter.

'Agnel, be careful of what you say,' warns Peter.

'I am mistaken then? Why don't you tell? . . .' Agnel says.

'I won't let you get away with this!' shouts Peter.

'Oh? What will you do? Come out in the front and talk!' taunts Agnel as he pulls Peter towards him. Peter is confused and all his fake bravado melts away.

'Just look at this man's strength! Show it to your wife!' Agnel declares as everybody laughs loudly at Peter.

Peter gulps down another drink, his head inflamed.

The train blows its whistle as it slows down and Peter cycles into the station. As Theresa gets down, Peter looks sharply at the compartment and spots the same young man, sitting by the window. As she sits on the bicycle, Peter senses that Theresa is exceptionally happy this evening. He gets even angrier.

'Pedro, I was so scared this morning. If he had not caught me . . .' Theresa tells Peter as they ride back.

Theresa cannot see Peter's face as she is sitting in front. She would have been surprised at the pulsing vein and bloodshot eyes. They both get down when the cycle reaches the house.

'Pedro, let's leave earlier tomorrow. Otherwise what happened today—'

Peter raises his hand and before Theresa can react, both her cheeks have gone red with the resounding slaps. She screams and her mother-in-law sits quietly, as usual, and watches the scene. Peter continues to hit and punch her relentlessly—on her back, stomach, hands, legs and cheeks.

Translated from the Konkani by Sacheen Pai Raiker

These Are My Children

Damodar Mauzo

Having finished watering the coconut trees named after Angela and Anthony, Rosalina took the hosepipe and stood before Abel. This young sapling was maturing into adulthood and was about to bear fruit. Tiny nuts could be seen clustered at the base of the crown.

The tinkle of a cycle bell outside the fence interrupted Rosalina. She hurried to the gate, leaving the water running out at Abel's roots.

'Rosalinmai, it's nearly noon and you've not finished watering the plants?' Vassu, the postman, entered through the gate, leaving his cycle to rest on the side-stand.

'You're right, son. I got delayed because I spent a sleepless night. I only dozed off at dawn and when I awoke it was bright and sunny outside.'

Even before Vassu handed over the letter, she knew that it was Anthony's. Thank God. She had been looking forward to it.

Rosalina was terribly upset ever since she had

received the land acquisition notice.

'I'm so thirsty, could you give me a glass of water?' Vassu asked, fanning himself with a bunch of letters.

'Of course! Come and sit in the veranda.' Rosalina went in to fetch water, muttering, 'No wonder you're thirsty. It's so hot and humid today.'

I wonder what he's written, thought Rosalina as she filled the glass. Must've received my letter. Has he decided to come, or has he written to tell me that he can't make it? She was anxious to read the letter, but her eyesight was growing weak and even if she managed to read, she found it difficult to understand some of the English words. As long as Diniz was around, she had not needed anybody's help. Two years ago, her husband had died of a sudden heart attack, and now she was forced to rely on others to read her letters.

As she came out with the tumbler of water, it struck her. Why not ask the postman to read the letter? Joaquim, her neighbour, would return home only in the evening, by which time her anxiety would have grown unbearably—so why not?

'Here, baba. Here's your water.' Handing him the tumbler, Rosalina asked, 'You have the time . . . do me a favour, son?'

'Fine. What's the problem?'

'Would you read this letter and tell me what it says?'

'Of course! Give it to me. No secrets, I hope!' he joked, as he slit the letter open.

Of late, Anthony had started typing his letters to make it easy for his mother to read them. But since Diniz's death, she was a broken woman. She'd lost her self-confidence. It took her a long time to read a letter and she still had to take it to Joaquim for confirmation.

Going through the letter, Vassu told her, 'It's from Anthony. He writes that at the end of the month he plans to come home with his wife and children. He says that Abel has written to him. He's engaged to an Australian girl and both Anthony and Angela would be going to Australia from Kuwait and Bahrain for the wedding in December. Anthony says he'll give you all the other details when he comes. Shall I read out the letter?'

Rosalina, her mind wandering, and finding it difficult to take in all the news, came back to the present. 'Uh, it's okay. Thank you, son. God bless you.'

Vassu went his way.

Rosalina slumped into the veranda seat.

So that's that. My last bird too is building his own nest. Abel went to Australia for a job. Now he'll be married there. He'll settle down there. Perhaps he'll visit Goa with his family. Perhaps he won't. No! He will come! Hadn't all three of them come home when Diniz died? They will surely come when their mother dies.

'Are you in, Rosalinmai?' someone called from outside. 'Your pipe is still running.' Shaking off her thoughts, Rosalina rushed out and turned off the tap. Disconnecting the hose, she rolled it and hung it up. She entered the house mechanically.

The rice water was bubbling on the fire. But Rosalina had lost her appetite. She decided to let the rice boil on and have it as canji. That saved her the trouble of making curry. All she needed now was a piece of pickled mango to go with the canji. After Diniz's death, she made curry only occasionally. And since that accursed land acquisition notice arrived some days ago, hunger too had deserted her.

When Diniz died, all the children had rushed home—Angela from Bahrain, Anthony from Kuwait, and Abel, though he couldn't make it in time for the funeral, had come from Australia.

Angela had stayed on till the Month's Mind. But both the boys had to return to work. Nevertheless they had stayed on for two whole weeks.

Before going back, Anthony had remarked, 'Have you heard, Mai, a new railway line will be passing by our house? It'll be great then—board the train here in the morning and by evening you're in Bombay!'

Angela had found the thought amusing—that Abel or Anthony would trade their flight for a train ride just because the line passed by their house! She'd even teased them about it. Nobody had then even imagined that this demon of a railway would intrude right into their own fence.

When the clerk from the land acquisition office came to serve the notice, Rosalina hesitated. As long as Diniz was around, she did not have to take any decisions. When the notice came, she felt that at least one of her children ought to have been with her. Seeing her hesitate, the clerk reassured her, 'Lots of people have been served with these notices. Why are you so worried? Yours is only a small strip. Many others have to give up large areas.'

'But . . . what, what will they do with this land?' Rosalina was confused.

'It's their system. Land is simply acquired on both sides of the proposed railway line. Why are you bothered? Just sign here.'

Hesitantly, Rosalina had signed. She knew nothing then. The coin dropped into place when Joaquim casually mentioned to her, 'It seems part of your fence and some trees are going to be cut.'

'Which part, baba? The official told me that the land was simply acquired on both sides of the line and now you're telling me that my fence and trees are to be cut!'

'Once the land is acquired, they are free to do anything with it. Can you stop them?' Joaquim said.

'Do you know exactly which part of my fence and which trees are going to be cut?' she asked apprehensively.

'The part adjoining our land. Twenty of our coconut trees, that mango tree, a banyan tree, and our cowshed too. Your front fence, along with the gate, those coconut trees and all the bougainvillea and other bushes . . .' rattled off Joaquim matter-of-factly.

But Rosalina's dazed mind was in no state to take in any more.

That day was a long nightmare. She tossed and turned the whole night long, sleep evading her.

All the three saplings planted in the names of her children had grown into healthy coconut trees. And all the maternal love that could not reach her children far away across the seas was lavished on these three trees. They were not just like her children. They were her very own Angela, Anthony and Abel.

Diniz used to tell her, 'Don't shower so much love on those trees, dear. After all, they're only trees. If tomorrow in a storm one of them falls down it'll only break your heart.'

Rosalina would get angry at this. 'Why should the tree fall? If it falls, may it fall on me! If any of them breaks, may I break with it!'

Sixteen years ago, her eldest child, Angela, had returned from school excitedly brandishing a coconut sapling.

'Mai, our local MLA was distributing coconut saplings. I too got one! Let's plant it in our yard.'

Diniz was home on holiday from Kuwait. It was then that Rosalina had told her husband, 'Let's plant this sapling. Soon Angela will grow up, get married and go to her husband's house. The sapling will always remind us of her.' Diniz had obligingly planted the sapling with his own hands. And, as it turned out, Angela was married even before the sapling started bearing fruit.

After landing a promising job in an American company, Diniz had sent a visa for Anthony while he was still in college. It was all too soon for Rosalina. Though Abel, who was still in school, would be with her, she would miss Anthony a lot. Not merely because he was her first son, or because he would support her in her old age: Anthony had taken after his father; he looked a lot like him and was as dependable.

Before Anthony left, Rosalina said to him, 'Anthony, my son, when you go, there will be a void in my life. I will miss you, but for the sake of your future I won't stop you. But do one thing. Get me a coconut sapling. I will nurture it. It will remind me of you.'

Anthony made a special trip to a Benaulim nursery and brought a coconut sapling. She got it planted before he left. Today that sapling had turned into a robust yielding tree. Veritably Anthony!

The year that Diniz returned on TR from Kuwait, Abel got a lucrative job in an Australian company to work on a farm near Sydney.

The coincidence of Diniz returning to Goa for good and Abel's departure for distant Australia evoked mixed feelings in Rosalina. As the day of departure drew closer, Abel on his own fetched a coconut sapling and planted it by the side of Anthony's. Abel's hitherto unsuspected concern for his mother touched Rosalina deeply.

Rosalina was content with her husband's protective presence at this old age. But she yearned for her three children. When Diniz went on his customary evening stroll, Rosalina, left alone, would be deluged by memories of her children. She would then go to the well and draw a dozen pitchers of water and empty them at the feet of Angela, Anthony and Abel.

And now these trees nurtured like my own children are to be cut? What then do I live for, she thought, bewildered and angry. After that sleepless night spent tossing and turning, she had got out of bed early and gone to Joaquim's house.

'Joaquim, are you sure that my coconut trees are to be cut?'

'That's what I hear. We've been asked to collect the compensation money. They're not taking it free. The compensation is quite good, it seems.'

Rosalina became highly perturbed.

'I don't want their money! What the hell do they know! How dare they put a price on my trees! Damn them! May they roast in hell!' Cursing them to perdition, she returned home.

Most people collected their compensation money

while a few, holding out for a better rate, received it under protest. Even Joaquim's father collected his amount. But not Rosalina. She did not go. But she did do one thing. She wrote to Anthony to come home urgently. She wasn't sure that he'd come. Of late, her children's eagerness to return to Goa had waned. Angela was involved with her own family. And Anthony was drifting away. Earlier, he would return home every two years, but ever since he'd fallen in love and married seven years ago, his visits home had become less frequent. He had met his wife in Kuwait, where she too was working. Since her entire family was in Bombay, the wedding was held there. Diniz could not get leave to come, but Anthony had taken his mother to Bombay for the marriage. His next visit home was three years later, with his wife and son. After that, he'd come for his father's funeral—this time with the addition of a baby girl. His two kids and wife kept him busy.

Now that she'd received his letter, Rosalina was sure that he was coming. She felt a sense of relief at the very thought of it. Anthony was like his father—very determined. Once home, he would take care of everything.

Despite such reassurances, she still felt uneasy and restless. She would then get up early and fix the hose to the tap. And treat Angela, Anthony and Abel with even greater affection. Ever since Diniz had brought her the hose on the day they got the PWD connection, Rosalina's burden of watering had become much lighter.

The solitude that her husband's death imposed on her suffocated her. There was no one to talk or open her heart to. She would then sit, running hose in hand,

and talk to her children.

'Remember, Angela, the lavish wedding reception your father threw for you—the drinks flowed just like this water!

'Anthony, my dear, just because you're in a foreign country you should not forget your home. Remember, your father built this house with the sweat of his brow for you, his children. Love your wife and children, but never forget your mother, my son!

'And Abel, my boy! Don't think that I love you less. As my youngest child, you ought to have been dearest to me. And you are. But . . . you know I tend to lean on Anthony, and you know why—he's so much like your father. That's all. But you are equally dear to me!'

Even after baring her heart thus, the hose invariably tended to sprinkle an extra dose of water on Anthony.

Abel's letter followed one week after Anthony's. He gave details of his fiancée and asked if Rosalina would come for the wedding.

Rosalina sighed deeply. Abel would some day visit Goa as a tourist with his family. She could visualize it:

This is the Basilica of Bom Jesus.

This is the famous Calangute beach.

Here is Dona Paula.

And this is my mother.

That is how I'll be introduced to his wife and children.

He'll take some photographs and take them back with him for his album . . . That day she sobbed at the trunk of Abel and blabbered on for hours, pouring out all her apprehensions.

Almost a month had gone by since Anthony's letter. He was already in Bombay and someone brought news that he'd be home next week.

Rosalina made mackerel parra, because Anthony loved this fish pickle. She arranged to get jackfruit from his favourite tree. The fisherwoman was instructed to bring the best available catch.

That morning as she was busy cleaning the house in preparation for her son's impending arrival, the neighbouring children called out to her excitedly, 'Mai, Mai, come out. They've come to cut your trees!'

She was momentarily stunned. She felt as if somebody had aimed an axe at her head. The next moment, she rushed out. Four labourers were waiting at the fence—axes ready.

As she reached the gate, one of the two officials peering into their files enquired, 'Shrimati Rosalina Fernandes—is that you?'

Rosalina nodded.

'We have to remove the front side of your fence. Those bushes and these three coconut trees will also be cut. It seems you haven't yet collected . . .'

'No!' Rosalina was trembling with fury. 'You can't cut these coconut trees. They are mine. You dare not touch them!'

'Listen, ma'am, we are government servants. We have our orders. We have to follow them. It's not you alone, several people's trees have to be cleared today. See there, the work has already started. The embankment has to be built here and we have to complete the work today itself. Please don't disrupt our work. Come on men, dismantle the fence from here.'

Cowed down by his authoritative voice, Rosalina pleaded, 'Dismantle the fence, take the land, I don't mind. But don't, for God's sake, please don't cut these trees. I beg of you!' She knelt down before the official.

'Don't worry, bai, your trees are really A Class— you'll get the maximum price for them. You can even claim to rebuild the fence.'

Rosalina once again lost her temper with the officials. 'Mister, aren't you ashamed to put a price on my trees? Would you put a price on your children's heads? Tell me! Would you? I'm warning you! Take your labourers and go back. My son will be here in two days' time. He'll deal with you!'

The official was furious. 'Look here, we have no time to wait for your son. We have to finish this work today. Ours is a time-bound programme. You have no right to stop us!'

Meanwhile, the labourers had dismantled the fence and were standing near the trees. The first tree they chose was Anthony. A feverish chill passed down Rosalina's spine. She shuddered at the sight of the glistening axe.

Suddenly transformed, like an enraged bull she charged at the labourers with surprising force. Caught unawares, both of them lost their balance and fell flat along with their axes.

The next moment she hugged Anthony tightly and shouted at the top of her voice, 'Come on! Raise your axes. Cut me first! Then kill my children!'

The unexpected attack from the old woman confused the labourers. At first they were embarrassed. Then angry. They got up from the ground and tried to drag her from the tree. But Rosalina clung to Anthony tightly. Even the two labourers could not prise her hands from the tree.

A crowd had started to build up. The official was nervous but refused to give in. As he could not use force against the old woman, he adopted a conciliatory tone.

'Ma'am, you're obstructing government work. It's an offence. However, I request you once again, please move away. Let the work proceed.'

But by now Rosalina had found a ferocious resolve. 'No! I won't move! I don't want your money! Don't you dare touch my trees!' she screamed.

Unwilling to give in to her, the official tried another tack. 'Come on, men, leave that tree, cut the other one.'

A labourer moved towards the smaller tree. Immediately Rosalina left Anthony and rushed to Abel's rescue. Before anybody could stop her, she had pushed the labourer down.

The official came running angrily. 'Hey! Hey! You've gone too far! We won't tolerate this any more, I tell you!'

But before he could take another step Rosalina shoved him violently to the ground.

'You're out to kill my children? I'll see who has the guts to touch my trees! I curse your children. May they all die! May you be worm food before you die!'

Fortunately Joaquim's father managed to pull her back in time. Or else Rosalina's kick aimed at the official struggling to get up would surely have landed on his head.

In a terrible rage, the official scooped up his file and the strewn papers, called his labourers and stomped off. 'I'll teach her a lesson!'

The crowd heard him swearing as he passed them.

The sound of a jeep starting and driving off could be heard.

'Rosalinbai, you shouldn't have done that. After all, he's a government official. You have a point but . . .' Joaquim's father, who was trying to pacify her, was cut short by Rosalina. 'So what? The government has a right to kill my children? Please tell them that they can take my land, even take my house. But tell them to spare these trees. These are my children! I need them. Please save them! Save them, please!' She rambled deliriously.

Within half an hour a police van arrived. The official, now accompanied by an inspector and two constables, strutted up to her. Aware of the crowd which had swelled by now, the inspector addressed her in a conciliatory voice.

'Look, you have committed an offence by obstructing and manhandling government officials on duty. However, considering your age and your state of mind, I'll persuade them to withdraw their complaint against you.' Sensing that the crowd was finding his words reasonable, he moved towards her. 'But promise me that you will not obstruct them. Let them carry on their work.'

Rosalina realized that she was cornered. This would be the last stand. Give in now and everything was lost.

In a frenzy she rushed to Anthony, embraced it tightly and shouted, 'No! I won't let you cut my trees. Cut me first, then cut my children!'

Realizing that her frenzied outburst could possibly lead to an ugly commotion, the inspector promptly signalled to the constables. The three policemen prised away her hands from the tree. Lifting her bodily, they carried her to the van.

Joaquim's father, along with some elders, tried to

plead with the inspector. But ignoring them, the police took Rosalina away.

That fateful day, all the three—Angela, Anthony, and Abel in his first flush of inflorescence—were felled.

The District Collector's office was jammed by a crowd of fifty-odd villagers along with the headman, all seeking Rosalina's release. She was let out around noon and taken home.

Despite the painful awareness of the fate of her trees, at the stark sight of the fallen, broken trunks, Rosalina blacked out.

With the efforts of neighbours and doctors, she regained consciousness only on the third day.

That day she received a letter from Anthony. It read:

'Dear Mai,

I've been stuck in Bombay for the last week. I just couldn't make it to Goa, though I wanted to come and see you. I'm going back to Kuwait. I've received a telex from my office and have to rush back. I'll try to come next year. Meanwhile, don't fret yourself over the land acquisition and those trees. I'll send you all the money you need. Please take care of yourself.

Your loving son, Anthony.'

With a sinking heart, she shut her eyes, praying for them to remain closed eternally.

Translated from the Konkani by Xavier Cota

What the Flower Foretold

Uday Bhembre

The musicians had just received the signal to start playing. The attendant moved around, lighting the wicks in the oil lamps and in the chandeliers in the courtyard, bathing the whole place in a mild amber glow. Outside, daylight was waning and dusk crept forward, setting tiny oil lamps flickering beside tulsi plants in courtyards all over the village.

Dasa Bhat sat before the silver lingam to the left of the square, worshipping it with tumbey flowers. His fair skin gleamed golden in the lamplight, set off to perfection by the purple silk dhoti he wore. A wet towel was bunched over his left shoulder and his eyes were trained on the work at hand. Suddenly he'd mutter aloud as though he were talking to some invisible deity. When the tinkle of bangles fell upon his ears, he'd glance out momentarily at the womenfolk making their sacred rounds of the shrine, but his eyes always moved back at once, for this was a special puja—it was being performed on behalf of Appu Shenoy.

Appu Shenoy paced the narrow corridor that surrounded the sanctum sanctorum, muttering holy verses, his head bowed in prayer. He'd been sitting beside Dasa Bhat all this while, his eyes fixed on the flowers adorning the lingam, and it was only now, after his leg had turned numb under his weight, that he had begun to pace up and down. This was always the case when he arranged for a puja to find out what God had in store for him. And each time he passed the lingam his eyes were drawn inexorably to the flowers that were perched so precariously on it.

In the early days, whenever a puja was arranged, Appu Shenoy would sit in silence, pleading with God to show him a favourable sign. But days passed and nothing happened. Perhaps it was his God who gave him the strength to endure. He had decided that he would not stop his obeisance until God granted his prayer, and it was this decision that helped him get through the doubt and uncertainty in the days ahead. So it was with a peaceful countenance that Appu Shenoy paced up and down till his feet grew tired. But his mind was still strong. He was angry with his God but this anger was almost obliterated by the profound love he bore, by the deep faith and reverence that permeated his being.

Throwing the free end of his dhoti over his shoulder, he paced up and down when suddenly Dasa Bhat's words—'Shenoy, a flower has fallen . . .'—fell upon his ears. For a second he didn't believe what he had heard, his ears had played such tricks on him many times. So he walked a couple of paces, and again Dasa Bhat's voice called out to him: 'Shenoy, a flower has fallen. Come quick!'

The tremor in that voice and the piercing clarity of those words touched Appu Shenoy's heart and he rushed forward as though it was God himself who was calling out to him. His eyes went to the lingam and a picture of Lord Damodar floated before his eyes. His body felt heavy, a curious weight seemed to have settled on his soul. And just as summer days turn hottest just before the rains, the confusion in Appu Shenoy's mind reached it's peak.

'God has bestowed the choicest flower on you. The fifth from the arch behind the lingam, and the third from the image itself.'

Dasa Bhat's words brought Appu Shenoy back to his senses. He cast a grateful eye over the paraphernalia of worship, wondering if it was true that God himself had granted him this flower as a token of blessing. But he collected himself in a moment, remembering that Raghu Hegde had spoilt the effect of his puja by expressing a similar doubt one day. This wavering of his complete faith in his God filled him with remorse, and striking his cheeks as a mark of apology, he prostrated himself before the image of Nandi that stood in the temple square.

'Shenoy, get up. Let me finish the rituals and bring the puja to a close,' Dasa Bhat called out to him and Appu Shenoy rose, accepting the flower that was held out to him. He touched it reverentially to his forehead and prostrated himself on the ground once again. Then suddenly he remembered his wife. She never failed to sit in the passageway beside the square whenever a puja was being performed on her husband's behalf. Thus she always heard what the priest said and it was never necessary for Appu Shenoy to relive the agony by having to tell her that God had not granted his prayer by dropping forth a blossom yet again. But she was nowhere to be seen today.

Appu Shenoy crossed the square and entered the raised mandap. There were a few people seated on the veranda adjoining the courtyard of the temple, but he didn't pay any attention to them. Calling out to the clerk, he told him of the divine blessing, and the relief and satisfaction that appeared on his face seemed to be mirrored by the happiness which the clerk expressed. Appu Shenoy instructed the man to pay the priest whatever he demanded. He also told him to see that coconuts, food and drinks were offered to the lesser spirits whose shrines stood near by.

He wanted to shout and tell the world that God had blessed him with the choicest flower, but the good news had to be conveyed to his wife first of all. So he hurried past the rooms that had been built for worshippers in the temple annexe and made his way to his own quarters.

Champavathi had just returned after a dip in the temple pond, so he did not quite see the emotions on her face when he gave her the good news. However, he heard her muttering something about God's grace as she hastily lit the oil lamp that stood before the photograph of Lord Damodar in its niche. Lighting some joss sticks, she shut her eyes and muttered incoherent prayers as Appu Shenoy also folded his palms in gratitude. Then, running an affectionate hand over her hair, he gave her the treasured blossom which she carefully placed in the silver box that stood before Lord Damodar's picture.

'Bring some sugar,' he said.

'What for?'

'Go and bring some.'

Champavathi returned with a tin of sugar, out of which Appu Shenoy took a small pinch. 'Open your mouth,' he said.

'Now?' she exclaimed, shyly. Appu Shenoy barely heard her as he dropped a few grains into his own mouth as well and set off once again.

'All right. So Appu Shenoy's puja has borne fruit. But all that about the extremely favourable signs shown by the position of the flowers that fell, that can't be true,' someone remarked.

'So God took pity on him after three-and-a-half years,' someone else said. By the time Appu Shenoy got to the veranda, the good news had travelled all over the temple complex and the clerk, the temple accountant, Vasu Bhat, and all the others who had gathered there asked him to treat them to tea. Some of them praised his constancy and his devotion. Others declared that hard work always brought rewards, while yet others sang of Dambaab's glory.

The sense of heaviness that had weighed Appu Shenoy down was all but gone and his mind and body felt unshackled and free. The hollow feeling that had grown within him over the last three-and-a-half years vanished as a sense of gratitude overwhelmed him. Hope danced before his eyes and every time he caught a glimpse of the deity Dambaab, his palms joined in reverence.

The demand for tea was nothing new, really, but today it took on a new significance, for Appu Shenoy had something to celebrate at last.

'Bhiku, tell Lakshman to send some tea, and let him keep sending as much as is required. Tell him I said so.'

Appu Shenoy said the words as he always did, while the temple reverberated with talk of Dambaab's graciousness, of flowers and portents, and of course of Appu Shenoy.

Appu Shenoy belonged to a wealthy family that ran a grocery shop in Kumta. He was an only son and when his parents passed away not too long after his wedding, the responsibility of keeping the family line going fell upon his young shoulders. But this was not to be. Though he knocked at the doors and filled the purses of innumerable village doctors and priests and sorcerers, his wife did not conceive. No cradle rocked in his house, and the creeper of new life did not take root at the foot of his family tree.

Appu Shenoy's dry and colourless married life continued thus for twelve long years before his wife took ill with fever and died. Appu was shattered. He had looked after her every need during the prolonged illness, and even as she approached the end of her life, it was she who had given him emotional support.

With these last few threads of sustenance severed, Appu Shenoy's boat was cast adrift. What if this boat capsized and sank as well?

This was what haunted Appu Shenoy all the time. His body would also be reduced to dust some day. Who would keep the Shenoy name alive, then? And who would offer oblations to the ancestors in the Shenoy household? The question gnawed at him. The desire for a happy family life surrounded by a wife and children was overshadowed by the overwhelming need to keep the family line going—this was the reason why man journeyed through life, he felt.

Thus it was that with his hair turning quite grey, the question of a second marriage threw his mind into turmoil. But then one day he quelled all his doubts and decided that a cradle must rock in the ancestral Shenoy home. He agreed once again to marriage.

Champavathi was dusky and attractive enough, and came from a family that was quite poor. Caught up in the full flush of youth, she no doubt resented the twenty-two years that separated their ages, but being docile and peaceful by nature, she gave Appu Shenoy no cause for complaint. On his part Appu Shenoy did everything he could to keep her happy, adorning her wrist with gold bangles, bringing fresh flowers for her hair and ensuring that she did not have to wait months on end for a festival to arrive before she could wear new clothes.

Two years passed in this fashion and Appu Shenoy was once again consumed with fear. The slivers of hope had long since died and he could only see darkness before him. Fed up with the prescriptions of the village doctors and weary of the fasts and religious ceremonies they had performed, his spirit wept within him as he watched Champavathi shower her love on the children in the neighbourhood. What is this, a curse of some sort? he wondered night and day.

'Go to the temple of your family deity, go and serve your God. Dambaab's grace is all powerful. He made Devray's mad grandson totally well again,' Narsu Shanbhag advised him.

Appu Shenoy's dejected spirits lifted considerably to think that God would grant his desire if he stayed in the temple and offered his service. He told Champavathi what Narsu had said.

'What does it matter whether we go to the temple to serve Him, or whether we stay at home and worship Him in our hearts. Whatever He has willed will come to pass. But you certainly need a change, you need some peace of mind. How many years is it since we set foot outside this house! Let us go and stay in the temple for a couple of months,' Champavathi said.

Appu Shenoy felt as though a cool, fresh breeze had blown over his mind and body as he prepared to leave that house which seemed darkened by despair, that neighbourhood where everyone glanced at them with pity, and that shop filled with dust and cobwebs through neglect. Handing over charge of the shop to a distant cousin, Appu Shenoy and Champavathi set out with renewed hope in their hearts.

Immersing himself totally in the rituals and activities of the temple, Appu Shenoy forgot for a while the sorrow that pressed against him like a barb. He placed all his cares and worries at Dambaab's feet and became one with the other pilgrims.

Champavathi's clothes and ornaments marked her out as a wealthy woman, so at first the poor villagers remained at arm's length. However, she did not let this gulf remain for long and did everything possible to become one of them. A woman of few words, and with a peaceable temperament, Champavathi succeeded in her efforts to a large extent, but the fact that she had no children automatically shut her out from much of the conversation and activity. So though she was accepted as one of them, she always remained a little apart.

Bathing twice a day in the temple pond, making

his sacred rounds of the shrines, opening out his heart to the Lord as he stood in the square accepting his offerings—these rituals became part of Appu Shenoy's life. At other times he'd sit in the veranda with the other men, sharing their joys and sorrows. Stories of how mad persons had turned sane once again or how the bedridden had become well, and of how Kushta Prabhu, heeding the words of the divine oracle, had struck a mine yielding high grade ore, only served to strengthen his faith. Dambaab will not send anyone back empty-handed, he reasoned to himself, but when will he act? he often wondered.

Janardhan Bhat conducted the various pujas in the temple. His grave face as he went about the rituals made one feel that he was indeed talking to the Lord. Appu Shenoy had great faith in him and believed he would certainly interpret what God had in mind for them. One day he received a flower as an offering. This was an indication that God would be merciful to him, he was told. Another time the flower indicated that Dambaab would watch over him and his wife. But the flower that would signify that their heart's desire would be attained simply did not come. The two months they had planned on stretched to five but no such flower came their way.

Finally Appu Shenoy decided that it was time to return home and Janardhan Bhat conducted a puja to seek Dambaab's blessings in this regard. But the flower that would indicate that Dambaab wanted them to go did not fall to their lot. God wants you to stay on and serve him for some more time, they were told. So Appu Shenoy stayed on. God doesn't want us to return empty-handed, he consoled himself, deciding to stay on till he received some other sign of divine will.

The leaves of the pipal fell to the ground and fresh ones came up in their place as Appu Shenoy served his God with selfless devotion. When he scraped off the lumps of candlewax that had melted on the ceremonial palanquin for distribution amongst the children, he became like a child again. When he sat on the veranda playing cards with the other adults, he was like one of them. Ladle in hand, he was sure to be seen serving the seated multitudes at any temple feast, or if it were Diwali he would be soaked in oil as he went about filling and lighting the lamps. At Dussehra he would help decorate the ceremonial staff surmounted by the image of the Lord; on Shivratri he would busy himself with the chariot. And every Monday, of course, he would lend a shoulder to the deity's palanquin. So even if Lord Damodar himself were to ever appear before Appu Shenoy, he would not be able to accuse him of ever shirking his duty.

During the rainy season that year, the temple pond filled up to its brim and overflowed on to the bank. That was the time when Janardhan Bhat took ill and was confined to his bed and his nephew began to conduct all the rituals connected with the puja. Dasa Bhat was fair and handsome, with light eyes, and though a number of proposals came his way, he was still a bachelor. He didn't speak much but he had a very melodious voice and whenever he sat down to sing and play the harmonium all the womenfolk, perched on the thresholds of their houses, strained to listen to him.

Appu Shenoy arranged for a puja once a week. Dasa Bhat performed it, while he paced to and fro. The flower that signified that his desire would be fulfilled had not fallen to Appu Shenoy's lot during Janardhan Bhat's time. But he hadn't got the Lord's permission to leave either. He'd lost count of the number of coconuts, the amount of food and drink offered to the lesser spirits. Nor could he remember how many rituals he had arranged, how many lamps, how many fasts. Of course, his life had stabilized here and he'd received much honour and respect, but no matter how much he served the Lord, that special, blessed flower still didn't fall his way. Would he receive it from Dasa Bhat's hand? Appu Shenoy paced up and down, pondering over the question.

Champavathi sat in the passageway near the door, her eyes clouded with worry. The bones in her neck showed up prominently as she sat there, like a wilted flower on a broken stem. Much of the money they had brought with them had been spent by now and she had to wear the same sari for more than one festival. Her eyes moved from the square to the puja that was being performed, and from there to Dasa Bhat's fair body, and then deep into his grey eyes. Then again she'd stare at the eyes of the idol, wondering if her desires would ever be granted. And on Mondays, after the palanquin ceremony, she'd accept a braid of sweet-smelling flowers from Dasa Bhat and wear it in her hair for two days—the Lord's offering, blessings from the deity.

The Shigmo festival marking the new harvest passed, Dussehra arrived, then Shigmo arrived again, followed by Dussehra . . .

Ever since he received the blessed flower from

Dasa Bhat, Appu Shenoy seemed to live in a totally different world of hope and joy. His faith had been strengthened and the belief that his family line would continue to flourish brought a new sense of peace. That afternoon as he entered his house after taking a dip in the temple pond, Appu Shenoy heard his wife retching. Throwing his wet towel on a line to dry, he began to rebuke her, 'Haven't I told you not to eat those gooseberries and other sour things? What did you eat now, tamarind?'

'It's not that,' Champavathi protested softly, a new mellowness in her voice, a strange sort of tremor.

'What do you mean, it's not that? This happens every day.' Appu Shenoy's anger was tinged with concern.

Champavathi remained silent but her eyes beckoned him close and he read in them the future that had been promised by the blessed flower. In the shy yet happy look on her face he sensed what was in store for them—the song of the cradle, the light from the family lamp as it burned bright and clear.

Appu Shenoy's mind whirled with joy, and just as a mother clasps an errant child close to her bosom, he showered all the love and affection at his command on Champavathi. He wanted to spread the good news, to tell everyone about Dambaab's graciousness, to offer sweets to all he met, but Champavathi held him back. Now he had to look after her, keep an eye on what she did, and he forgot the world.

It was only thirteen days since God had blessed him with the flower and already the fruits of his devotion were evident—it didn't take long for the people in the village to get to know of this. But if

Champavathi hadn't held him back that day, he'd have announced it at once, and with a whole lot of fireworks, too. What bliss! What peace! What a lot of new hope!

A whole lot of people drank tea at Lakshman's shop that day. Appu Shenoy paid for it all. Even that brought him satisfaction, it was a matter of pride. That evening as Appu Shenoy did the rounds of the shrine he saw Dasa Bhat leaning against the door. Pressing a piece of granulated sugar into his hand, Shenoy whispered into his ear, 'The flower has spoken . . . She is due . . .'

Dasa Bhat turned his face towards the deity, shutting his eyes and muttering some prayers. Appu Shenoy did the same, then calling heaven's choicest blessings down on Dasa Bhat, he moved away to the mandap. He seemed to see peace and happiness reflected in everyone's eyes, where did he have the time to read what was written in the grey depths of Dasa Bhat's eyes?

Appu Shenoy had spent four-and-a-half years at the feet of his Lord but he had never noticed how time had passed. The nine months of Champavathi's pregnancy, however, crept past like ants moving; he felt as though they were nine years, so heavy was the weight of responsibility that rested on him. He had to ensure that she did not go to the pond to take a dip, that she did not eat a gooseberry or two. He had to prevent her from sitting up all night to watch the plays that were enacted on full moon nights. He had to reason with her and shelter her like a fragile, much-loved bird.

The lamp of the Shenoy family was in her care, it had been lit by Lord Damodar himself. If it were allowed to go out, Shenoy's world would be besieged by darkness. And then, when nine months had finally passed and Champavathi gave birth to a baby boy, there were fireworks in the village, the likes of which the villagers had never seen before. Everyone spoke of Dambaab's grace as they had never spoken before. More people drank tea at Lakshman's shop that day than ever before.

Appu Shenoy seemed to be touching heaven almost, how could he ever make his gratitude to Dambaab evident? A golden image? A ceremonial one? Dambaab astride a horse? That would be done, he decided . . . Champavathi had plenty of gold ornaments. A Maharudra yagna? That too would be done. A feast for the whole village? Rewards for the priest? A shawl for Dasa Bhat . . . Appu Shenoy's generosity welled out of his deep faith and happiness and even Dambaab must have been overwhelmed.

It was Appu Shenoy's son's cradle ceremony, and he was named Damodar. 'May he grow up to be like Damodar, the Lord,' everyone said, as they partook of the sweets that were on offer all day. Everyone in the neighbourhood got a fresh look at Appu Shenoy's generous nature, and a wave of happiness spread all around. Fate had smiled on the Shenoy household after a very long time . . .

It was the midwife who struck the only discordant note. Appu Shenoy is dark, she observed, and Champavathi is dark too. But the baby is extremely fair, and grey-eyed too, looks like Dasa Bhat, she said. But Dasa Bhat had been missing for the last fifteen days. He'd gone off to Sangli to visit his sister.

Appu Shenoy couldn't wait for him to return. He

was so full of happiness that his feelings seemed to radiate from his eyes, casting a glow on his face. Nothing else could enter his ears and mar his bliss. He was longing to return to his ancestral home, to see the cradle rocking in that house, to hear Damodar's laughter echoing through those rooms, lighting up the house. So Appu Shenoy waited impatiently for Dasa Bhat to return. He wanted to receive the flower which would signify that Dambaab would let him go.

He did not have faith in any of the other priests. It was through Dasa Bhat's hands that Dambaab had delivered the blessed flower and everything he desired had fallen into his lap. The lamp of the Shenoy household was lit, the flower of farewell would also have to come through Dasa Bhat's hands. Dambaab would surely grant that soon; Dasa Bhat was so very good at his work.

Translated from the Konkani by Vidya Pai

Lord Vatobha and
Aunt Radha

Naresh Kavadi

I don't deny it. My grandfather left the green coastline of the Konkan and settled down in the green pastures of a village named Hivre in the hinterland. They say that he left the Konkan to seek his fortune. Well, so they say, but it is difficult to understand why God should create some people for the Konkan and leave their fortunes scattered all over the interior. Anyway, those wily fellows always seem to know exactly where their fortunes lie. My grandfather was no fool.

You could say that the wheel had turned full circle. My grandfather's grandfather had once left the hinterland and come to the Konkan to seek his fortune. Or misfortune, if you like. Why do I say that? Well, the story goes that my grandfather's grandfather used to be called over to a wealthy man's house to conduct the occasional puja. As it happened, one day he returned from the puja with one of the most beautiful slave girls of the house. There were so many slave girls there!

One missing beauty—would the wealthy man even notice that she had gone? As it happened, the wealthy man did notice. He was known for his sharp sense of observation. Someone must have ratted on him! He must have been quite sure of himself, my grandfather's grandfather. My guess is that he knew the wealthy merchant would notice the absence of the girl, but he must have thought that there would not be such a rumpus over a mere slave girl.

But the man had not gathered so much wealth by being overly generous. The fellow hit the ceiling. 'Lord, husband, why must you take such a trifle to heart? Don't I know the girl? Such a libertine! Our pujari's such a handsome man, and a gentle soul too. She must have held him in her clutches. Why, we could look for another beauty for our Lord now, could we not?' That consolation from the wealthy man's only wife (so they say). But there was no consoling the owner of the missing property. He dispatched a constable to arrest my grandfather's grandfather. Before the constable could get there, however, my grandfather's grandfather had abandoned the Konkan with the slave girl and the wife and kids in tow. Now it is not for me to vouch for what the wealthy merchant did next. Did he replace the missing girl with another or did he make do with one slave girl less? I cannot say.

Where exactly my grandfather's fortunes lay I do not know, but I do believe kidnapping beautiful slave girls from wealthy men's backyards was not on his mind. For, when my grandfather was ready for such swashbuckling deeds there were no wealthy men's backyards left. Actually, the backyards were there, but the wealth had gone—the one in question into the hands of the Topikar family, as a matter of fact. No question, then, of a backyard filled with beautiful slave girls. Why then this pull towards the interior? My grandfather ran a small household. The red triangle, that symbol of a planned family in modern India, had not been conceived of yet, but my grandfather was a man of principle. A daughter and a son. *Buss.* That was it. He might have gone on a bit, perhaps, but my grandmother let him down. A wife dying young was not unheard of in those days. Neither was marrying again and producing more children. But Grandfather had resisted. He would have resisted less had it been difficult to get a decent meal in the house and had it not been for the fair-skinned beautiful widow next door who did the cooking. But poor Grandfather! The beautiful cook also died on him. God should grant such obliging beauties a longer life, don't you think?

Grandfather had treated her right. As soon as he learnt that she was unwell, he saw to it that she got her medicines. The best of drugs, and in the right doses too. In fact, he had first-hand knowledge of how efficacious these drugs were. He had seen them work on a number of young beautiful widows. But, alas, the beautiful cook succumbed to the treatment. I suppose it was this unfortunate incident that prompted Grandfather to leave for the interior to seek his fortune.

No sooner had Grandfather stepped on that soil than he saw a pencil of light. Now this is where the old village kulkarni comes into the story. Old Kulkarni had a palatial mansion, and in matters of conducting personal businesses with efficiency, he could put Grandfather in the shade. Old Kulkarni had a daughter, his only child. She must have been of marriageable age. Certainly the marrying kind. The father and daughter decided that it would be a good thing to have my grandfather and his children stay with them.

It did not take long for Grandfather and old Kulkarni to become the best of friends. They, however, were not content to remain friends for long. Old Kulkarni decided to give his daughter's hand in marriage to Grandfather's son. (That's where my father comes into the story.) Marrying his son off to old Kulkarni's daughter was a matter of no great importance from Grandfather's point of view, but old Kulkarni did not leave the matter alone. He had found the ideal solution for Grandfather's daughter (my aunt) as well. Her wedding would also have to be thought of, right? Old Kulkarni decided that he would make the best offer to the young girl—himself. You will agree that if old Kulkarni had a daughter she would have slipped into the role of playing my grandmother in the story. That would have settled the score at both ends. But no, there is no grandmother in the story.

Old Kulkarni marrying my grandfather's young daughter did not go unnoticed in the village. You know how it is. People will talk. Of course, only the ones who have nothing better to do. As far as I recall, this was the time when no one had heard of our very own Govindrao, I mean Govind Ballal, and his controversial play *Sharda*. Even if he had already written it, I don't think it had seen the light of day yet. And even if it had, at least both my grandfathers had certainly not seen the play. Even if they had seen it, they had certainly not liked it . . . Whatever the truth, here was a man who had come all the way from the Konkan to the interior to seek his fortune. He must have known what he was doing, don't you think?

These people who gossip, who have nothing better to do, surprise me sometimes. Grandfather Kulkarni must have had some reason for marrying. He must have given it considerable thought. After all, only the young marry without giving the matter much thought. This was the action of a wise man, mature in years and experience. He might also have advised Grandfather to do the same. I should not be surprised if Grandfather Kulkarni had actually started the ball rolling in that direction. If he had enough time, that is.

Poor Grandfather Kulkarni left for his heavenly abode less than a year after marrying my young aunt. Well, he was old. Bound to die. Aunt became a widow. A childless widow at that. It wasn't on account of his age that she was childless. No. Haven't you heard of young wives bearing children even if the husband is past his prime? She just had not quite become a woman yet. (In fact, she started to become one a year after he died.) How could she have borne him children?

I was born the year Grandfather Kulkarni died. A distant cousin of my mother's had turned up from somewhere to assist my mother with the baby. She, like my widowed aunt, was also in white. She simply stayed on. I used to call her Aunt Radha. Grandfather adored her. Mother hated her. Mother hated everyone anyway. She was not the sort to give her children the occasional hug either. When I felt like it, I would cuddle up to Aunt Radha or my other aunt and sleep. Both my aunts loved me. They would even fight over whom I should spend the night with! I would settle the quarrel by snuggling up between their warm bodies.

When I was thought of as being of age, I was sent off to a gurukul to learn the art of official begging.

Guruji loved me. He parted with his most treasured secrets just for me and I became his favourite pupil. I often took his place at the pujas he did not feel like attending. That pleased him the most. When I did not feel like attending school, he would come over to the house. He enjoyed his chats with Aunt and Aunt Radha.

Now Aunt Radha simply took off one morning and went to live at the temple of Lord Vatoshwara at Pimpri. The Lord is also called Vatobha out of affection. What an active god he was! Some gods are like that. (Some seem to be asleep at all times. Incomprehensible, isn't it?) No doubt about it. A real livewire, this god. Would Aunt Radha have been swept off her feet like that otherwise? It was the year Grandfather died, but what had that got to do with it? Had Aunt Radha been left with a choice? She had to go. Lord Vatobha's wish was her command. I was miserable. Heartbroken, really. I wept openly, without fear or shame. Mother was not too pleased with me. She snapped at me, 'Damn you, what's come over you to cry like that? It is a good thing she's gone or she would have been your ruin as well.'

Soon after Aunt Radha left, a gentleman named Nagorao came to live with us. They told me that he was a sort of brother-in-law to Aunt. Distant, of course. I hated him. Not because he always glared at Father and Mother when he spoke to them. Not because Aunt stopped taking me close to her breast at bedtime . . . Aunt Radha had left for Lord Vatobha's temple; perhaps if I prayed hard enough, Lord Vatobha would make this horrid man go away. Believe it or not, the Lord heard my prayers. Mother must have prayed to Lord

Vatobha just as hard, for one day, after a fight, Nagorao left. Sadly, Aunt also left the house that day. I did not understand a thing. When I asked Mother, she screamed, 'Go to your Father and ask him where she is. She has not left her address with me, you hear that?'

I would have asked him if I could. Even when I was little, he seemed always to be in a trance. They say he had divine powers. I never saw any but that is what they said. I only saw him nodding on the balcony all day and then sometimes, when he was in the mood, he would say something. Who could understand that gibberish anyway? I could not, that's for sure. The simple village folk said they could. They wouldn't flock to see him, now would they, if they didn't understand? And fall at his feet even? I never saw Father do a stitch of work. He must have, at some point of time. But what? With his epilepsy, he could not have been of much use.

Mother was always quarrelling with Father. She must have cared for him too, for she always saw to it that he got his medicines. Not that the medicines helped him at all. Unknown to us all, it was Lord Vatobha who had the answer. One morning, as Father lay in his chair dozing, the Lord came to him in a vision. I heard Father shouting from his chair, 'Coming! Coming! I'm coming!' I got the shock of my life. Then I understood. Just as the Lord had summoned Aunt Radha, he had now sent for Father. After all, if Father wanted to be cured of his epilepsy, Lord Vatobha would demand his dues. It was a summons from the Lord himself. No doubt about it. Father left for Pimpri the next day and I was left alone and defenceless at the mercy of Mother. Praise the Lord!

Must have been a moody sort, this Lord Vatobha. For Father had served him for about a month when he sent him back on home leave. Poor Father! Then again, the Lord would not do without him, so off he went again. Father spent the rest of his life between the temple at Pimpri and his home with us. All Lord Vatobha had to do was call him and off he went. All Lord Vatobha had to do was grant him home leave and in he came. People say this Lord Vatobha had depth. Nothing of the sort! I always knew when Father would be called again. Mother would raise a shindy one night and I knew that Father would make his way back to the temple the following day. I was brave enough to speak my mind one morning and said, 'Mother, why do you quarrel with him? Don't you see that Lord Vatobha comes to his rescue almost at once?' Mother almost attacked me, 'Why do I quarrel with him, the man says! Damn you, you should have been born a woman and then known why I quarrel. Mind your own business!'

I shut up like a clam. Mother clearly did not know what she was talking about. Why on earth would one want to be born a woman to know how to fight? All one had to do was marry one. But I learnt that the hard way.

Not that I married her just to learn that one lesson. Our wedding too was one of Lord Vatobha's arrangements. Grandfather died before I was old enough to marry. Father hardly belonged to this world. And I hadn't dreamt of such a thing as marriage. I feared the very word. Not that our next-door neighbour Gangu or the other girl Godi did not come into my dreams when I was asleep. Well, Aunt Radha and

Aunt too appeared in my dreams. So what? It did not mean that I was ready for marriage, right? Anyway, Lord Vatobha made our Guruji the instrument of his desires. I hadn't dreamt that Guruji's love for me would bear such fruit.

One morning Mother screamed in my ear, 'Damn you, arranged your own wedding without so much as a by-your-leave, eh?'

What was that? I did not understand. I bowed my head and in the most respectful tone asked her, 'I don't understand what you're saying, Mother. Father may have had something to do with it.'

'He must have had something to do with it, the man says! Does he know that he's a married man and that he has a son? He's going to arrange for a match for you, eh? You've been up to something . . .'

One could never argue with Mother. I held my peace. I was certain Lord Vatobha had an explanation. Guruji arrived in the afternoon and confessed that he had personally arranged it all. I was overcome with his love for me. It did occur to me, though, that it might have been nice if someone had asked me if I wanted to be married. But would I have said a flat no if someone had been that nice? Can't vouch for that. It pacified Mother somewhat that I had nothing to do with it at least. The matter did raise a few questions, however. So when Mother wasn't about, I approached Guruji and asked him, 'Guruji, I don't think I'm ready for it.' My Guruji, always so gentle and affectionate. But now his appearance was more like an enraged Sage Jamdagni and he screamed, 'You ass! Twenty years old and don't know if you're ready for it? Planning to remain a bachelor then? That won't do! You will *have* to be married. I have given Gopirao Deshpande my word.'

Given Gopirao Deshpande his word! I nearly blacked out. Gopirao Deshpande had just one daughter who might be of age. I had had a look at her while conducting a Satyanarayan puja once. One does not forget a girl who sits in front of you cross-legged on the floor and slaps the book open so the pages fly all over. I am an understanding man. I would not hold it against her. It is not a crime to be born ugly. Not her fault either that she was born with a handicap. But what had I done to deserve this?

But one must keep one's sense of humour intact under any circumstances. Grandfather had come to the interior to seek his fortune, but what had poor Aunt done to be saddled with a dying man? What was Father's crime? It's all Destiny. That Grandfather should find this tiny village of Hivre out of all places, that Father should be so distracted, that Guruji should belong to this village and to our particular sub-caste . . . Destiny, what else? And one must live out one's Destiny.

I had learnt over the years that self-consolation was the key. I said to myself, 'A beautiful wife only gets you into trouble, she is like an enemy within. Have you not heard Guruji say this in class? You're not exactly a great looker yourself, are you? You're not fair-skinned, handsome, tall and beautiful like Mother. You're more like your Father . . . short, dark and not exactly well proportioned. Everyone fears Mother. People fall at your Father's feet. But until today no man offered you his daughter's hand. Guruji is quite obviously a man of vision. How wonderful to have a wife who is lame! No fears of her ever running away.

Such a wife would remain docile towards you and your Mother. Don't forget! To fall from Guruji's favour would also spell disaster. Lord Vatobha must have a plan.' I was quite pleased with myself. I was now ready for life with my better half. Yes, I would be the lesser half.

Mother seemed to accept things as they were. Father was, as usual, a world unto himself. He would not have noticed had I plastered myself with red oxide instead of the ceremonial turmeric. An auspicious hour was selected and I placed my neck in the noose. I don't know if anyone sent invitations to Aunt and Aunt Radha. Perhaps they were invited, but they did not come. I did not dare ask Mother. She would have been quite happy if people had thought that I had a speech handicap. She did not once lose her temper during the ceremonies. She must have known that she would have all the time in the world once the wedding was over.

Father and I had grown used to the lashings of her tongue. I was a little afraid for the wife. But I had no cause for fear. The wife turned out to be the type who could hold her own. Her tongue was as sharp, even sharper. Perhaps it had been handed down through the generations or perhaps that one leg shorter than the other had something to do with it. She turned out to be sharp-tongued and sharp-witted too. Well, Father being the way he was and Mother being the way she was and things being the way they were, one should have been grateful that the wife was willing to give up home and family for a life with me. I had not realized it, but the wife made things quite clear to both me and Mother. Not that Mother had accepted defeat yet, but she had certainly met her match.

I did try and intervene but the wife had surpassed Mother in every aspect. Mother had denied us her love, but even in her blackest moods she had never denied us a meal. The wife had beaten her to it. Even in the middle of a tantrum, Mother never ventured out of the kitchen if there were visitors with Father. The wife had no such compunctions. In fact, the presence of visitors seemed to egg her on. I can't be certain if I had agreed to the wedding in the hope of replacing Mother's regime with another's. You know that I hadn't given marriage a second thought. Peace in Mother's lifetime was an impossible dream. Now I knew that peace in my lifetime was unthinkable. Must pat Father on the back! Problems concerning his wife and child had never disturbed his peace. What chances did the virago have—he could see everything that went on but he never let it show; he hardly ever said a word. Who knows what went on in that mind?

Then one day he suddenly said something out of the blue: 'I have the secret of the eight superhuman powers. Want it?'

I should have said 'Yes' at once. Instead, I said 'No' without a second thought. I must have known what I was doing, for if having the secret of the eight superhuman powers had made such a zombie out of Father, that secret was of no use to me. Father never brought the subject up again.

One night I decided to head for the Konkan just like Grandfather's grandfather had done. Just like that, on the spur of the moment. When we were alone, I told the wife about my decision. With her razor-sharp tongue, she said, 'Doesn't seem to be a family tradition here to ask the wife's opinion. Looks like a summons from Lord Vatoshwara to me. Then how does anyone else's opinion matter?'

I tried to keep my voice down, 'No such thing as summons. But Mother and you . . .'

The wife interrupted me harshly: 'If not today, you'll receive the summons sooner than you think.'

I held my peace. I told Mother about it with great reluctance. Her happy reaction took me by surprise. Just when I was wondering about it, she said, 'Go to the Konkan in peace, son. I'll take care of your wife.'

I looked first to the left and then to the right. Such a relief to see that the wife was nowhere around. I abandoned my plans for the Konkan with a sigh and went about the business of the day.

It was Father's turn now. That night he lost all power of speech and by morning had embarked on the last journey. He must have known it was coming. Why else would he have wanted to share the secret of the eight superhuman powers with me? Father had not said it in so many words, or I would have been a little more receptive. Praise Lord Vatobha!

Father left and a stranger came into the house. I would never have known but for the quarrel between Mother and the wife. I overheard them quarrel and I held my head between my hands. What else could one do? A quarrel always preceded bad news. What was in store now? Surely Lord Vatobha must have a plan? Perhaps a bachelor has to be kneaded like dough to bring out the right to exercise his husbandly duties? The good Lord couldn't have found another way of doing it.

And what next? Wait around while another

generation was being born? I was not sure I was ready for an attack by reinforcements. Would things have been different if I had taken the secret of the eight superhuman forces from Father? Had they been of any use to him? If they had, he would not have had to rush to Lord Vatobha so often. Father had slept through a whole lifetime and at the end of it, dozed in his armchair to pass the time of the day. Perhaps that was the secret of the eight superhuman powers. Did one's fortunes lie in getting two square meals a day without lifting a finger?

Speaking of two square meals, even this was to be denied to us soon. Guruji, always the harbinger of bad news, brought tidings that Nagorao Kulkarni had made a claim (on behalf of Aunt) on the house and the lands in the court. I had clean forgotten about Nagorao's existence. Quite appropriate that Guruji, the bringer of that gem of a daughter from Gopalrao Deshpande's house to ours, should bring us this sort of news. I was in a mess. Hardly in a position to face Mother and the wife. Hardly capable of fighting it out in the courts. Mother made no bones about it. With the wife standing right there, she turned towards Guruji and said, 'This nincompoop won't be able to do anything. You need brains to hold on even to an estate that's been handed to you on a platter. You can't doze your way through a crisis. What fresh spark is going to save us now?' Mother looked towards the armchair. Well, just as well that Father wasn't in that chair now. The wife glared in my direction. I did not dare meet her eyes. Mother did not let the matter rest.

'Here! Take these papers and throw them on that Naga's face. This is my father's property.'

For a minute I thought that Guruji might refuse to get involved and my heart sank, but then he was only pretending. He made a great show of scepticism at the scheme succeeding and then took the papers. The baton had been passed. For me, it was the death knell.

I realized that there was no other road for me to take except the one that led to Lord Vatobha's. If I were to loll in Father's armchair, would Lord Vatobha take kindly towards me? From then onwards, I took to dozing in Father's armchair. Wonder of wonders, it happened. Lord Vatobha appeared before me! He came to me in the form of Aunt Radha. What god worth his salt would not display his miraculous powers? It was like a slap in my face. At first I did not understand and then I knew what I had to do. Lord Vatobha had sent for me.

Once I knew the Lord had sent for me I did not see the need to seek Mother's or the wife's consent. One morning I just left for Pimpri. I must have arrived in the evening. There I learnt that Aunt Radha had built a two-room tenement for herself in the vicinity of Lord Vatobha's temple so she could serve the Lord in the best possible way. When I went up to the tenement, I saw her sitting in the front room. I must have seen her after ages and yet I knew her at once. How beautiful she was, Aunt Radha! Her skin was fair and it glowed just like Mother's did. The white sari clung to her body. She had stuck a large white hibiscus in the big bun on her head. I was stunned. Would she know me?

She turned towards me. I saw the flame of recognition in those great big beautiful eyes. She dropped everything and ran towards me and held me close to her chest. Her voice trembled as she said,

'Come to me, my little Lord Krishna. I have been waiting for you. Lord Vatobha had said you would come.'

Confused, I wondered if Aunt Radha was saying all this in a trance. I said, 'Arrey, Aunt Radha, don't you know who I am?'

'I? Not recognize you? My crazy one! Do you know who you are then? Come. Come right in.'

Aunt Radha had my hand in her's. She looked me in the eye and said, 'How you've grown, and so handsome!'

Was she laughing at me? I could not say a word. It was some time before I told her the whole story. I told her about the vision and how Lord Vatobha had appeared before me in her form. She said, 'Fits in then. Lord Vatobha always appears before me in the form of Lord Krishna. The last time he appeared before me only to say that I would meet my Lord Krishna soon and that he would not come to me after that. And now you today!'

I did not understand everything that she said, of course. I was simply happy to listen to the sound of her voice. She'll explain, I said to myself.

After dinner Aunt Radha spread my sleeping mat on the floor in the front room. She spread her own mat in the inner room. I lay on the mat and Aunt Radha bolted the front door. Then she went in and brought the copper tumbler and placed it near my pillow. With a gentle touch, she brought the flame of the latern down and then came and sat by my side on the mat. The journey had left me exhausted and I wanted to call it a day. I said to Aunt Radha, 'Aunt Radha, go to bed. We'll chat to our heart's content tomorrow. I'm sleepy.'

'I'm sleepy too,' she said with a soft laugh.

She turned her back to me. She drew up the end of her sari and started undoing the buttons of her blouse. I started trembling. What on earth was Aunt Radha doing? Aunt Radha lifted the blouse till it rested against her neck. Baring her beautiful fair skin, she said, 'Scratch my back like you used to when you were little. That's how I used to be able to get a good night's sleep.'

'Aunt Radha, I was a little boy at that time!'

'My crazy one, what I said earlier is true then. That you do not know who you are. You were not little then. For was my Lord Krishna little for his Gopis? He was little and yet he was big. For me, you were never little. Now scratch my back and no excuses.' Aunt Radha did not look at me as she said this and with a trembling hand I started scratching her velvety back.

Translated from the Marathi by Heta Pandit

Tatoba

Vithal Thakur

Tatoba had done nothing all his life. Neither was he a man of means like the revenue collector, Sardessai, nor did he have a shop of his own. In fact, people often wondered how he managed to run a household at all. No one had ever heard a quarrel in his family. No one had ever seen him beg anyone for a loan of a few rupees, and yet he and his children seemed to be doing quite well for themselves. Of one thing they were certain, that there was not a soul in the whole village who did not know him. In his long loose pyjamas, his hands in those wide, gaping pockets, a brightly coloured shirt hanging over his back, Tatoba was indeed one of the village sights! Here was a man who looked like he had just been let loose from someplace and would probably do anything to get someplace else. To put it in a nutshell, people avoided him.

Well, there dawned this day when that poor Shivlya mahar simply could not put this man off. He was what you might call a simpleton, you see. And a hard worker too. Of course, like all the other mahars of the village he was good at skinning and curing dead cows and goats, but he went a step further. He would fashion a few crude-looking sandals out of the leather and sell them to the villagers. So here was Shivlya on his way back from skinning somebody's dead cow. He had moved heaven and earth to make certain that the cow's owner should give him the carcass. Even promised the owner a pair of sandals free of charge.

His head was filled with the length and quality of leather he'd be able to get from the carcass when he bumped into Tatoba.

'How are you, friend? Where to, then?'

Shivlya was taken aback. This man had addressed him as an equal! No one had spoken like this to him before, except when they needed a pair of sandals—and now this . . .

'I was at Ram Putya's place. His cow passed away . . .'

'I see. They must have sent for you to skin the animal.'

Shivlya looked at him in amazement. Tatoba wore an expression of dead seriousness.

'Well, then, there's one thing you can do,' Tatoba continued in a conspiratorial tone, drawing his lips closer to Shivlya's ear. Shivlya didn't want to hear anymore. He was certain that this gentleman would order a pair of sandals in the next breath. He looked down and started measuring Tatoba's feet with his eyes.

'You know Sardessai sahib, don't you?'

Well, you might say that there was nothing startling in the question. After all, Sardessai was one of the wealthiest men in the village! And everyone knew that he'd been living on and off in Pune these past five-six years. Such a God-fearing nationalist! He used to visit the village once a year, if only for a day.

Without waiting for a reply to the question, Tatoba went on. The sahib had sent him an urgent letter, he said, asking him to arrange for a heap of bones from the carcasses of dead cows or bulls as manure for the trees in the orchard. Since Tatoba had been asked to make the arrangements, it had been his duty to seek the most hard-working of all mahars and he had sought Shivlya out.

'Well, then? What do you say? Ready to take up the challenge?' Tatoba asked Shivlya, making a clicking sound with his tongue against his single false tooth.

'Respected sir,' Shivlya said, his mind already on the job, 'what can I say? It would be an honour. Only, you know how expensive things are these days . . .'

'Out with it, man! Be reasonable and don't waste the sahib's time!'

'Twelve annas is all I ask, sir!' Shivlya spoke as he would to the sahib himself.

'Take sixteen! But I want the best bones for the Sardessai's orchard, mind! Here, take two for the moment. You'll get the rest when you deliver.'

Shivlya nodded and shoved the money into his vest-pocket.

Sixteen annas! He must deliver the bones from at least twenty-five bulls for that much money! What a pleasure this task would give him.

Shivlya was up early the next morning and before the cock crowed he had dumped the bones from twenty-five bulls at Sardessai's front gate. He had just finished dumping the last bag of bones when he saw Tatoba stride across to meet him.

Tatoba stared at the massive heap of bones in front of him and screamed, 'Shivlya! Stop! Stop, my man, stop! Oh, I have not wasted a moment rushing across to give you the news! The sahib has just sent a letter to say that he does not need the bones anymore.'

And then, as if the skies had fallen upon their heads, Tatoba looked straight at Shivlya and said, 'And I've sufferred the loss of a whole two annas . . .'

Shivlya stared helplessly at the heap of bones and thought of the labour he had put into this contract. He couldn't possibly spend the rest of the morning lugging it all back to the house. It would break his back! He wiped the sweat off his brow and made his way back to his house, a sad man.

And after that, whenever Tatoba bumped into poor Shivlya he'd recall how he had suffered the loss of a whole two annas and how irresponsible the revenue collector had been and so on. Until Shivlya had parted with the two annas . . .

Then one day the Sardessai came on a visit from Pune. Tatoba made it a point to meet him at the station. After all, Tatoba had been a sort of retainer for the family all his life. He had taken it upon himself to receive the head of this illustrious family each time he came on a visit.

It must have been about eight in the evening. There wasn't a horse carriage or any sort of carriage in sight. You had to rely on your God-given legs to get anywhere. It is interesting how a cool night's air can loosen one's tongue. Walking back from a station, Tatoba began to fill the time with the kind of stories that would appeal to a religious man.

A man hit another man. The other man vomited blood. Died on the spot. Then, of course, the story of how someone had placed a bundle filled with the guts of a dead cow at the wrestler's doorstep. In the morning when the village awoke, all they found were the wrestler's bones on his bed. Tatoba saw that he had caught Sardessai's imagination. He then plunged into his ghost stories—headless ghosts, ghosts who carried their own heads in their hands, tall ghosts, short ghosts—endless lines of ghosts.

One cannot say if it was the long walk home or the rich supply of ghost stories but Sardessai seemed to have broken into a sweat at the end of the walk.

When they reached the house it was quite dark. The sahib needed a light to be able to unlock his door. Tatoba flicked his cigarette lighter on and the Sahib turned around to get the keys out of his suitcase when . . . he saw a massive heap of bones in the light! He thought of the unfortunate wrestler, let out a blood-curdling scream and held on to Tatoba for dear life!

It must have taken Tatoba a good fifteen minutes to calm the sahib down. Such a devout, God-fearing man need not fear such things, he said soothingly. In fact, one need not be superstitious at all, what with one's education and all. And in any case, even if there was such a thing as black magic, one could always counter its effects with a series of prayers and pujas, could one not?

Exhausted though he was, Tatoba spent the next hour and a half explaining all the details of what pujas could be done and what these would cost. Then there was the additional benefit from slaughtering a few roosters, that last counteraction being entirely optional of course. Finally, they both dropped off to sleep after coming to the conclusion that the sum of two hundred rupees would settle scores with the Devil.

The sahib left for Pune the next day. He had been convinced that the pujas would be cheaper by far if Tatoba made all the arrangements and had entrusted him with two hundred rupees. The money safely in his pocket, Tatoba made a beeline for Shivlya's house. 'Get those bags of bones to my place,' he ordered.

Then Tatoba went home to his wife and children and said, 'Wanted a few bones to enrich the coconut trees, didn't you say? Well, I had told you to be patient, right? You'll see them at your doorstep tomorrow.'

Not waiting to answer any of their questions, Tatoba went into an inner room and hid the two hundred rupees in his cupboard. Then he lay on the mat on the floor and began to snore. You could say that here was a man who was sleeping the sleep of the innocent.

Translated from the Marathi by Heta Pandit

The Legacy

Subhash Bhende

The house was in one of those crowded parts of Margao town. Narrow, cramped doorways, with little light and air and the whole house in ruins. It had windows, of course, but not the big wide open ones. Hardly any width, and no decorative grilles or wire meshes. One of the houses in the neighbourhood did have electricity but such advancements of science were prohibited in this house. Someone had presented the house with a radio once but the batteries had died a long time ago. Now the radio stood in its corner with layers of dust for company. Dense smoke from the kitchen rushed out in panic, swirled around the living room, sought the opening of a window and fled out into the big wide world. As it departed, the smoke left its territorial markings in every corner of the house.

There were six members in the family. Kaveribai, her three sons and two daughters. They ran a grocery store in the bazaar. Each of the sons had imbibed just enough learning to be able to do the accounts in the store. The father, oblivious to Life, had passed on to the Other World, content in the knowledge that the three sons had sworn to sell themselves short for profit at the store. The eldest, now thirty-five, turned out to be a picture of his father—irascible and ill-tempered. The last time he had laughed was when he was a child and still in his mother's lap. He had stopped smiling the day he realized how selfish, greedy and unforgiving the world was. He did not trust it. Neither did he trust anyone who said that there was anything in it that could make you smile. And since the eldest could not bear the sound of laughter, the younger boys, two and four years apart in age from the eldest, made certain that they did not smile or laugh out aloud. If things got too unbearable and they could not help themselves, they got in a good snigger, but only on the sly.

The eldest would sit at the counter, near the cash box, silent and unsmiling, making the bills. The middle one and the youngest would sit up front, wrapping the cumin and the asafoetida in small packets. The middle one was quicker at that sort of thing. The younger fellow, though he had been trained to wrap the cumin seeds and asafoetida for four years now, still made hard work of it, and the quick-as-lightning temper that he often became the target of did not improve relations with the eldest. But if people in the know heard the eldest scold the middle one, they came to all sorts of conclusions.

Whatever their differences, the three brothers had one thing in common—they were all equally dejected when it came to a Sunday and they had to shut the shop by law. Not that there was nothing to do on a Sunday. Behind closed doors, the three brothers would be busy. Slabs of jaggery had to be broken, rotten potatoes separated from the good ones, and worm-infested chickpeas thrown out. After this was done, they would spend the rest of their day wondering how best to spend it. Then they would eat early, go to bed and put out all the lamps by ten. You did not have to look up a calendar if you were in that neighbourhood on a Sunday! While they slept, the eldest dreamt that his cash box had grown beyond proportions; the youngest dreamt that he could make the cumin seed and asafoetida packets with express speed and great efficiency. The middle one did not dream at all.

Kaveribai, the mother, had a fixed schedule. She always got out of bed at the stroke of six to make chapattis. With the chapattis, there would be a chutney on some days, ghee and sugar on others, and on some days a lump of jaggery with a little grated coconut. Once in a while she would indulge in a little dry potato bhaji, but she knew that this annoyed her eldest son; afraid that she might overdo things, she never made the bhaji more than once a month. In a large vessel, there would be water that had the scent of coffee. There wasn't any milk in it. Only the eldest son was served real coffee with milk in it, in keeping with the family tradition. The rest had to make do with a morning meal of a few chapattis washed down with a glass of coffee-flavoured water.

As soon as the boys left, Kaveribai would get to work. By eleven, the youngest would run into the house with fresh fish from the market and run back to the shop again. The daughters were in charge of cleaning the fish. The boys would come home to eat a hurried meal and then go back to the shop. Then until about nine at night there would be nothing for the women to do. Every evening Kaveribai would call out to her neighbour Vainibai from the window without any bars. They had been neighbours for forty years now and yet all their communication had always been through that window. Neither had seen the other's home from the inside. They could talk this way for hours, mostly about the fish they had eaten that day and then about the ups and downs of fish prices these days, followed by another attempt at getting to the root of the problem of rising prices. Then there would be the story of the lunch laid out by Keni's daughter-in-law, as first heard from Kamti's wife; a little light shed on the latest fashions as sported by Talaulikar's daughter who had just returned from Bombay after her graduation; an analysis of the difference, in height and width, between the young couple that had just passed by the front door. This went on until it was time to light the evening lamps. Then a little rice gruel and, when the boys returned, some supper and then bed.

Kaveribai's two girls were ten years apart in age. The older daughter was twenty and still wore a skirt and a blouse. She was built small and looked every inch a teenager. Nobody in their right minds would have considered her ready for marriage. 'Nothing to worry about . . . not for another ten years,' they said to themselves. The younger one was an accident, and a nonentity in the house. Her status in the family could be compared with the drooping udders of the she-goat in the shed.

There was no place for family chatter in this house. Nobody spoke unless they were spoken to and they were spoken to only if absolutely necessary. The youngest son, of course, had been clumsy enough to make a light remark at the well one night. 'Mother, aren't the papads smelling delicious tonight?' he had said, washing his feet. That had been his last casual remark over anything. After that he had only spoken with a purpose. The eldest did open his mouth now and then, if only to let forth a volley of abuses. He heaped curses on all their relatives when he had nothing better to do. They were a cunning, scheming lot, his relations. He wouldn't trust them with their own grandmothers. They were only fit to receive kicks, to be thrown into ditches and shoved into the burning pits of hell. That was how the eldest put himself to sleep. Then he would snore in his sleep.

It just never seemed the right moment to encourage a little talk about his wedding. Heaven knows, he might hit the roof if one broached the subject at the wrong moment. In any other house, it would have been a normal thing. A casual proposal for a marriage alliance and the whole house would be all abustle. In this house, however, despite the absence of bars or grilles on the windows, even a fresh gust of wind was reluctant to come in.

And then, one night, Kaveribai took ill all of a sudden. The eldest daughter had been trained only to clean the fish and knew nothing beyond that. The house was in a shambles. The morning chapattis stopped. They had to make do with pao from the local bakery. The eldest had to get used to the taste of coffee without milk. In the evenings, there was far too much canji. It was time for the eldest son to take matters in his own hands. He made a thorough assessment of the situation and after an age of near complete silence, asked his mother a question. 'What shall we do now, Mother?'

'We must look for a good cook.'

'A good cook? Are you out of your mind? Will she be able to cook our dinner the way we like it? Will she fit into our lifestyle? Won't she be wasteful? Will she be thrifty?'

'Then what do you suggest we do?'

Kaveribai shifted her head, from the right cushion to the left, deep in thought. Then, with her illness and her helplessness as armour, she took courage and asked her eldest son, 'Will you marry? That will bring in somebody who will look after things the way we want. We will have a right over her.'

It was a precarious situation. There was no time to waste. Marriage, considered a useless, purposeless activity until now, took on a hue of utmost importance. Why, even a trifling thing like a marriage could have many advantages! One would have never thought of it!

Kaveribai took the eldest's silence for affirmation. She turned to face him and said, 'Have you seen Nadkarni's daughter? He's been making those fruitless visits . . .'

'Have you seen her?'

'Yes, I have. Once. At the festival in Nageshi.'

'All right, is she?'

'Hmm. Not bad looking.'

'Then let them know at once.'

'Oh! But don't you want to . . .?'

'I said let them know, didn't I? We like the girl. Find an auspicious hour. Start at once so things can be finalized.'

'But your . . .'
'Mother!'
'All right, baba, I shall let them know.'

The wedding over, the house had a daughter-in-law. Plain to look at but a veritable bulldozer at work. Now all Kaveribai had to do was lie on her mattress and direct her daughter-in-law from her sickbed, just to show her who was in charge.

It was a Sunday afternoon. The men of the house were outside, yawning and taking in a bit of the sun. In the inner courtyard, the daughter-in-law of the house was winnowing the rice and humming a song.

> *Radha has lost her mind over Lord Krishna . . .*
> *Radha's crazy about her Lord . . .*

Kaveribai could not believe her ears. A song? A song about Radha and Lord Krishna? And in this house? While the men were right there, outside? The walls of the house seemed to quake with the shock. Kaveribai lay in her sickbed, trembling. 'Daughter-in-law . . .'
'Yes, Mother? Need anything?'
'Stop that prattle before you say anything to me!'
'The singing disturbing you, Mother?'
'My dear girl, if they hear you outside, that husband of yours will bring the whole house down.'
'But what harm can a little singing do?'
'Listen to me, you! The women of this house do not ask questions. All they are allowed to do is reply when questions are put to them and if they are not used to it, they just have to live with it and learn the hard way!'
'Oh, forgive me. I did not know this . . .'

After this, sifting through the rice became a difficult business. How in the world could one see the stones in the rice if one's eyes were brimming with tears?

There was nothing she loved to do more. She had taken pains over her lessons with Waikarbua. Waikar would say, 'Some day, girl . . . you'll make a name for yourself! The Lord has blessed you with a wonderful voice. Don't ever forget to practice your singing every day!' And then the prizes and awards she had won for singing at school! And the merit marks earned in the singing class! Should she now forget it all? Sing the bhairavi before even attempting the malkauns? She had plans to bring her tanpura back with her after her next visit to her mother's. Would that tanpura be condemned to a corner in the house, gathering dust? It had one string broken—would the string remain broken for ever? In this house, they might even suggest breaking the rest of it!

Darkness fell upon the house. The eldest pored over his accounts books under a dimly lit lamp. He looked at no one and nobody disturbed him. He was in the midst of writing up his debtor's accounts.

'Can we go to the movies next Sunday?'

'What? The movies?' His voice sounded like a sliver of ice from under his starched collar.

'Hmm. There's a Meena Kumari movie in town. She's one of my favourite movie stars, but you wouldn't know that, now would you? I simply love the way she talks on the screen—she can really set your heart pounding, you know. Do you know what her voice sounds like? Well, to me, it sounds like a voice coming from the core of a deep, dark secret place . . .'

'We are not accustomed to this kind of talk . . .

about such drama.'

'All right then, I shall stop being the cinema critic! But you'll take me to the movies?'

'I? Take you to the movies? A couple out in the open . . . It's shameless!'

'Oh, no! How can the world think of us as being shameless? We're married.'

'Such wisdom is best suited to people in big cities like Bombay and Pune.'

'Oh, but what's shameless about a married couple . . .?'

'It is not the tradition of this house to explain things to the wife! Not yet, anyway. Once this sort of thing starts, there's no telling what it might lead to. The wives are going to think no end of themselves. They'll dance on their husbands' heads . . . wrap them round their little fingers. When I was fifteen I was taken to see a documentary film about a saint. After that, the custom has been dropped in our house.'

'But . . .'

'As for the women of this house, your mother-in-law and your sister-in-law have never, never in their lives seen a movie. And if you don't see a single movie from now onwards nothing's going to change, I can guarantee you that!'

That night she could not sleep. Meena Kumari . . . Vyjayantimala . . . strands from popular films ran through her mind. And that rapier sharp voice which could only have come from the core of a deep dark secret place. She had never thought that a human voice could sound like that! What of it now, though? She must forget about all that completely—she must allow the curtain to fall.

Restless the next day, she asked her sister-in-law, 'We can go for a short walk, then? I'm bored in the house all day.'

'Where can one escape to?'

'Oh, somewhere. We could go up to Damodar Shala or to the Kamraj Garden. They say you can listen to some new film music somewhere there.'

'Who knows? Have I ever been to the Garden? All I've seen of it is what one can see from a passing vehicle.'

'Well, in that case, today you shall see it from the inside.'

'Oh, no! Good God! The women of this house go out but once in a year for the festival at Nageshi. This year was an exception. On account of your wedding, we were able to step out of the house twice! You may not believe it, sister-in-law, but we haven't even seen our own shop in the bazaar . . . not really, I mean . . . both Mother and I . . .'

'Not go out? Then how does one spend the evening?'

'One stands at the window. Watching people passing by . . . you'll never know how the time has flown!'

'But doesn't one get bored out of one's mind?'

'Sister-in-law, it must be boring for you, not being used to it, but if you do it often enough you'll hate leaving the house even for a minute!'

Two years went by. The eldest son's wedding was no longer news. Kaveribai still lay on her sickbed. She spent most of her day complaining to her daughters and her daughter-in-law about her aches and pains, peppering her complaints with some exaggerated symptoms. You could say that she was in love with her own illness. As long as she could lie on that sickbed she was content and happy. The only thing that caused her some anxiety was the possibility that she might get better some day. The thought of leaving her beloved bed and walking about worried her sick.

One day the eldest went to his mother. He stayed with her long and talked ceaselessly. What he wanted to say could have been put in a nutshell. That it was time for the middle brother to seek a bride. That every member of the house should be treated as an equal. That no one should be given cause to complain. No one should nurse a grudge against the other. He left it to his mother to speak to her middle son on this matter.

Her middle son was outside, in navy blue shorts, shirtless. Every now and then he would wipe his sweaty bare chest with the end of a filthy rag. When his mother called out for him he jumped out of his skin, as if struck by an electric shock, and ran into the house.

'You sent for me, Mother?'

'Hmm. To ask you about a match. You're old enough to marry now . . . best got over and done with.'

His mother had startled him. He rubbed his chest vigorously in confusion. So vigorously that a few loose threads fell off the filthy rag. Then he spoke, 'But must I?'

'Yes. It's best done with! His was done and therefore yours must be done! It would have been a different matter if he had not married at all.'

'All right then.'

'There's a girl in town. Salelkar's daughter. I don't suppose you want a this or a that in a girl? . . .'

'Just one thing . . .'

'What?' Kaveribai shot out of her sickbed and sat upright.

'That the wedding should take place on a Sunday, so that there's no need to shut shop more than is necessary.'

Perhaps for the first time in his life, the middle one went out that day and bought himself two new vests from a shop in town. He was never seen without a vest after that day. Both his mother and his elder brother were convinced by this act that he had taken his imminent wedding quite seriously. As he had desired, the wedding was gotten over with on a Sunday morning in the Nageshi temple at the auspicious hour.

The sun had set in the hills. The elder daughter-in-law of the house stood at the window, engrossed in conversation with their neighbour Vainibai's daughter-in-law. They made quite a pair.

> *Just where the river meets the sea . . .*
> *I shall wait for thee . . .*
> *I shall wait for thee . . .*

The middle son's wife sang in a strident voice. The eldest daughter-in-law nearly jumped out of her skin. 'Sister-in-law! What in the world are you up to?'

'What? What do you mean?'

'Why! Throwing questions back at me, are you? You were singing just this minute, weren't you?'

'Liked it?'

'We'll see about liking and not liking later! Today, I see you're singing in front of me. Tomorrow you may sing when the men are home!'

'But what of it?'

'What of it?' The eldest daughter-in-law put her face close to the middle daughter-in-law's and shouted, 'Nobody's allowed to sing in this house! Nobody! Such shamelessness is simply not permitted here, understood? The men don't approve . . . our mother-in-law does not approve. I do not approve.'

Kaveribai listened to every word. Tears of sheer joy filled her sick old eyes. At last! She could now pass on the baton to the eldest daughter-in-law and go on to the Next World. Here was someone she could trust to uphold the strict traditions of her household. Her happiness knew no bounds.

Translated from the Marathi by Heta Pandit

The Hour's End

Laxmanrao Sardessai

A wedding invitation! Rambhau's hands shook as he held the card in his hands. Anantrao's daughter to be married! Why, that beggarly slave! How did he manage to find such a wealthy, talented bridegroom for his daughter? This sort of thing could make anyone's hair stand on end, he muttered to himself. Rambhau's own daughters, both of them, had made rather modest matches. 'That beggarly Anantya's fortunes have turned—that's all I can say!' he burst out.

There are some people in this world who simply cannot bear to see others succeed. Rambhau was one of them. Envy was one emotion that ran riot through every fibre of his body. To keep this fire ablaze, he made it his business to know everything about everybody. Who was to be married, who had just had a son, who had done well in the examinations, who had won a lottery . . . He simply had to know. And once he knew all there was to know, he would do everything in his power to cloud the fortunate receiver's joy.

His community folk had nicknamed him 'Venom'. They feared his poisonous gaze. Mothers would cover their children's faces with the end of their saris at his approach. Neighbours would cover the clusters of ripening bananas on their trees for fear of his evil eye. Village girls returning from the bathing ghats, fresh as the morning dew, were terrified of his gaze.

Rambhau was the self-appointed harbinger of bad news in the community. A dark messenger of bad news. If a person passed away in the village, he'd be the first to know and the first to pass the word around. He seemed to have an abundant supply of energy for such matters. Ah! A loose woman had abandoned her husband! Here, a widow had given birth to a child! There, a young virgin had been led astray! That's how Rambhau spent all his time.

You did not need to be awfully clever to expect news of an imminent disaster or a crime committed if you saw Rambhau on his rounds in the village. If he was at your door, you could expect the worst. With Rambhau, it was never a casual visit. Everyone knew that. Prepare for an auspicious ceremony and Rambhau would be on your threshold, bringing some inauspicious tidings and deriving supreme satisfaction if he succeeded in putting a spanner in the works. You had to exercise immense caution. You had to look for grooms for your daughters and brides for your sons outside Goa—even as far as Nashik and Pandharpur, well out of his reach.

Rambhau was in his element when it came to ruining the lives of the young and the underprivileged. Now there must have been over a thousand young people, scattered all over the country in search of work—to keep track of the private lives of so many! Yet, Rambhau knew exactly what each one was worth. He knew how much property each of those youngsters had a claim to.

As far as his own family was concerned, Rambhau had found the ideal solution. At considerable pain, he had drawn up a family tree. It began with a gentleman named Kushtojirao and ended, at this point in time, with an infant in the cradle named Subhash and included small children such as little Sarojini. Here was the personal history of several generations of his family in a nutshell. If they saw him seated before the family tree, his eyes fixed on the chart in front of him, in deep concentration, they knew for sure he was plotting somebody's ruin. He had committed to memory who in the family was the sickly one, who was on his deathbed, which women would be due for childbirth and when. This traffic of information crowded his mind today. Rambhau looked at the wedding invitation again. Through his jumble of trivial knowledge, he had to find a way! Suddenly he saw the light. It was quite clear. He had set his sights. It was none other than that poor old asthmatic in the Sabnis household.

Rambhau could not wait to finish his meal. He got dressed as fast as he could. Margao was some miles away; the sun was high, and the road undulating. It was also lonely. Rambhau was well over sixty but age was no hurdle to a man with a purpose! He would make light of such an arduous journey. It would also give him the opportunity to work out every detail . . .

Today was Saturday. The wedding was scheduled for Monday at the auspicious hour. There wasn't much time left. How he wished for a death—anyone's—in the family! Even a birth! For the birth of a child in the family could also signify ill-omen, could it not?

It was a noble task, his dharma, to inform people that they could not proceed with the wedding at an hour like this. He was certain that the old asthmatic Mukundrao of Margao would not let him down. After all, had the asthma not taken a toll of the man for months now? Had the sickness not sapped him of all his energies? In Rambhau's register, his days, indeed his hours, were numbered! He was certain the old fellow was on his deathbed. This added a spring to his step.

When Rambhau stepped into Mukundrao's house, it was dark. 'Rambhau at our doorstep at this hour!' exclaimed the household. What could be worse? Even Mukundrao's long illness was bearable compared to this! What alternative did they have but to welcome him into the house? One elderly gentleman had called on another to enquire after his health. They were duty-bound to offer him their hospitality.

It was true. Mukundrao was dying. There was no doubt about it. Strange thing this, this asthma, a treacherous disease indeed, thought Rambhau. Mukundrao had almost breathed his last twice before this. Even as the news of his imminent death had travelled far and wide, it was soon followed by the announcement of his recovery! You couldn't trust a man to die properly these days.

Mukundrao spent a restless night. Would the old man keep on breathing then? Rambhau listened to the dying man's tortured chest and let out a sigh.

Morning broke with a smile. The skies burst with

sound and colour. The dying man's chest still heaved with life. Rambhau felt cheated. What tenacity! He could have strangled the old dotard himself! If he had decided to die, then why the delay? What difference would two days make? How else could Rambhau's scheme succeed?

All day, Rambhau did not stir from the room. Outwardly he made a convincing show of concern for the dying, elderly gentleman—administering medication to the patient and solace to his sons—his behaviour befitting his age. One more day like this and his scheme would come to nought! Anantrao's daughter would be married and all would be lost!

In the bright light of day, hope had dawned in Rambhau's heart, but by nightfall the slight movements of that heaving chest and those frail hands put paid to his plans. He left the sick room in disgust.

Another dark night. At the first sign of light, Rambhau stepped into the sick room. He had made up his mind. There was no point staying on in this house. Then, as fate would have it, he saw Mukundrao lying there very still. Rambhau convinced himself that this was indeed the end. In any case, even if there were any signs of life left in the old soul, it would only be a matter of minutes. The hour's end! No doubt about it, this was the result of his untiring efforts. His heart swelled with pride as he slunk out of the sick room.

There was not a moment to be wasted. He could not afford to stay on for the last rites. What if the wedding ceremonies should commence? Anantrao's daughter would garland the bridegroom. That was all it would take for his scheme to fail. He grabbed his coat and handkerchief from the clothes peg on the wall. He must proceed to Panchwadi. He had not slept a wink these last two nights and had not had a decent meal.

An eight- to ten-mile-long journey lay ahead . . . But this was not the hour to waver. He tied his dhoti firmly around his waist and set about his business for the day. What if the old asthmatic should come back to life? The possibility made him quake. But he did not allow his steps to falter. Whatever the consequences later, he must first have the wedding called off . . . What if no one believed him? What then? At times like these you needed the support of a man of reputation. It was the rule of the game—convince four people of the man's death and the 'truth' would take care of itself!

When Rambhau reached Borim, it was eight. It was a cool morning. The air was filled with smoke from cooking fires. A few village boys had lit a bonfire of dried leaves on the edge of the road to keep themselves warm. Fisherwomen had set up shop with their baskets of fish. A few people were returning with fresh, glistening fish.

Panchwadi was a good distance away. Rambhau was tired and hungry. He saw a shabby teashop by the roadside. He knew he'd have to make do with that. All of a sudden, he heard someone call out, 'Rambhau! Rambhau!'

It was Yashwantrao Kosambi calling out to him from the veranda of his house. Rambhau turned towards the house. Ah! To kill two birds with one stone! Here was the prospect of a meal and moral support!

'Why the rush? Where were you heading, Rambhau?' Kosambi asked with suspicion. Yashwantrao Kosambi had seen Rambhau at a distance. It was odd, someone out so early in the day and walking at such speed. He could not be up to much good! His suspicion grew because it was he, Yashwantrao Kosambi, who had, after considerable effort, made the match.

Besides being clever, Yashwantrao was also very talented. A lawyer who fought for the poor. He may not have made a fortune but he enjoyed immense satisfaction. Anantrao was one of his clients. Five daughters to be married off and not an anna to give as dowry for the girls. Yashwantrao's kind heart understood this. It was this sympathy for Anantrao that had made him find a match for Anantrao's eldest daughter.

The young man had come on a visit from Belgaum to Goa to see the temples. He was both wealthy and talented. He had spent his vacation with Yashwantrao, who knew the family and liked the boy. Yashwantrao knew that the boy was looking for a bride from Goa, and it wasn't long before he had found the ideal match for him in Anantrao's daughter Sushila. After the matchmaking, Yashwantrao had also helped set a date for the wedding. He had spent all of yesterday at Panchwadi and had promised to be back by ten this morning. In fact, he was getting ready to leave when he spotted Rambhau and called out to him.

Rambhau came up the front steps and walked into the veranda. Yashwantrao insisted that he sit down and then called out to the servant to fetch the hookah. Rambhau had, like many others, heard great tales of

Yashwantrao's lavish dinners. Two birds in the hand! A full meal and Yashwantrao's support. No fear now of being disbelieved.

Yashwantrao asked, 'Where were you headed, then, Rambhau, in such haste?'

Rambhau grabbed the hookah from the the servant. He pushed the end of the smoking pipe into his mouth, took a few greedy puffs, exhaled, coughed and said, 'Off to Panchwadi. Coming?'

Yashwantrao's suspicions were well-founded, after all. It became clear to him that Rambhau was all set to ruin the wedding. Oh, poor, unfortunate Anantrao! To get a daughter married to such a fine groom and without the burden of paying a dowry—would this devil want that to happen!

But Yashwantrao did not allow his anxiety to show. He said casually, 'Panchwadi? Anantrao's place? Oh, all right. I suppose I must go too. They did insist . . . there was this invitation.'

'But this wedding will have to be called off, Yashwantrao,' Rambhau said slyly.

'And why is that?' Yashwantrao asked.

'Why do you think I am rushing there? After all, one must observe the tenets of our dharma, don't you think?'

'But, of course! What is it that has happened? Do tell,' Yashwantrao asked with great curiosity.

'Oh, sir! The things that happen! Life is but birth and death! Can a wedding take place if there has been a death in the community?'

'True. What sad tidings have you brought with you?'

'Oh, a member of our family—Mukundrao—passed

away this morning. He breathed his last and I left the house forthwith.'

'Oh, oh . . . in that case you'll have to make it to the wedding before the end of the day. They must be informed.'

'Now you know why I'm in such a hurry, even in this cold weather!'

'I understand. I think I can accompany you,' Yashwantrao said.

'I was hoping you would.'

'Oh? Why?' Yashwantrao asked.

'Well, you know, they might not take my word for it at the wedding pandal. It will be a smooth operation if I have your support,' Rambhau said frankly.

'How right you are. Why don't we leave after breakfast?'

Yashwantrao went into the house. Hastily, he wrote a note and quickly dispatched a servant to Panchwadi. He then instructed another servant to go to the riverside and fetch what fish was available there.

Rambhau was dazed by the splendid choice of dishes at the breakfast table. 'Come, Rambhau! Let's have a bit of tea,' said Yashwantrao. They both went into the drawing room. Rambhau dispensed with his coat, washed his hands and his feet and then proceeded to attack the food on the table.

At the table, he spoke incessantly—about the late Mukundrao's family life, the family's joys and their sorrows, their material possessions, his own children, Anantrao's poverty and so on. Yashwantrao listened to all of this calmly. Inwardly, he was seething. What a shock it will be to poor Anantrao if the wedding is called off—a wedding that had been favoured by good fortune. This is certainly not going to improve Anantrao's wife's illness. He imagined the scenario— the wedding called off and the good-looking, modest Sushila married off to some ugly moron!

Yashwantrao held his composure. He was not the region's leading lawyer for nothing. He was both intelligent and cunning. It did not take him long to work out a plan that would release Anantrao from this man's clutches. Yashwantrao beamed. Smile for smile, story for story, he matched Rambhau's cheeriness with his own.

Satiated with the morning meal, Rambhau relaxed. Just then, the servant appeared with fresh mullet. Rambhau rushed to examine the catch. His mouth began to water. How many dishes one could make with this lot! His imagination took culinary flight. Yashwantrao noticed this and said, 'Do we have to leave right away for Panchwadi, Rambhau? How can we just abandon this bounty and leave!' Rambhau's salivary glands had been activated. On the one hand, the call of duty and on the other, the promise of such tasty fresh fish! He was caught in a whirl. Finally, he gave in. 'In that case, why don't we eat early and then leave?' he said weakly.

'I shall make the necessary arrangements right away. Relax.' Yashwantrao then went to the cook and whispered, 'Under no circumstances must lunch be served before noon. Four or five of your best dishes, mind. Fried fish, fish curry, fish masala and so on.'

After that, Yashwantrao and Rambhau spent the whole morning chatting. Rambhau stuck to his favourite topic—who was doing what, how and where. Somiya the boatbuilder had made fifty thousand in the boat business, Fati Gabtya had minted a lakh of rupees fishing, his neighbour Zillu Phatya had sold his canoe and built himself a new house and bought a rice field. What was most amusing was that Rambhau knew each person's earnings right down to every paisa! As if each one of them had appointed him as his accountant!

When in company, Rambhau always talked about everyone's success stories. The truth was, he envied them all.

It was ten in the morning and there was a nip in the air. A morning bath would have been ideal. Yashwantrao said that the hot water would be ready soon and called out to the servant, 'Bring the oil!'

A servant appeared with a can of oil and began to massage Rambhau's head. Rambhau was in raptures. This man certainly knew his job! His fingers danced on Rambhau's bald head and Rambhau was soon in a trance, his eyelids dropping like curtains. The tense muscles on his face lost their firmness, the scent of coconut oil filled his senses. He could see nothing, hear nothing, smell nothing else. All was complete contentment.

An hour passed. As the ritual came to a close, the servant led Rambhau to his bath. There he briskly poured hot water from the big copper pot on to Rambhau's head. He then scrubbed Rambhau's body with soap. The maidservant came in with cool water and poured it into the pot of hot water every now and then. A kerosene stove burned brightly under the big copper pot. The servant continued to pour scalding hot water over Rambhau's forehead, his shoulders, his back, just as Rambhau directed, just as he desired. And so it went, with Rambhau sighing in supreme satisfaction.

At the end of the oil massage, the bath; and at the end of the bath, total mental and physical indolence. Total languor, insatiable hunger! The tasty dishes he had stuffed down his throat in the morning had fizzled out. He felt as if he had not eaten for days. The aroma of the fish frying pervaded the air. The floormats had been laid in readiness for the afternoon meal. Rambhau had been given clean white clothes to wear after his bath. His own dhoti, soiled by the red earth of the road he had taken, had been washed clean and put out to dry by a servant.

Rambhau was offered the seat usually reserved for the guest of honour. The dishes were all gastronomical delights prepared under Savitribai's personal supervision. Mango juice, pomegranate salad, kokum curry and other specialities of the region. Rambhau laid into the food. There was no other way to quench the fire that raged from his belly to his brains. Besides, where else had he experienced such hospitality!

They finished their lunch and then went into the drawing room. When would he be able to lie down, Rambhau wondered. Relaxed, he could hardly utter a word. He lay on the couch and then, suddenly, the realization that this did not quite fit into the scheme of things dawned on him. He shot up. Seeing this, Yashwantrao said, 'Why, Rambhau! It's just struck one! Let's take a nap before we leave. Does anyone expect us to go anywhere on a full stomach? A cup of tea by three would be nice. The auspicious hour has been set for seven-thirty. We should be there by five.'

Yashwantrao did not wait for Rambhau's reply. He shut his eyes and pretended to be fast asleep.

Rambhau slept for a good two hours. He awoke with a start, massaged his eyelids and looked around. There was nothing but darkness. He pinched himself. Was he dreaming? He let out a few curses. How could he have been such a fool? How could he have ignored the call of duty? How could he have given into such a temptation as food at a time like this? This Yashwantrao had betrayed him! His plot had failed miserably! He called out in desperation.

No one answered. He could hear people moving about in the house. What's this? Where was Yashwantrao? Beads of sweat appeared on his brow. What ill-wind had blown him to this house? Curse his fate! Neglect your duty and this is what you get! This is the result of not exercising enough caution! That wretched Yashwantrao must have some motive!

Rambhau was on the brink of despair. He saw some light coming through the slits in the window. It must be the light from the evening lamps, he said to himself.

Rambhau ran to the window in panic. His heart thumping, he opened the window only to find bright sunlight outside the room. It was as if sunlight had streamed into his heart. He cried out in joy. All was not lost! He called out to Yashwantrao. There was no reply. Rambhau looked at his watch. Just past three! Four hours at his disposal! He could make it to Panchwadi quite easily. He went towards the door, calling out for Yashwantrao.

Rambhau tried to open the door. What's this? The

door bolted on the outside? Had he been locked in? Rambhau began to hit the door with his bare hands. He clanged the bolt, made a lot of noise and even kicked the door but no one came anywhere near the room. He was shaken to the point of tears. No doubt, this was a trick! Yashwantrao had insisted on his staying on, had offered him a meal and had coaxed him into taking a nap. To what treachery? In desperation, Rambhau gave vent to his lungs—shouting and crying as loud as he could.

Ten minutes passed. Rambhau sounded like a prisoner in a cell. How would he escape? By now the servants had collected in the veranda outside the window. On their faces was a mixture of curiosity and bewilderment. Yashwantrao's strict instructions were not to open the door under any circumstances.

Shortly, Yashwantrao himself appeared outside the window. He glanced casually into the room. Rambhau in his coat, with his handkerchief stuck in his front pocket, seemingly all set to embark on his journey . If Yashwantrao had opened the door for a split second, Rambhau would have made a dash for it and made a beeline for Panchwadi!

Rambhau saw Yashwantrao and instantly became the paragon of virtue. All at once, he was the penitent, troubled soul. 'Yashwantrao! You have stabbed me in the back! Why? You have acted against the social order, against dharma itself!'

Yashwantrao stood there unmoved. In a calm voice he addressed his elder: 'What is my crime, Rambhau? I offered you my hospitality. I offered you the best of fare—was that my crime? How have I upset you?' Then he gave Rambhau a look as hard as stone.

Yashwantrao's composure and the hard tone shamed Rambhau momentarily into silence. Then, he said, 'Yashwantrao! Have mercy on me! Open the door. Let me go!'

'Where will you be headed, then, Rambhau? To destroy the wedding of a good-hearted, simple, innocent girl? A girl already under the shroud of poverty? What will you achieve by that?'

Yashwantrao was now overcome with emotion. He foresaw a happy married life ahead for Sushila. This creature who had charged himself with the task of destroying an innocent girl's life was as devilish as he was pathetic, he thought.

Yashwantrao continued, 'Rambhau, it pains me to behave in this fashion with a guest in my house. But what else could I have done? You will not be released before eight tonight. You can bring the roof down if you like. I shall represent the two of us at the wedding, and shower our blessings on the young couple—yes, blessings on your behalf too. I trust you will find the bed in your room quite comfortable until then. You have been through so many sleepless nights these last few days. You will be given tea, the hookah . . . Through the window of course! On the dot of eight, the door will he opened. After that I shall be at your sole disposal! We can sample the fish left over from lunch. Do stay the night and leave in the morning.'

He left Rambhau and walked towards the palanquin. As soon as he sat in it, the bearers lifted him up and sped towards Panchwadi.

Translated from the Marathi by Heta Pandit

The Africa Boat

Laxmanrao Sardessai

'A ship! A ship!'

A cry rose from the black corporal's lips. He was trembling. He spun round and thumped his musket on the floor. He looked through the sea mist, his eyes peeled, and then, as if to dispel any doubt, he turned to me and said, 'Don't you see the Africa boat?' Through the thick mist, I could see the faint dark outline of the ship.

Imprisoned on alien soil, these black soldiers jumped and danced at the sight of a vessel—however big or small. The approaching ship conjured up an image of Africa—a lush green paradise, a snug cottage thatched with bamboo and dry grass, a granary, and the company of young women. Huge, clumsy alligators in the Zambezi. These images grew in their mind's eye and then, the excitement, the waiting and the wanting overwhelmed them. That's when they called their black comrades from their scattered posts in the Fort and danced with joy. They clapped and whistled, drumming on empty tins to express their longing to return to their homeland.

Nicolav seemed to be the only one disappointed by the sight of the ship. He gripped the bars of the window and with a sad expression, turned to me and said, 'The two years of our contract are over. We'll be going back next week.' His tone implied that he did not want this to happen.

The scene before us was the usual frenzied dance of the blacks, mad with the prospect of seeing their homeland once again; yet there was something more precious than that pulling Nicolav away.

He pushed his hand through the window for a cigarette, put the musket down on the steps and sat down. He lit the cigarette I had just given him and then looked at me like a caged animal. After a while, I asked him, 'You don't like Africa?'

'I love Africa but I don't want to go there just yet.' His broad face darkened, but I detected a hint of tenderness in his voice.

Could Nicolav be in love? The thought went through my mind like a dart. But the love escapades of these corporals had become legend over the last few months. No sooner had they laid their hands on their wages, they ran to the lanes where they could buy love and paradise for a few days. There were some twenty-five odd prostitutes who had set up shop under small thatched roofs just outside the Fort walls. For a few days, these men would call the chosen ones their wives and even boast about their beauty and skills. As the month came to a close, the thatched roofs of those houses seemed to come apart. Came the new month and new wives replaced the old ones. The roofs came up and went down as passions rose and fell. Through all this tidal wave of passion, however, they never once lost sight of their homeland and the boat that would take them there.

Nicolav did not reveal his innermost feelings to me that day. I gave him a little advice: 'If you don't want to leave on the Africa boat you could make an application addressed to the superior officer. He'll be happy to allow you to stay on, I'm sure.'

He took my advice and wrote out an application immediately. He signed the document, then folded the piece of paper neatly and put it in his pocket. He seemed satisfied with this new development. We could see the ship quite clearly now and the dance of the corporals before us reached a frenzied peak.

Days went by. I saw a sea-change in Nicolav's behaviour. When I was first taken prisoner along with some of my friends and interned at Fort Aguada, he had been cruelty itself. When he was on guard duty, we could not hope for any kindness. He would never chat with us, never ask for a cigarette. He would not even allow us to talk except in whispers. If we even so much as exchanged a sentence in Konkani or shared a joke, he'd think we were laughing at him. That would really get to him and he would swear and curse and thump the butt of his gun on the floor. One day, while we were at our baths at the well, he had even attacked one of my comrades. We had taken our complaints to the Commander and he was severely punished for his brutality. Naturally, that had not helped improve relations. We had seen the inhuman side of him for about three months. It was only in the last month that he had suddenly changed. He would often go into raptures over the beauty of Goan girls. After that, he would allow us a little more time for a stroll. Sometimes he'd even help us draw the water from the well for our baths.

When the bugle went off at the stroke of six, all the soldiers held their tin plates in their hands and stood in a queue for dinner. It was a fare of half-cooked or burnt rice and fish soup, served and eaten quickly. Those who were too ill to eat or too sick of the Fort food would throw the leftovers into the sea and then watch the fish fight over it.

Nicolav was the only one who did not do any of these things. He would save the leftovers on his plate in a small tin bowl and then disappear with them from the Fort. I watched him do this over fifteen days. A picture had emerged before me that probably explained everything. The Africa boat, his application, the sea-change in his behaviour over the past month and his stealing away with food after every meal could only mean one thing. But I was determined to find out the whole truth from the man himself.

When he was not on duty, Nicolav spent all his time on the Fort wall with his fishing hook and line. At high tide, the waves would lash the Fort walls and in the rains the water cascaded over the rocks. Even in the rains, Nicolav never stopped fishing. He'd throw his line, wait for a bite and then pull the line up with a whoop of joy. He would then release the creature thrashing about in the throes of death, and push it into his bag. He often caught five or six fish this way. He would even give us two or three through the bars in our windows, before slipping out through the back stairs. His comrades would nudge each other and laugh behind his back but it did not seem to bother him.

A few days after the Africa boat had come in, Nicolav arrived on duty looking ecstatic. He looked at me and said, 'They've accepted my application. I shall be able to stay on for another year now.'

The poet in me tried to guess what noose it was that had bound him to this land which was not his. The Bombay boat was making its way into the Mandovi. I could see the sandy beach across the bay. The row of coconut trees there seemed to touch the waters of the sea. On my right, the wide open sea had spread itself out. Some ships could be seen moving in from the direction of Siridao. There must have been a hundred or so Arab fishing dhows, lying in wait for the night's catch. Then the water's edge and the green shade seemed to take a turn on a curve and disappear into thick darkness.

'Would you like to see my wife?' Nicolav said suddenly, catching hold of my hand.

'Wife?' I must have sounded shocked. After all, I was familiar with the 'wives' of the black soldiers. Nicolav saw the surprise and the suspicion on my face. 'No, no. Not that kind of wife—a wedded wife,' he said.

I looked at him in amazement. He spent a good part of the day telling me his story—the marriage, the love between them. A young girl, true love, undaunted courage, supreme sacrifice—all this came together in Nicolav's love story.

The object of his affections was not a black girl. She was a young Goan maid called Marie, attached to the household of a rich Catholic landowner. Nicolav and the girl had at first had a loose, unconditional relationship. Then they got to know each other and fell in love. When the rich landlord showed exactly how cruel and violent he could be, she ran away from his household and came to Nicolav for shelter. Nicolav built her a small hut near the Fort walls and she began living there. It was for her that he saved the food from his plate and it was for her that he spent all his time catching fish.

After that day, Nicolav shared with me all the little incidents that had brought them together. He told me how his comrades teased him about the clandestine match, how he faced up to all the odds, how his Commander gave him his support and how he had managed to shut his comrades up after the wedding.

His sincerity was transparent. I gave him all the encouragement I could. In turn, he allowed me and my compatriots all the freedom he could give.

One day he said, 'We will go out for a stroll tonight.'

I was stunned. He said, 'I trust you completely. I'm quite certain you will not make any attempt to break out.'

I had often dreamed of taking that stroll on the free sand of the beach, of going out of the walls of the Fort. We did have the freedom to spend an hour along the bastion walls of the prison cells, but we could see little from our cell windows. We could see the sea but could not touch it, we could hear peoples' voices but could not see them. I trembled at the idea of a walk outside the walls of the Fort. From somewhere deep inside me, came the courage to do it. I told Nicolav that I would come.

Nine o'clock. It was pitch dark but there was a sparkle on the sea. The row of coconut trees along the opposite bank formed a thick black outline on the edge of the water. The beacon light from the lighthouse of Aguada swept the sky, wiping it clean. The forty or fifty cannon of the Fort had sealed their lips and gazed out at the ocean. Out in the open and in their barracks, those hundred or so black soldiers went about their business, weary with the waiting, singing or playing on some sort of African musical instrument. The waves lashed the wall that stretched from the main gate to the rear exit of the Fort, as if calling out to us.

The cell door opened. I got out. I followed Nicolav out through the back door. There were lights in the thatched huts by the side of the Fort wall and some activity too. About one furlong from the door was a raised wall. We climbed gingerly over this wall until we came to a strip of clean sand. We could see some old guards of the Fort in silhouette. The beam from the lighthouse swung relentlessly. I was out of my prison cell and the Fort and yet I was still a prisoner. Even so, the joy of walking, running on a sandy beach! Of being able to feel the trunk of a coconut tree! Nicolav was a good distance away from me. I had forgotten he was there!

After about an hour he came close to me and said, 'Come, I shall take you to see my wife.'

I followed him. It would have been impossible to dissuade him. All of nature was silent; only the waves lapped ceaselessly. The darkness was thick and still and the skies lay wide open over us.

Soon we came to a thatched hut. We had startled her. Nicolav assured her that all was well. She did not look a day over twenty. There she was, this twenty-year-old girl who had only a few months ago sold her body to a rich landlord, and yet now on her lips danced the smile of unspoken love. Brown-skinned, she had small sharp eyes with the innocence and simplicity of the blacks in them. Nicolav's hair had such a kink—as if his head had been covered by a tight coarse blanket!—but Marie's was long and straight. The light of an inner beauty shone through her. I could see why Nicolav was in love with her.

After I had settled down, Nicolav began extolling the virtues of his young wife. I nodded my head in agreement. He pushed a cup of wine before me which I declined with a laugh. He polished it off in a few gulps. The warmth in his tone seemed to get richer as the evening went by. His voice filled with ecstasy, he said, 'Some day I shall take her with me to Africa.'

'But only after you've become a father!' I said, indicating the swelling of her belly.

'I shall be a father four months from now! Step by step!' He caught her in his arms and started rocking her gently by the shoulders. He kissed her cheeks and caressed her long hair. He must have thought that the joy of having a loving wife was his alone in the whole wide world! He began to extol the virtues of India, the land that had given him this precious gift.

'The day your Marie lands in Africa, your land will be filled with my brethren!' They both loved what I had just said.

I heard the gong strike eleven. We got up to leave. 'Come and see us before we leave for Africa,' she said shyly.

A few minutes later I was back inside my cell. Their nationalities, their religions, their languages had not stood in their way! That thought ran through my mind.

Nicolav was changing a little every day. He appeared to be shedding his old bad habits like so many layers of skin. He had even learned to read and write Portuguese and had started paying attention to his clothes. He would not now dream of paying a few annas for the pleasures of the flesh, or get involved in a drunken brawl. His mind focused only on his wife and the baby growing inside her womb. His whole being seemed to be waiting for that event—the birth of his baby. What would this child be like? A love-child from the womb of an Indian girl? What would its eyes be like? And its hair? What colour would it be? These thoughts kept his imagination alive. He would watch the antics of his comrades at the Fort and wonder what it was that had changed his own life, made it so different from theirs.

All he was waiting for was to go back home and show his brothers and sisters, his relations, this wonderful, precious thing that he had gained in the East. How he yearned for their congratulations! Now he had started making enquiries about the boat to Africa. He had appealed to the government on behalf of his wife. They had given him permission to travel with his new family.

And then one morning he came to my cell window and burst out, 'Marie's had a son!' He was clearly overcome by his emotions.

I had seen his personality grow over the past year. In any case, I could do very little else in the prison cell but read and think! I had seen a clumsy oaf turn into a happy man. He could not wait to get back to Africa now. Anxiously, he waited for news of the boat.

Finally, a boat named the 'Zambezi' arrived at

Mormugao port and he decided he'd leave with his wife and child in the next two days. That evening he said to me, 'I am very keen that you should come and see my son. We shall go out tonight.'

In the face of his emotions, I could not but agree.

The door opened at the stroke of nine just like it had done the other night. I got out of my cell and left by the back door.

This time there was a full moon. Nature seemed to be decked with jewels and all the creatures of the night sang her praises. The waves lapped the shores in whispers and disappeared on the sandy bank. The beacon from the Fort lighthouse swept over the waters and the forests.

Nicolav's family life was brimming with his love. Marie had her three-month-old son in her lap. The child had all the features of a black. I picked him up. This robust little child would surely bear the long journey to Africa, I said to myself

Nicolav offered me a drink made with mangoes. He had made arrangements for some fruit for me.

I must have been there for an hour. Nicolav would be on that boat in a day from now. Another band of soldiers would come and he would hand over charge of the guard to them.

As we got up to leave, Nicolav said to me, 'Go to the seashore. Sit between the two poles there. I will be with you in an hour.'

I came down the slope to the seashore and walked briskly. The Fort and Nicolav's hut became two dots on the horizon. They must have been at least half a mile away. There was no one about. Even the coconut fronds were still. The waves lapped the shore in near-silence. In a flash, a thought entered my head. I had gone far beyond the limits of the two poles on the shore. I had just gone on walking. I could see a few houses under the shadows of the coconut trees and Candolim village before me.

There was nobody who could stop me now. I could be free! Free of prison and the boredom of it! I could shock the world! *'Political Prisoner Escapes from Aguada Fort Jail'*, the Bombay newspapers would say.

My trial had not even begun yet. They had held me here without so much as a trial. I had a few friends in Candolim village. I could spend the night with them and then go underground the next day. I started walking faster. No one could even see my shadow as I walked under the coconut trees.

The courage to escape had been hitherto dormant within me. It was as if something or somebody was pulling me towards the village. Just then, my eyes fell upon the light from the lighthouse and I saw Nicolav's hut. I saw in that light Nicolav, his little family, the Africa boat and his dreams.

I stopped in my tracks and looked at the shoreline. I saw a happy picture of Nicolav and his little family on that shoreline. I turned back.

I went up to the two poles and had barely sat down when a shape appeared from out of the darkness. It was Nicolav.

He had been running. I stood up. He hugged me. Overcome with emotion, we headed towards the Fort. That night, every line the waves made on the mouth of the Mandovi river looked to me like a smile.

Translated from the Marathi by Heta Pandit

Salvation

Raghunandan V. Kelkar

'*Hoi! Hoi! Aiyee! hu . . . ud!*' The sounds from the riverside were loud and harsh. The source of those sounds? Four men driving fifty animals to the city slaughter-house. Men and animals had only just emerged from the other side of the river. Trussed up in pairs, the animals merged into the river's haze. Through the raging water, they had tugged and pulled at one another and at the ropes that bound them together. Their mouths, their noses were full of water. Bound into one tight mass, they struggled to breathe. Was relief on its way? No, but the loud, hard lashings of the stick on their backs were. Blows rained on bare wet backs. What pain! Pain that drove some to empty their bowels in the middle of the street. Pain that found its way to their bladders. Fear and hysteria clouded their vision. Was there anybody there that night who could see? Not on their lives. Battlelines had been drawn. The helpless animals, bound and lashed, on one side of the lines and the men from the slaughter-house on the other. Truck drivers, passersby, each offered their own

brand of advice. 'Oi! Plug the bastard's tail into his
arse and slam the stick over his ear!' A big bull reared
his head. What? Defiance at this hour? All hell broke
loose on the unfortunate animal's head. Thwack! There
was a lesson to be taught here and at once. A lesson on
his ear. Thwack! A lesson on his back. Thwack! On his
belly. Thwack! On his horns. Thwack! That would
teach him. That would keep his panic still. Now was
the time to grab the animal's tail and twist it.
Indescribable pain. Panic and paralysis. That was the
only way to get the big bastard on his way. They gave
it a twist so hard, the tail would have come right off
the bull's body had he been a lesser animal. Blow
followed blow. His great big body trembled from head
to hoof. He was exhausted.

The caravan-on-hoofs headed for the city.

There could only be one word to describe this.
Hell. For could Hell be a place worse than this?

They had just gathered momentum when passenger
buses from the bus-stand came out of their nocturnal
dens, growling. Shouts from the drivers and conductors
of the buses added to the din. 'Hey, you! Can't control
a few cows, eh, you lot? Hold the buggers by their
horns and use your sticks, dammit! Clear the road,
fellows! Or I'll drive the bloody bus over their bloody
arses!'

The men from the slaughter-house lost their temper.
Their sticks landed on the animals' backs like bolts of
lightning. The animals thrashed against one another.
Hide pressed against hide. Horn enmeshed with horn.
Now, as ill-luck would have it, the devil himself had
placed a municipal tap on the way. Water flowed
freely from the leaky tap. In a stupor, a bull walked

towards the flowing water, his dry mouth open, his parched tongue sucking the air.

Th . . . chaak! A rock landed on his head. Darkness enveloped him. The tongue that had come out to taste water went right back in. The whip replaced the stick. It came down on the back of the creature just as the temple bells resounded. Devotees moved up and down. Passersby walked to and fro. The herd went past a bungalow. The lady of the house emerged in her fancy clothes and yelled at the men from the slaughter-house. They must mind their cattle, she warned, or else the animals would bring the compound walls down and cause severe damage.

The herd became fair play to a group of urchins. They threw a few stones, aiming for the eyes, the nose, the rump, just for a little practice. One hit a cow's head, missing the eye by an inch. She raised her head and shook it. The small children laughed. Such innocence!

A bus came close to the herd. The driver turned the bus towards the pair of bulls at the far end of the herd. Nudged them just a little with the bumper. The conductor didn't want to miss his share of the fun. He stretched a long leg out of the bus door and kicked a cow violently.

The herd slowly made its way up the hill. To their left, a deep ditch and to their right, a bare slope. Fear gripped the animals as they drew into a tighter bunch. A bus or a truck had merely to come down that slope and they knew the whiplashes would follow. No bus and no truck and yet a few blows from the stick and a few lashes from the whip for good measure. They had reached the top of the hill and had taken the wide, tarred road.

At the top of the hill, a different sight altogether. Green grass and a few cows placidly chewing the fresh green grass. A fighter bull in his prime tossing a few tufts of grass into the air with his large, perfect horns. Saliva rushed into the mouths of the animals on their way to the slaughter-house. Over the past four days they had forgotten what it was like to feed on wet, green grass. What possible harm could a few shreds of grass do? How much time did they have, in any case? The men from the slaughter-house looked tired, didn't they?

Animals and men, exhausted after their long journey on hoof and foot, took the turn towards the grass. A few animals plucked at the grass underfoot. A few took bites of empty air. Were they not hungry? Had they forgotten the taste of food? They had spent the past four days lumbering over the ghats of Kankavli, Kudal and Wadi without much food or water. They had already passed on to the land where there is no thirst and no hunger. They had been made to walk all day and all night. They had been made to run with whatever dregs of energy they might have had left in them. They had been walked through purgatory and into the gates of hell.

On that patch of grass on the hilltop there was no knowing what each animal might do. A few of them licked their wounds. A few stared at the others, uncomprehending. And some, still with a little life left in them, reared their heads in a display of defiance. The other cows and bulls on the patch stopped eating. The fighter bull came close to the herd, head erect, chest out. And then came mute compassion. They came close to the herd on its way to the slaughter-house. What a sight that was! The free cows and bulls nuzzled the bonded animals in sympathy—they seem to be like us, they have the same marks on their bodies. They too have shared man's burden and yoke . . . But why were they being beaten, whipped and tortured? Where were they being taken? Well, there were so many things they did not understand about men.

The men from the slaughter-house had their smoke. The shade of the mango tree seemed to have revived them completely. They straightened the turbans and scarves on their heads and reached for their whips. The herd was on the move again. The sun was high. The flailing whips cracked down on the dry hides like salt on open wounds. 'Hey, Moo . . ve! Uh! Let's go!'

They were in a hurry to get to the city. The new supervisor was a man of principle. Believed in the importance of punctuality. Time seemed to fly, and with it, the ends of the whips. The devil had taken possession of this group of men. They flailed their whips and waded into the herd with their sticks, screaming abuse. A trot replaced the trance-like walk. Where had the energy come from? Perhaps the animals thought that this sudden speed would bring them their freedom. Perhaps they thought that if they ran fast enough they would find the pathway to escape.

'A few paces more, Unman!'

'Hurry! Hurry! Yakub, use the bloody whip!'

They could see the limits of the city. Mapusa. Like crazed dervishes, the men lashed at the animals. A mass of skin and bones. To add to their misery, they now had to confront snarling traffic. On the one hand, the terror of being crowded out by buses, rickshaws, cars, scooters and people, and on the other, the shower of abuses and whiplashes.

They turned towards the slaughter-house. The men and their animals had finally arrived at their destination. Scarves were loosened to wipe the sweat from the foreheads of the men. The supervisor put his bag down and came towards them.

'Fifty, are they? Not one missing?'

'No, Sa'ab!'

'You're a day late.'

'Old hags we got here, Sa'ab. Can't move their arses fast enough.'

The supervisor ground his teeth. He went into the slaughter-house. They could see him speak to a man inside. The man inside handed eight hundred rupees. The supervisor came out from the slaughter-house. He held out just two hundred and fifty rupees to the three men in front of the herd.

'Here! Split this up!'

'Is that all, Sa'ab?'

'Motherfuckers! Swines! Come a day late and want more, eh?'

The supervisor was in a temper. They could not afford to stay there any longer. As they left for the city, they saw the man inside take each animal into the slaughter-house. There was no protest, no defiance, no fear this time. The animals went in meekly. They had come home, to the last and final cowshed.

An hour later, a small stream of blood ran by the side of the slaughter-house. You could hear a few muffled moans, a suffocated cry. The animals had finally made their escape.

Translated from the Marathi by Heta Pandit

The Sign of Ire[*]

Orlando da Costa

As the harvests of the vangana appear along the meadows and the wind ripples the green horizon, the still-damp earth shivers with an intense, fertile joy. Even the fieldworkers are dazzled by the sight. They feast their eyes on the stalks, patiently hoping that the grain will become so fat and golden that it falls of its own accord.

The nights seem to hover lower, coming to rest on the sleeping face of the land; and when the sun breaks through, the stalks twist and turn in the wind. Day after day their colour deepens; soon it will completely fill the eyes of the landowner and his tenants.

As the glow of the sun reaches the grain, turning it golden, dryness flattens the land, leaving it hard and cracked like the scab of a wound. The sun pierces the

---

[*]An excerpt (Chapter 6) from Orlando da Costa's novel O Signo da Ira set in 1940-41, depicting the feudal rural society in Goa during a year of drought, aggravated by the Japanese occupation of parts of Eastern Asia.

workers' backs; dry dust rests on their burnt skins like clouds of restless insects. After the rice has been harvested, the ground will agonize with the bristly nakedness of mutilated stalks; the land, after a night like so many others, will awaken tragically illuminated by a sun that grows hotter and brighter by the hour.

Small hopes either die or barely survive the obscure tragedies that involve both the land and the men who work it in the same circle of fire. Plants burn or dry up. Their roots seem to wither, crisped during three months under the earth's parched crust. Even the rocks that had been softened by rain and humid fog end up blazing in the midday sun. Sweat drips from burnt faces; bodies glisten until the arrival, in June, of the angry monsoon rains.

Bent over the grain, the women once again felt the rigid stalks move beneath their weary hands. The sun had gone down a little and another hot breeze was blowing, rustling the palm trees set along the road to Nuvem.

'I can't go on,' Natel repeated, almost inaudibly. Her hair was matted to her forehead.

Piedade, working beside her, answered without looking at her. 'Only a little further . . .' Her left hand grasped a clump of ripe stalks, which she calmly and firmly cut with the blade of her scythe.

From hillock to hillock the meadows were being stripped, trampled, saddened. Sheaves of grain lay about. As they accumulated in piles, they were taken, by cart, to the threshing floor.

With each step she took Natel felt the earth give way beneath her. In her lower back, stroked by the soft afternoon wind, the sensation of pins-and-needles became a painful jabbing. She felt nothing except the ache in her middle, as if the rest of her body, the very arms she was trying to control, belonged to someone else. If only the sun would go down right now, and the meadow be completely cleared. Then she would be able to see the faces of the other women, their heads and bodies once again erect. Then she could return to the village, where, lacking even the strength to get a drink of water, she could throw herself on the floor mat and fall effortlessly asleep. But she still felt the sun shining brightly in the sky; she knew that they must harvest every inch of rice. She looked up, trying to see how far the ripened stalks extended, but her eyes only encountered an opaque barrier.

A long, faint sigh shook her tired, perspiration-drenched body: 'Saiba.' Those working with her had moved on. From time to time they stopped the mechanical movements of their arms and, still bending over, their eyelids leadened by beads of sweat, looked at her and said: 'Let's go, Natel . . .' Her comrades' words of encouragement disheartened her even more. She knew that the landowner's overseer was watching, noting who was getting behind in her work. At the same time he kept a close watch over the number of sheaves being left for the carts. She would never want baab Ligor, or her grandfather, or Bostiao to find out that she had not been able to work as fast or as hard as the other women.

Piedade was more than a yard ahead of her.

'Hey, girl, let's go! I'll wait for you . . .'

To Natel's eyes, the distance seemed to increase; the reapers were fading away, as if their image was being reflected on the faintly rippling surface of a lake.

The rustling of the palms had lessened; only a gentle breeze seemed to cool the women's sunburned faces.

The harvesting was finished at nightfall. The carts took to the road even before the reapers had left the field. The sun illuminated the land until the last moment; its efforts were such that it seemed to be bleeding. Then, suddenly, the air darkened; bands of fleeing birds began to cross the sky. The devastated field seemed to be regaining its strength from the tired, still-warm land.

Baab Ligor's face still had a sombre, impassive expression, as if he were in mourning. But under his wrinkled forehead the thick, greying brows were showing signs of irritation. With his hands in the pockets of his starched coat, he walked through the halls of the huge house, speaking to no one. His voice was heard only at night, at the hour of the evening prayer when the family and servants gathered before the oratory. Then, in a cold, reserved tone, he would begin the first words of the prayers. He would pause, silently listening to the confused voices whirling about him, droning through the familiar prayers. Before the echo of the voices had died out in the small room lighted only by altar candles, he would raise his voice again, commanding the others to follow in his wake. Something in his voice transformed those prayers into a strange penitence that he seemed to be inflicting on himself and on the members of his household. When he finished the prayer and closed his eyes, his words seemed to hover above them all like the last agony of a condemned man. With his fingers interwoven, he would pull his hands up to his chest, cracking the numb joints. He would get up slowly and extinguish the candles himself. He was the last one to leave the small chapel.

After the ripened grain had been separated from the sheaves, it was left on the ground outside his house to dry in the sun. Once dried and husked, the rice promptly disappeared into the black market.

'It was a good year,' said those who understood such matters.

'But where is the rice?' others, who were neither landowners nor field labourers, would ask.

'It was always that way!' Jaqui was often heard to say from his seat at Rumao's tavern. 'There were always those who gave orders, who got what they wanted . . .'

'No one orders me around!' Pedru shouted from his corner where he'd been squatting for hours. No one answered him. His eyes were dim; his words came out all mixed up, as if his mouth was full of kernels. 'Ligor baab's the only one who tells me what to do,' he went on as the others continued to ignore him, 'and I hope he's completely ruined.' He'd been to the landowner's house that very morning, and had been treated with unusual harshness. Pedru had concluded that it was his daughter's fault, which was why he had not even talked to her but had returned instead to the village and come straight to Rumao's.

'What's the news from town?' Rumao had asked him, filling his cup with fenim. He would have liked to loosen Pedru's tongue, get him to talk about Coincao. Rumao had never seen her again after her departure to work for the landlord. But he had dreamed of her. He wanted to hear about her so that later, in his dreams, he could imagine all that her body suggested. 'So, what's new?' he had insisted calmly, in a tone capable of eliciting a response from even the most withdrawn of listeners. But Pedru's thoughts were elsewhere. His wild eyes were aflame with a vague desire for vengeance.

'Baab Ligor's fields are all mortgaged. That's the news from town,' he had answered wryly. 'They've been mortgaged for a long time, even before the last harvest. Any day now, he'll be ruined!' Having no more to say Pedru had slowly begun to drink his fenim.

Jaqui entered the tavern, followed by Bostiao and Gustin. Rumao greeted them vaguely as he set cups before them.

'Well, I've got some news that you don't have, even if I don't go into town all the time like you do!' Rumao's eyes were shining. With a steady hand he filled the cups and continued. 'Ligor baab's rice, you know, was stolen from the husking machines. That's the last we'll see of it because it's disappeared!' He paused slightly and, since no one interrupted him— they were all too stupefied to say anything—continued, 'The owner of the husking machine compensated baab Ligor for the loss, but the rice that you planted and your womenfolk harvested the other day, that's gone forever.' He gave a sarcastic chuckle, as if it were a very private joke. But he was really laughing at the dumb, confused faces before him.

The men quietly looked at each other.

After a long pause, looking first at Rumao and then at Jaqui, Bostiao finally asked, 'But won't Ligor baab complain to the authorities?'

'Why should he?' Rumao burst out laughing. 'You don't understand . . . if he were to complain, he'd never find the thief or the rice . . . the husking operations would have to be halted for some time . . . and baab wouldn't make a red cent.'

The men stared silently into space. Gustin's throat was dry, as if it had suddenly been filled with sawdust. He picked up a cup and drained it in one gulp.

'So,' Rumao went on with his explanation of the mystery, 'at least Ligor baab didn't lose everything.'

'But what about us . . .?' Gustin's voice was troubled; the alcohol still burned his throat.

'You? . . . It's a matter of putting up with another few months of hunger . . . and waiting.' Rumao was serious now. He rested his hand on Bostiao's shoulder. A dark, heavy shadow passed over the villagers' faces; their dull eyes awaited a word that would again give them hope.

Jaqui still said nothing. Very quietly, Gustin moved towards the door. Pedru, trying to regain the use of his legs, made an effort to get up. Bostiao looked at Jaqui but saw only a hardened, ominous look.

The men wandered along the roads, carrying their axes and knocking on every door in their search for work. Often, dusty and discouraged, they ended up in town where they encountered groups of low-caste labourers from many different villages. They would stare at each other suspiciously. As their search continued they were followed by the burning sun whose brightness only served to deepen their despair.

'There's no other way . . .' baab Ligor had told them. 'This year God cursed my fields and my harvests!'

'But the harvest was a good one,' Gustin wanted to

tell him, remembering Rumao's words.

'You'll just have to knock on others' doors. There's plenty of work around,' the landowner continued. 'There's always wood to be cut, roofs to be repaired . . . jobs of that sort to help you earn a living. I can't do anything else for you . . . of course, I release you from all obligation to me.'

He had planned to dismiss them with a little smile, but his face maintained its look of guilt and disgust. They were all standing in the entrance hall, in the same place they had been the night that baab Ligor, as patron of the festival, had given them bottles of fenim in return for their homage.

Baab Ligor was wearing a white linen suit with mother-of-pearl buttons down the front. His neckband was unbuttoned; he had on leather sandals. Although he was fanning himself, a long thread of sweat, like a vein, ran down his forehead and disappeared under his heavy brows.

'God willing, there will be enough work for you.'

'But what about the rice, baab . . . for our children?' Zuao Domingue had asked his question with lowered eyes. Baab Ligor flashed them an impatient look, as if he'd been waiting for just such a question.

'Rice, rice!' he yelled, infuriated. 'And whom will I ask for rice?' The men had never seen him so angry and cruel.

'I don't have any rice either . . . and I'm the landlord!' His voice became calmer; it acquired that peculiar firmness, the special tone in which masters sometimes address their servants. Without letting anyone answer him, he continued: 'It even seems as if you're not used to being short of food . . .' A spark of cynicism shone through every word. 'During these last years we haven't eaten high quality rice in my house; we've been using jaggery instead of sugar. The war has created many shortages; the maids complain about their wages; servants spend all day in long lines, just to buy a bit of coal oil.' He walked up and down the room, taking large strides. Every few seconds he fanned himself. Stopping, he added: 'Don't think you're the only ones making sacrifices, because you're not! At least you have small plots of land for gardens; you have a roof over your heads . . .'

He scrutinized the sunburned faces that he'd known for so long. Some since they were children, although he couldn't remember exactly how they had looked then. Nevertheless, their faces still showed the same meek expressions he'd always seen there. Large, rough feet, sunburned skin, eyes shining in humble supplication.

'And you owe what you have to me, and only to me! If you weren't my tenants you'd be a lot worse off . . . Your fathers and grandfathers worked these lands for my father and grandfather. So we have to accept this year's losses the way we'd rejoice in a good year.' A faint softness seemed to creep into his eyes. 'To be sure, this year is worse than usual . . . I was robbed, my entire harvest was stolen from the machine . . .' His eyes brightened, his eyelids trembled as he implored, 'Who was it? Can't you tell me . . . It had to be the tenants of some other landlord. The devil convinced them to steal instead of working and enduring the hard times. Just let any of my tenants even think about stealing . . . I'd kick him out, once and for all,' he added vehemently.

Jaqui stood chewing his dry lips. He raised his brows, giving himself a clearer view. Baab Ligor was standing before him, his hand still raised in an interrupted gesture. Drops of sweat shone on his reddened face, and they slid slowly down to his chest which was still trembling from the force of his words. Without moving he confronted Jaqui's cold, knowing eyes.

'But . . . our share of the rice,' Jaqui began, without lowering his eyes, 'baab Ligor kept that separate from the other; it didn't go to the husking machine.'

'No!' The reply was very quick. 'But don't depend on that. You'll get a portion of it . . . for your children . . .' The men standing around him had raised their eyes, which now showed an unusual spark. For the first time the faces seemed capable of being changed by a new force, whether of vengeance, hate or simple protest. Baab Ligor managed to overcome that moment of surprise and hesitation; he raised his voice again, his tone quick and decisive.

'I'm telling you now that you'll only get a small amount, a very small amount . . .'

'My wife is expecting a child,' Gustin burst out. An increasing rage was mixed with the pain of seeing all his hopes shattered.

'I'm sure she'll get her share . . .' baab Ligor answered. 'The division is up to you. Distribute it as you see fit.' His handkerchief mopped his wet face and vigorously rubbed his forehead, which had become dry and reddened. 'I also have many mouths to feed in my house. Or do you think I'm lying?' Baab Ligor felt himself in control of the situation again; the fire that he had seen in his tenants' eyes must have been the result of despair; it had completely died out now. 'I need money so you can carry out the next planting. This isn't the first time such a thing has happened to my land. And the other landowners have even lost their seed fields. Almost every year, you know it as well as I do, there's some catastrophe. Either it rains too little, or it rains too much . . . In the past we could make up for it because we imported rice. Now . . .'

He looked steadily at Jaqui and, pointing to Zuao Domingue, said: 'You two come back in a week. I'll have your rice set aside for you.' He loosened a few more buttons on his jacket, revealing the greyish hair on his chest. A gold chain and a dark scapular hung around his neck. Baab Ligor had spoken his final words. A sudden vacuum separated him from the men lined up in front of him. No one moved; no one lowered his eyes.

The landowner had remained motionless, unblinking. In the midst of this embarrassing silence, a honeybee flew very close to baab Ligor's face. With a sure blow of his fan he knocked it to the floor, next to Zuao Domingue's feet. Zuao Domingue killed the insect with his naked heel. Looking indifferently at the flattened body, baab Ligor had left without saying another word.

On a beautiful sunlit morning the villagers sombrely witnessed the distribution of the rice. Quitru, her eyes filled with tears, looked at the three measures that had just been poured into a corner of the grain-bin.

'Saiba!' she implored the yellowed image leaning against the wall, 'what will become of our child?'

'This rice,' Gustin pointed with his foot to the almost empty bin, 'is for you alone. You must eat well

so you'll have enough milk for our child. Meanwhile
. . . the rains will come and perhaps things will
change.'

'Perhaps things will change . . . How, Saiba? How?'

Quitru knew very well that Gustin's heart was
breaking. The hopes he had held for the harvest had
been completely destroyed. He tried to smile in her
presence but she saw that his courage had given way
to a sense of helplessness; his eyes were dull and
lifeless. Those eyes brightened sometimes, but only to
release the glow of his hatred. What had become of
their soft, sweet look?

'Saiba! What will become of us?'

'Perhaps there is a way to get more rice . . . or
money,' Gustin muttered.

'How, Saiba, how?' she asked anxiously, hopelessly.
'It's useless for us to kill ourselves working during the
next few months. And I can't even get a job, not in my
condition.'

'Calm down,' Gustin answered a bit coldly, turning
towards the door. His wife's sobs pierced his heart.
The seriousness of his expression deeply frightened
Quitru. She wanted to embrace him, to whisper tender
words that might comfort him and reawaken in him
that joyous confidence he'd always shown her. But
Gustin had already left, leaving the door open behind
him.

The sun beat down on the courtyards. Even the
voices she heard seemed to be suffocated by the heat.
She rested her hands on her stomach, as if to feel her
child moving inside. As she stood there, cold, silent
tears streamed down her face.

Translated from the Portuguese by Pat Williams

Hope

Vimala Devi

Torrential rains poured down. Through the low roof, water trickled down monotonously on to the dung floor. Pedru, squatting listlessly by the door, watched the river as the watery curtain blurred the scenery before him. Other than the noise of the water gushing down from the heavens, there was only the sound, an equally monotonous one, of the grinding stone with which his sister crushed the masala. His mother, ensconced in a corner, grumbled softly. Pedru could understand nothing of what she said. Silently he gazed at the choppy current of the river. Intermittently, a gust of wind would blow a spray into the house.

'Shut the door, Pedru,' murmured the mother. 'It's cold.'

'It gets stuffy in here!' retorted the son, bending forward.

'Oh yes, stuffy, but that's not because of the heat . . .'

They fell silent again.

It was the first monsoon shower, and it compelled

everyone to stay indoors. Pedru shook his head, despondent.

'Do you think I should go, Mai?' he asked.

'Go where, Pedru?'

'To speak to Mitzibai?'

The old woman didn't answer. Morgorit was still at the grinding, as if nothing else mattered to her. She stopped abruptly.

'When there's a break in the weather, it would be good to find some dry palm leaves to reinforce the roof,' she said. 'The coconut tree branches have become too thin and porous . . .'

Pedru didn't say a word. It was his mother who retorted indignantly:

'A-la-la, Morgorit! Pedru can't go about repairing roofs. He has passed out of the Lyceum and has to find himself a good job.'

'Hss, I'm tired of working only to see Pedru spend his days at home without earning a penny . . .'

'He doesn't like to go with us to the fields, Morgorit,' insisted the old woman. 'He wants to become a government employee.'

The girl held her tongue and the grinding could be heard once again. But it was not long before she broke her silence.

'I work, don't I, Mai? I worked from dawn to dusk so that Pedru could study at the Lyceum. I did so without ever complaining for years on end so that Pedru might become a big man like Robert baab. And now Pedru doesn't even care to find himself a job whereas I keep on slogging! Just because Pedru hates to step into the fields. Do you think it's fair, Mai? And now I have no dowry for myself, yet I have to go on killing myself here and let Pedru stay at home smoking his viddi. For how long, Mai?'

The old woman fidgeted in the corner. She understood her daughter and knew that she was right. But it was worth all the sacrifice for Pedru. He would find himself a job. He was clever, and with a little more patience . . . She bent forward and tapped her son gently on the shoulder. The boy started and for a moment turned his eyes away from the rain outside.

'Go! Go and speak to Mitzibai, Pedru! Go and have a word with her. She is a good landlady. She will surely help you.'

'But they are poor, Mai. As poor as we are. What can they do? A few days ago Vithal's wife, Mogrem, saw them having chapattis with tea for lunch! They are poorer than we are, mother. But do you think Mitzibai would still be able to . . .?'

The old woman passed her fingers slowly around her tobacco-cone and then put it in her mouth. She lit it and sucked in some smoke.

'But they are brahmins, Pedru. Very old brahmins. Whether poor or not doesn't matter. They know all the top people in Panjim. They have relations in the government. They are cousins of all the big people with influence. They are paupers now, but once upon a time they were the richest bhatkars of Orlim. I still remember Teresinbai in the big house, beautifully dressed, welcoming the pakle. And their mother, Rejinbai, was a wealthy bhatkan. Very generous people! In her time nobody went hungry in Orlim. There was rice and coconut for everyone. Her godown was always open to anyone in need. That was the cause of their downfall. And the gala parties they had! They lasted upto four days and were attended by government officials, and even the Governor himself. In my young days I worked in the grandmother's kitchen. And the father, what a handsome man he was! Robert baab has his features but not the same temperament. Anyhow, he is a good boy . . . Then the father died, and they began selling their things; then the grandmother passed away, and now they are poorer than we are. You are right, but don't you realize they are still our landlords? Everybody respects them, because they are good landlords. Very different from landlord Dias who robs us of everything—short of our soul, as that belongs to God . . .'

Pedru smacked his lips, moistened by the raindrops brought in by the wind.

The old woman continued, 'Let us pray the Rosary, Pedru, that Mitzibai will find you a job. The sacrifices the two of us have made will be rewarded. Remember that you are the first one from Orlim to have graduated from the Lyceum. That is a matter of pride for us. It was worth all the sacrifice, wasn't it, Morgorit? Let us pray to Our Fathers for the soul of old Rejinbai, that she may rest in the peace of the Lord . . . *Amchea Bapa, Tum sorgar assa* . . .'

A loud crash of thunder drowned out her voice. Raindrops, thickening, began to fall in through the thatched roof.

'And at the eleventh hour, it's this!' exclaimed Mitzi. 'Roberto now says he won't come with us.'

Teresa smiled and looked at her son.

'Do go, Roberto. It's your duty to escort your sisters. Don't you see they have to arrange a match for themselves?'

Mitzi, nineteen, wheatish-complexioned, fumed. 'We're going to miss the best dance of Clube Nacional because of him. And the money I've spent in stitching this dress! This boy now wants to play truant. Is it fair, Mai?'

'They only go out to dance with those pale faces and my friends begin to gossip,' burst out Roberto. 'They've gone crazy . . .'

'Don't believe him, mother. I dance just once or twice. It is Lena who dances much more. But what's wrong with that? Look,' she said, turning to her brother, 'they say the buffet this year is going to be better than it ever was, so the loss will be all yours . . .'

Roberto sat in the armchair, rocking, not looking at Mitzi.

'Now Lena has gone to Jeronima's who has a special way with hairstyles. When she comes back she too will be angry, I hope you know . . .'

Roberto kept rocking quietly. Their mother was at the rear end of the house. The two of them were left to themselves. Mitzi caught sight of the serious look on her brother's face. She went up to him and sat on the floor by his chair. Roberto pretended not to have noticed her until she took his hand and began to stroke it.

'You remember, Roberto, when granny died,' she began. 'You're right, we were very badly off then, and now we have to take care to save the name of our family. I know well enough that we're being watched all the time. They're waiting to catch us on the wrong foot and then have a good laugh at our expense. Of course, it's difficult for girls who are poor and without a father to escape from the claws of gossipmongers. But we are sensible girls and lucky too to have you for a brother. Very well, then, let's stay back home tonight. Would you like to play cards, Roberto? Let's send for cousin Alzira and have a great time.'

Roberto looked all perplexed at his sister, not knowing what she was up to.

'Well, that's not what I meant to say. It is just that I don't like you to dance with the pakle. Why can't you dance only with our boys? These pakle don't have a good reputation and they give the girls a bad name, you know it!'

'You're right,' said Mitzi, seriously. 'Our boys are so different from the pakle. Do you think I would marry any one of them? Well, they cut a fine figure here, but back in Europe they're only scum. And stupid too, don't you see? Our boys are quite different and when they marry, it's for life. I'd rather marry a sudra than a paklo! They change wives like shirts. And oh, talking of sudras, guess who came here a little while ago requesting us to find him a job? . . . Imagine, Pedru! Yes, Pedru, son of Salubrancar! These people are simply impossible. Now that he has passed out of the Lyceum, he thinks he is somebody and wants a job. They think they are on equal terms with us, you see? He came here with all that bai-fai, treating me like his equal. Anyway, I put him in his place. He wanted me to speak to cousin Josinho to employ him in the Fazenda, imagine! His mother and sister work in the fields and he thinks he is some gentleman only because he has graduated from the Lyceum. The cheek of it!'

Roberto nodded gravely in agreement. Then, turning to her, he said, 'Well, go and get dressed! You're still keen on going to the ball, aren't you? When is Lena coming?'

Translated from the Portuguese by Oscar de Noronha

Shanti

Epitacio Paes

'Eh Shanti!' shouted her mother from the corner where she was grinding some chillies and bits of coconut for the midday curry.

'Get up, girl, the sun is high up already. Give some canji to your father! How lazy you are! Aren't you ashamed of sleeping so long when Rohini and Pandu are already out with the buffaloes? Look, your father is waiting for his broth.'

The man had woken up early, his head still groggy from the previous night's drinking. He sat on the rough banister of the veranda, singing an obscene song about women. His body, bare except for a triangle of red cloth around his private parts, swayed to the rhythm of the grinding-stone. His tiny pigtail jiggled. The rising sun warmed his parched, wrinkled skin, under which his muscles, weakened by heavy and frequent drinking bouts, sagged visibly.

Shanti woke up, rubbed her eyes and yawned. Then turning to her little brother who was still asleep, she pulled him by the feet. He slid down like a sledge on the mat which had a high sheen to it as a result of constant use.

The little boy, so abruptly woken, burst into tears and went to seek refuge in his mother's lap. She promptly uncovered one of her breasts and let him suck it. Shanti in turn ran up and demanded the other, but her mother slapped her on the buttocks and drove her away.

'Go, see if the canji is done and give it to your father.'

Shanti ran inside and began to blow on the fire. From the rim of the boiling pot, a white, foamy wisp spilled down.

'We have to buy the girl a blouse,' said the wife, interrupting her grinding. 'She's growing up and it is a shame to let her go about like this, bare-chested. I myself never covered my breasts until I was fifteen and no one noticed, but times have changed. In those days we would go to town without a blouse on, with nothing more than one capodd round our bodies. But now nobody does that anymore. Shali wears a petticoat underneath her blouse and other stuff over it! The other day, when the cloth seller came, I didn't even have a few paise to buy a yard of rough cotton. You waste all your money drinking . . . how on earth are we going to clothe our daughter!'

'I drink! I drink, all right, but I drink a little. If I don't I have no appetite for food and if I don't eat I can't work. What am I to do? Let her carry on as she is. If all the girls from our quarter go about bare-chested, why should we alone bear the luxury of covering her body? She's only twelve, I presume, I'm not sure—she was born during that small-pox epidemic which killed my brothers and my mother . . . You say you didn't cover your breasts until you were fifteen? Eh! Eh! It must have been quite a sight.'

'You know nothing and you see nothing around you. Don't you know that nowadays children grow up faster? Some days ago, Santu asked me if we were willing to give her in marriage to his son.'

'Eh! Eh! Only if he takes her free.'

'Free! Fifty bangles, three copper vessels, gold earrings and a silver necklace. The usual.'

'Fifty bangles, three copper vessels, gold earrings,' he sang. 'Give it to him! Is that all he wants?'

'You would have made similar demands if you were him!'

'We must get her married sooner or later.'

Shanti appeared with a metal dish filled with steaming rice broth and laid it by her father's side. He began to slurp it down with obvious relish.

'Would you like some, girl?'

Shanti nodded and began to gulp down the rice while her father tilted the dish for her.

'Shanti, what are you up to? Go inside and help yourself to your heart's content,' said her mother. 'Give some to Munu too.'

They did not wait to be told again. They sat down and competed with each other to eat as much as possible.

'So, what do I tell Santu?' asked the wife.

'Tell him that we only have the girl, nothing else.'

'He won't agree, I'm sure.'

'Tell him to hold on until we manage something. The girl is still young. She is the same age as Anna Rita's daughter. She is not bothered about it like we are.'

'They are Christians. Our customs are different. We must marry her off in the course of this year or the next or else the neighbours will laugh at us. Melu has already married off three daughters and Bhima two. You ought to be ashamed of facing them!'

'But I married you when you were over fifteen.'

'That was because I had nobody except my aunt who was deaf. They used to tell me that I was past the marrying age.'

'I was your salvation, ha! ha!'

'I was forced into it in spite of knowing that you drank so much! I don't want my daughter to meet the same fate.'

'What do you want me to do, woman?'

'You could do with drinking less and saving a few paise. Your father never drank.'

He began to sing his favourite song once again to drown out his wife's tirade. He had a quick wash and went to check the spades which he had left in a corner. About an hour later the wife finished making the rice and the curry. She filled the tiffin with enough to go round for two. And both set off for the day's work: the tilling of the paddy fields scorched by the fury of a blazing sky. It was a job undertaken by virtually every man and woman of their quarter on a seasonal contract.

Along the road, the line of men and women thickened. Scrawny men, ravaged by alcohol, their wrinkled chocolate-coloured nudity seeming to blend with the earth, moved ahead. They moved in measured steps, as if conserving their energy, their thoughts all centred round the paltry coins they would collect at the end of the day. Scantily clad women, their brass bangles and anklets jingling with every movement, walked with their married children who had barely crossed puberty. They kept tripping over their clothes, exhausted by the violence of the previous night.

'Shanti! Mind Munu!'

'And don't fight with Antonio.'

Shanti had told them not to worry, since Antonio would be away at school and would only return in the evening. She would sit under the tamarind tree and play with Butu. And she would shut the door behind her. And she would go nowhere near the stream. And she wouldn't eat the rice before the church bell tolled at noon.

When, a little later, Butu called her out to play she went to the temple's cemented yard, where Munu rode on her as if on horseback. They joined the children who usually gathered there, playing all kinds of games while the procession of fathers and mothers continued on its way. Little boys would hold branches of trees and jump around striking poses, while a few others uttered sounds in some unknown language, imitating the dancers who came year after year for the celebration of some religious festival.

As for the girls, the majority of them brought along their infant brothers and sisters. They would put them down on the flagstones and then dance around the sacred plant.

Munu would come in the way, and Shanti would pick him up, set him down on a pillar from where he couldn't come down by himself, and once again begin the endless merry-go-round.

Shanti would vanish once in a while. She would enter her house, open the rice pot, and disobeying all her mother's strictures, scoop a few spoonfuls into her mug. Filling her mouth, she would run back to the yard without as much as wiping her face.

Her mother returned only at nightfall, exhausted, carrying besides her own her husband's spade. The latter staggered behind her on wobbly feet, his ponytail clearly visible. The mother would at once sit down to grind the spices for the night's curry, her movements hampered by Munu who sucked at her breast.

'Was everything all right, Shanti?'

'Yes, mother.'

'You didn't fight with anyone?'

She twisted around, her arms wide open, a picture of innocence.

'Why is Munu so dirty?'

'He was playing with mud and kneading it with Prema's brother's piss.'

'Couldn't you have washed him, lazy bones?'

She then made for the well, accompanied by her husband who followed her like a thirsty buffalo, craving for some water down his body burnt by a whole day's sun.

Shanti loved to draw water from the well, but her mother feared that she might fall in. Shanti would whine and stamp her feet. Finally the matter would be settled with the man of the house pouring water over them all. The cloth tied round their bodies dripping wet, Shanti would split her sides laughing, while her mother, though smouldering with fury, remained silent.

Shanti turned thirteen. She had grown taller, though her body was still scrawny. A flame-coloured blouse covered her flat chest on which two fleshy buds seemed to sprout. Her legs were thin, and her hips had not yet matured.

One day her mother bought her a new piece of cloth to replace the blouse and the skimpy wrap-around. She taught her how to make the pleats. Then, when the bangle merchant showed up, she covered her bony forearms with fifty-odd brass bangles.

'We're getting you married next week, girl. The boy's parents are coming to see you. No more play from today.'

From that day onwards Shanti's friends noticed that she had turned somewhat more discreet, conscious of her new attire, drawing water from the well and carrying baskets of rice on her head. She walked along the road with a grave demeanour, no longer laughing as she used to. They all envied her for her cotton saree, her bangles, her anklets and her luck. She took upon herself such chores as the grinding of cereals and the plastering of the floor and the walls with cowdung. She insisted that her mother lie down after returning from work in the paddy fields. She looked after Munu. She washed bundles of clothes down in the stream.

'Father, don't drink so much!'

The man would allow her to take the bottle away and would sit in a corner waiting for the food to be served.

'Munu! Don't eat so much rice, your tummy might burst!'

She would wipe his distended belly, cover his private parts with a handkerchief bought at the fair, and send him off to play.

'Mother, don't you go to the grinding mill. I have nothing to do today.'

She would hitch onto her head the rice basket, run to the grinding mill and return with the unhusked rice which was their daily bread.

They got her married.

She had never set eyes on her husband, not even on the day the temple priest pronounced them married. Only after the usual ceremony did she have the courage to look at him. She was seized by a longing to get rid of the flaming red attire, run into the cashew grove and remain hidden there. She was on the verge of tears, while all her friends stared at her with envious eyes. The musician's trumpets seemed to stammer. It was all like a bad dream she had once had.

But when the feast was over, the bridegroom left for his home with his retinue, leaving her at her mother's. Shanti picked up the life she led before, shuttling between her mud hut with its unpainted walls and cowdung floor and the hamlet well, between the leased cashew grove and the sun-scorched field. Her mother had given up many of the household chores which were now Shanti's responsibility, while her father indulged her every wish, only too happy to obey her. It was she who, before sunrise, filled her parents' tiffin with rice, swept the hut, gave Munu his food, untied the buffaloes and tended to many other things. Meanwhile, according to tradition, things were being finalized for the day when she would join her husband.

'He won't hurt me, mother, will he?' she asked, her heart pounding under the new saree whose numerous folds sat awkwardly on her lean, childlike body.

Her mother smiled and replied: 'What an idea!'

'I want to stay here, mother.'

'Are you mad? We didn't get you married to have you live with us. I also joined your father as soon as they married me off to him.'

'I don't want to . . .'

'They will laugh at you. Every girl goes to her husband's house. Look at Lila, Milan, all the others.'

'I don't want to.'

And she burst into tears.

She was taken to her bridegroom's home in a glittering procession. It marched to the monotonous sounds of the shehnai and the cynical beat of the drum. The women and children of the village came dressed in their ostentatious best, their heads covered with flowers, while the men, normally unkempt, dressed immaculately. Seven vessels of the largest possible size filled with sweets, two water pots, a pair of golden earrings, silver necklaces and needles were also being taken, according to the unreasonable demands of an inhuman mother-in-law. Judging by all this pomp, the ceremony promised to be a grand affair. The bridegroom was there in European clothes, showing no trace of conventional timidity. He smiled among a group of friends who praised the bride's beauty. From time to time he would look at his new watch. A gold pen gleamed in his shirt pocket. His abundant hair, profusely plastered with vaseline, reflected the strong light of the pressure lamps. His eyes had a lewd glint in them as they devoured Shanti. The feast began. Food was served on banana leaves. Everybody began to eat, the silence punctuated only by some remarks, usually referring to the bride's charms, to the bridegroom's suitability. Three men holding enormous pots in their hands made sure that no plate remained empty. The arrack pots kept in a corner were finished off in no time. The atmosphere perked up considerably.

The bridegroom drank too. He bragged about his mines to the gang surrounding him and they reacted, laughing uproariously. He was no longer a manual worker, had they heard? He had taken on contract the mining of a very good site at a favourable rate. Would anyone like to work for him? He would pay them well, better than the others, give them extra tips besides the salary! It would all be on paper, signed. He had a pen. Eight hours of work per day, exactly eight, timed on his watch, and wages at the end of the day. Money would come, that would be no problem. If they were interested in working for him they should say so at once, since he preferred to employ people from his own village.

Suddenly the music began, shattering the rumble of voices with its throbbing drum beat. As for Shanti, she was put in the tiny bedroom, the private room of the house, which was windowless, suffocatingly hot and reeking of freshly applied cowdung. A brand new bamboo mat, covered with a sheet, was spread on the floor. A profound silence, sporadically broken by the snoring of her mother-in-law who was sleeping in the adjoining room, prevailed all around.

'I wonder what Mother and Munu are doing,' she thought, seated on the mat, thoroughly exhausted, feeling choked inside the narrow cubicle, her body drenched in perspiration. She was seized by a strange sort of fear which made her nerves contract painfully while her mind churned with confused, vague thoughts and forebodings. She sat there for hours, wrapped up in her clothes, until, unable to control her fatigue, she fell forward on the mat.

Minutes later she heard someone coming towards her. Who could that be? Perhaps he. A shiver went through her whole body. She wanted to run away, crouch in a corner and cry loudly, but found herself unable to do anything of the sort. A few seconds later, the room was filled with the stench of liquor. She sat down on the mat with her head hung over her chest, her hands gripping her knees.

She lay down on the mat. Groping in the dark, he dragged himself on the floor in every direction till he laid his hands on her. He fell over her ferociously and clasped her in his arms like a drunken satyr.

Translated from the Portuguese by Muriel Faleiro

Senhor Eusebio Builds His Dream House[*]

Victor Rangel-Ribeiro

Eusebio Pinto, a man of modest beginnings, but now 'Euseb baab' to his social inferiors and Senhor Eusebio to his peers, had gone to the Persian Gulf at the end of the Great War in 1918, having heard that the Turks had been ousted and great things would be afoot. Then aged forty, he had wound up accepting a position as a low-salaried clerk with a British oil company prospecting in Mesopotamia, but the word that his fond mother spread around Tivolem was that he was there because the feringhee had sent for him. From his modest paycheck he unfailingly sent his aging parents a monthly stipend, intending they should spend it on their food or other essentials. Instead, his mother bought a candle a day, which she burnt at the

---

*An excerpt from the novel Tivolem, set in a mythical village in Goa in the early thirties.

altar of St. Cornelius, imploring his blessings on her son. Her prayers bore fruit: Eusebio's diligence earned him promotions, though not large salary increases; however, as he had found no place in which to spend his earnings, and had absolutely no vices, his savings mounted. When his parents died, he transferred to his now substantial bank balance both his attention and his affections. He retired and returned to his native village thirteen years after he had left it, saw the tiny house he had been born in, and, shrewd manager that he was, looked for land he could acquire.

The search did not take long. A great stretch of the village, running alongside the nullah, belonged to Dona Esmeralda. Her tenants included Forttu the tavern keeper, he who sold not only choice coconut-palm liquor but also Johnny Walker Scotch ('Still going strong', as a faded sign proclaimed); the shopkeeper Atmaram and his family; Mottu the postman, his wife Annabel, and their son, Little Arnold; Govind the carpenter, his wife Amita, and their five small children; and Kashinath the barber, with his wife and children. Dona Esmeralda had been their landlady since the 1890s, as her family had been for generations before that; with the Great Depression, however, the old widow had fallen on hard times, and it did not help that, like their ancestors before them, her tenants paid no rent, but gave payment in kind—in produce, and in services.

Senhor Eusebio needed an intermediary, and paid a call on Senhor Eduardo and Dona Elena. He was met at the door by the maid. 'The master's not in,' she said immediately, standing squarely in the doorway. 'Actually,' he said, embarrassed, 'I'm sorry to have missed him, but I've come to talk to your bai.'

Reluctantly she ushered him into the vast living room, inviting him to sit while she went to fetch her mistress.

Hat in hand, he sat somewhat nervously on the edge of a heavily carved chair. His childhood home, too, had had old chairs that his parents had prized, but the one he was sitting on was a precious antique, made of the finest ebony, and, like the rest of the furniture here, a couple of centuries old at least; he was not sure how it would hold up under his weight. A large crystal chandelier that hung in the centre was used, he gathered, on rare social occasions, as were the sconces high on each wall, light being usually provided by the ornate oil lamps that were placed around the room. Six tall windows overlooked the garden; from the facing wall the portraits of bearded ancestors glowered down at him with fierce intensity. He had seen those same types of portraits in other homes—even the women seemed grim. That was the generation Dona Esmeralda belonged to; he hoped Dona Elena, whom he knew but slightly from meeting her casually at church and on the street, would be more accommodating.

He found her to be pleasantly sociable. She apologized for her husband's absence. She remembered both of Senhor Eusebio's parents, though they had lived on the other side of the village and had been dead some years. She asked him about his years in the Gulf. And she offered him tea in elegant diminutive china cups, and raisin cake on exquisite dishes.

He had to wade through minutes of small talk before she allowed a moment of silence to develop. She was sitting upright in her chair, cup in hand, waiting for him to speak.

He decided to come right to the point. 'I'd like to build myself a bigger house,' he said, 'and I need land.'

'That could be a problem. The village is heavily built up, and all land around here is already owned.'

'I realize that. People will not easily part with what they hold.'

'There are sentimental attachments that develop,' Dona Elena said. 'And reluctances. Status—you'll understand . . . It's not like selling off a bit of furniture, though heaven knows that too can sometimes be traumatic. But there are roots, and memories. Quite aside from which, none of our properties are up for sale.'

'Your land is working for you, and that's not the land I'm after,' he said. 'But your friend Dona Esmeralda has the largest tracts around here. Perhaps on my behalf you could ask if she's willing to sell.'

'Dona Esmeralda is more attached to her land than I am to mine,' Dona Elena said. 'Besides, she is deeply involved in the lives of her tenants, and they in hers.'

'With all the respect due Dona Esmeralda, the times are hard,' he said. 'The Great Depression, it has not treated people kindly. Me, I've been fortunate; I had nothing, and went where the oil was. I saved up some money. She on the other hand is in dire straits; that's common knowledge, but she need not know that I know. Sooner or later she'll have to sell. In telling her I'm interested, you'll be doing your old friend a favour. Look, I've looked into the land; I'll pay five thousand rupees for it. That's a fair price, and in these times, it's quite a lot of money.'

As Dona Elena had foreseen, Dona Esmeralda's

initial reluctance to sell ancestral lands to a nouveau riche was compounded by concerns for her tenants and fears for the future.

'My son, I'm thinking of my son,' Dona Esmeralda said.

'Of course,' Dona Elena said.

'Artistic, but shiftless. No, don't protest,' Dona Esmeralda said, as her visitor made a move to interrupt her, 'the whole world knows it is so. Barnabe has a wife and child, has been married ten years, lives in Goregao, is almost fifty years old, and still he comes to me for money. You've seen his business—antiques and clutter, that's what I call it. Nobody buys the stuff he has. Without land to fall back on, what will he do when I'm gone?'

'You still have vast properties in Aicona,' Dona Elena said.

'But that's a far-off village.'

'May be so, but the land there is valuable. More valuable than the parcels you have here.'

'If only Romualdo were here!' Dona Esmeralda cried. 'What a mess! What a mess! You have your Eduardo, but I? Why do our men die and leave us with a mess?'

'You need time to think,' Dona Elena said, embracing her old friend and comforting her. 'I'll come back tomorrow.'

When they met again, Dona Esmeralda was visibly perturbed. 'Word has gotten around. My tenants are greatly distressed.'

'That's understandable. Over the years you have been more than generous with them.'

'No more than Romualdo would have been. Or his

parents and grandparents before him. But the truth is, they can't hold on to me for ever.'

'Fortunately, most of them have grown children.'

'Except for Govind and Amita. Of their five children, the oldest is just six years old. And all those goats! Govind and Amita depend on me for everything. They came to see me yesterday, bringing their little ones, pleading that the land that they were on not be sold. Govind fell at my feet. "You are my father and my mother," he said. "Do not abandon us." The children began crying. What am I to do? Eusebio's right—I need the money, and if I don't get it today I'll need twice as much tomorrow. But those children! I hugged them, and they cried and clung to me, not knowing why they were crying. On this I am adamant—I will sell Eusebio the rest of the land, but not Govind's patch. No. Those children . . . Never.'

Senhor Eusebio was upset. 'I'm from this village, too,' he said to Dona Elena. 'I feel for the people here. What makes her think I'll be rough with her tenants? Does she think I'm an ogre? That makes me angry.'

'But do you see her point?' Dona Elena countered. 'She has known their parents and their grandparents; has celebrated their weddings, rejoiced at their births, mourned at their funeral pyres. She has been their protectress and their benefactress for longer than you and I have lived.'

He would not be mollified. 'And probably spoils them rotten, while they rob her blind. If I can't have Govind's plot, I must reduce my offer. Or withdraw it completely.'

'And then you won't have your house. The five thousand you offered, and she gets to keep Govind's plot.'

'You are tough as an Arab sheikh,' he said.

'And alas! not quite as unctuous.'

'Tell the old bat I agree to her terms,' he said. 'She can keep her Govind, her Amita, and all the kids, both two and four-footed.'

The deal concluded, on an extended idle lot he set about building himself the second largest house in the village, as large arguably as Dona Elena's, though neither as large nor as grand as Dona Esmeralda's, and, as all could see, not quite as elegant. Her house, after all, was three hundred years old; people knew how to build houses in those days, as she once remarked to a visitor, the gossip Josephine Aunty, under rather extreme provocation.

Senhor Eusebio knew just the kind of house he wanted. Not for him the sloping roofs with interlocking rows of curved mud-brown tiles found in every village in Goa; those tiles tended to break if any hard object fell on them; but even if they didn't, they had to be removed and reset each year, since they shifted with the action of the wind and the sun and the rain. Besides, he wanted a house that would be unique— made not just out of red laterite rock but with outer walls made of poured cement concrete, a flat roof to match, and a terrace on top that would be open to the skies.

Tivolem had not seen so much activity in decades. The labourers worked in long lines, the men picking up the large red rectangular stones as the lorries brought them in from the quarry to the mouth of the narrow lane, then carrying them on their heads to the worksite; the women carrying sometimes stones, sometimes mortar, sometimes sand, but more often two large gleaming copper potfuls of water, one on the head and one at the hip, for the mixing of the concrete. Like so many busy and conscientious insects, they then retraced their steps, picking up yet other burdens to deliver.

People came from as far as Vasco in the south and Pernem in the north to gawk at the work in progress. Reaction in Tivolem itself was mixed. Forttu rejoiced in that, after a hard day's work, most of the workers stopped by his place for one or more shots of feni, even though the foreman and three others did not touch a drop of that cashew liquor. Govind, too, rejoiced; since much lumber was needed, he found himself sawing and planing as never before, and sang as he went about his work. His wife Amita was happy that the foreman and the three teetotallers drank only goat's milk. Kashinath, however, had cause to complain—none of the workers ever seemed to want a haircut, though anyone could see they needed them badly. As for the design of the building itself, Senhor Eusebio's new tenants showered it with praise, but were inwardly concerned, wondering whether their new landlord would take some of its cost out of their hide.

Other judgements were made on less subjective grounds. It was Dona Esmeralda's habit to go on a ritual stroll through the village, with her three black wirehaired terriers running ahead of her in single file, to receive obeisance from her former vassals. As the new house took shape, she was disturbed by the style of construction. Yet she kept her own counsel, confiding only in Dona Elena when the latter paid her a courtesy visit and they both sat down to tea: 'An ugly monstrosity—it does not belong. The man has much money but absolutely no taste.'

Dona Elena agreed. 'But there's good and bad in everything,' she pointed out soothingly. 'Let's thank God for the money and blame the bad taste on the devil.'

Dona Esmeralda was not amused. She was even less amused when a bustling Josephine Aunty stopped by soon after Dona Elena had left, demanding an audience. After a proper wait, Dona Esmeralda met her on the balcony; not everybody got to see the inside of her house.

Josephine Aunty wasted no time: 'Wonderful news! Senhor Eusebio is enlarging his plans. He now wants the terrace on the roof to be large enough so a dance band can fit in one corner.'

'A band!'

'Not a very big band. But he says he finds the village is much too quiet. Once in a while, he'd like to see some dancing and revelry in the evenings.'

So shocked was Josephine Aunty by Dona Esmeralda's highly emotional reaction to this bulletin that she reported the conversation verbatim to Senhor Eusebio, adding a few turns of her own.

Senhor Eusebio was in a charitable mood. 'Let her be,' he said. 'I'm not troubled by her criticism of my architectural plans. She should talk! Her roof leaks.'

'He says your roof leaks,' Josephine Aunty reported to Dona Esmeralda, salvaging what mischief she could out of the mild response. It was a damaging blow, because true. Come the monsoon rains, Dona Esmeralda's roof leaked not just in one place but in several. No sooner had a bucket been placed by a servant to catch the rainwater dripping through at one spot, than other servants (she had three) had to scurry to place pots and pans where other leaks had begun to sprout. 'I'm told the drumming of raindrops on various metals in her house is like a percussion concerto,' Senhor Eusebio had added. This too Josephine Aunty had reported.

Dona Esmeralda stopped speaking to Senhor Eusebio, and Senhor Eusebio continued to provoke her by raising his hat and bowing slightly each time she passed the construction site. Her dogs, sensing the mood, bared their teeth and snarled at him. In time, she passed that way less and less often.

The house was completed in January of 1932, and Senhor Eusebio moved in immediately.

Josephine Aunty revisited Dona Esmeralda. 'New furniture in every room,' she reported happily.

'Couldn't afford antiques?' Dona Esmeralda wanted to know, her eyebrows arching over the top of her lorgnette.

'Now he's added some,' Josephine Aunty came back to say a week later.

'Probably fakes,' Dona Esmeralda said. 'One does not know antiques until one has lived with antiques. All of one's life.'

'Dona Esmeralda should know, she has lived with herself all her life,' was Senhor Eusebio's somewhat ungallant reply.

Josephine Aunty, fearing for her own safety, still reported that sally.

'I do not trade personal insults,' Dona Esmeralda said, retreating to moral high ground. But in time she got her revenge. In the monsoon that year, one of the most severe in memory, her roof leaked water like a squeezed sponge, but Senhor Eusebio's leaked worse still. The flat roof and open terrace acted as giant receptacles where rainwater accumulated; it seeped through the ceiling, and ran in great streams down the insides of the walls, continuing to come down into the house long after the squall itself had passed.

'If my house is a percussion concerto, his is a misplaced discord. It just doesn't fit—and the worst is yet to come!' Dona Esmeralda quipped when Josephine Aunty told her of the floods in the enemy camp.

Dona Esmeralda resumed her leisurely walks through the village, preceded by her feisty terriers. Senhor Eusebio now did his best to avoid meeting her in public, but this became difficult, since each time they saw him the dogs rushed furiously at him, barking their heads off. She, however, remained the model of propriety, forcing him to acknowledge her presence by lifting her silver-knobbed cane in salutation and nodding her head in a most gracious manner.

Angel Wings [*]

Victor Rangel-Ribeiro

The car sped through the sleeping village like an ill wind, its engine groaning as it climbed the rutted road that would take it towards the city of Panjim. But even more than the straining engine, the startled villagers remembered that other sound—that high-pitched crying-out and keening that sounded somewhere between a long-drawn-out 'Ma-maa!' and the panicked bleating of a goat. Who was it, and why?

It was a child from Goregaon, the baker told them next morning, a child who had boarded at a school in that neighbouring village, a child who the previous evening had climbed a jambool tree to pluck the luscious fruit, had filled his pocket and climbed higher still to the topmost branches, where one had snapped, sending him crashing to the ground. They had found him at night, semi-conscious, his skull fractured, and it was his moans the village had heard as he was being rushed to hospital.

An excerpt from the novel Tivolem.

'You will wonder why,' the vicar said from the pulpit that Sunday, 'God allows such things. For you have all heard that the boy died. One might as well ask, why did He not create trees with iron limbs? Why did He put in boys the quickness to climb trees, in men the lust to climb mountains from which to fall? We cannot begin to understand the ways of God, and must trust in His infinite mercy. Other than that, I have no answers. All I know is, when a dear one is struck down, whether young or old, infant or grandparent, it is always too soon. Much too soon.'

Carefully, he adjusted his vestments, knowing that all eyes, following the movement of his hands, would be reminded whence he derived his authority.

'De mortuis,' the vicar said, and paused, leaving the words hanging in the air. 'They say the child was good, and we know he was good; children are the stuff that angels are made of. But of others, who are older and not quite so innocent, do we not also say the same thing? When we hear a man is dead, do we not praise him to the skies? And if that person turns out to be alive, do we not sometimes wish him dead? The same man, to be judged evil or good—is death the deciding factor? How twisted, how hypocritical then our judgements and our praise!'

The vicar's hands were white as they clasped the pulpit's marble rim. 'Many good things will be said about us, too, when we are gone,' he continued, 'but only we and God will know whether we deserve such praise or not. And if we don't, by then it will be too late.'

To Pedro Saldanha, standing just inside the crowded church, it seemed as though the vicar had singled him out for that sermon and that admonition. Others in the congregation felt the same way; the vicar's eyes, when he turned their way, bored deep into their souls. But Pedro Saldanha was overwhelmed. A deeply religious man, he was known for kneeling during long stretches of the mass, his knees burning through the hard stone floor, his arms outstretched in a symbolic crucifixion until he felt them no more, feeling only the pain. That Sunday, following the sermon, he remained kneeling, and self-crucified, long after all others had gone their way.

His sister waited lunch for him, anxiety replacing irritation as the hours passed and he still did not appear. She took the large wooden ladle from the pot and gave the curry another stir, feeding a bit of it to the scrawny tortoise-shell cat that turned and rubbed itself insistently against her shins.

'Yes, yes,' she said, when the cat turned away from the food. 'So you'll wait for him, too. That's the way it is with the three of us, all growing old together, he perhaps fastest of all. But we too, cat; yes, even you, with your nine lives.'

The woman moved to the window.

'Sometimes you'd think I'm his mother,' she said. 'Perhaps our mother would have wanted that, that I should look after him so. But he . . . we're stuck, unmarried—end of the line. No one after us, to mourn our passing, pray in our memory. No one but you.'

The cat jumped on the sill and looked down the lane, its tail swishing. 'All right, so he's coming,' said the woman. 'Now I see him too.' She went to the hearth, and blew on the ashed-over wood to bring the flame to life, feeling the heat flare against her face even as she drew back from the sparks and flying cinders.

Hellfire, she muttered, remembering the vicar's sermon at the early mass she had attended. Not that he had mentioned Hell—he seldom did; but he spoke of the hereafter, which was close enough. But the priest who had been vicar before him, that old priest had been able to work Hell and hellfire into every sermon he preached, no matter what the text for the day. She had been a young woman then, terrified by the vastness of the hereafter, sleepless at the thought both of eternal bliss and eternal damnation. When the present vicar arrived, what she had liked best about him was that he kept Hell in its place. Somewhere over there, but out of sight.

The garden gate creaked, and as she pushed the one chair back to the kitchen table her brother entered the room. Silently she placed the two pans on the table, and he sat and helped himself. He glanced approvingly at the curry—it was his favourite. Yesterday's fish curry, cooked in a sauce of spices, dried chillies, and coconut milk, boiled down to a rich, paste-like consistency; a little would go a long way. He ladled three heaping spoonfuls of rice onto his platter, then slowly put some back.

She turned to face him. 'It got to you that bad? Are we going to have fasting and abstinence now, in addition to prayer?'

'That vicar's got me thinking,' Pedro Saldanha said. 'You must have heard him at the six o'clock mass. Most priests would be happy to preach just one sermon a week, but not he. And what he said today is true! What will they say about me when I'm gone, Geraldine—and how little of it will be true? I never thought of it that way, not ever, and I've thought a lot about passing on.'

'So? You are a good man; you've led a good life.'

'I've got to go through the whole thing,' he said. 'I've got to see myself dead. Not really dead, but in my mind. Dead in my mind. And I've got to hear what they—you and they—are saying about me, now that I . . . I'm gone. Then I've got to match the two, see if I have deserved the praise. Change my life, if I have to.'

'Shall I heat the food again?' she asked.

'No, it's fine cold; yesterday's curry tastes better this way.'

But in a moment he pushed the platter away and rose from the table.

'I must go to the city,' he said. 'I'll be a while.'

'If you're walking you'll be gone a good four hours,' she said.

'It may be five,' he said. 'I have much to do. But I'll be back before sundown.'

But it was not quite three hours later that she heard a crunch of tyres in the lane, and looked out the window in time to see a coffin being taken off a hearse. 'Mary, Mother of God!' she cried, her heart pounding as she raced through the house and down the steps into the garden. But her brother was one of the two who were jockeying to get the coffin through the gate.

'Hold the gate,' he cried, and with careful shuffling steps they carried the coffin up and into the house. Into the sitting room they went, and set it on two chairs right in the middle of the room.

'Are you mad?' she cried, following her brother about the room, 'inviting bad luck on us like this, no one dead and this awful thing in the house?'

'I want to see myself in my own coffin,' he said. 'I want to get the feeling, now, while I can do something about it.' He paid off the driver of the hearse.

Outside, they heard voices at the gate. Josephine Aunty rushed in, breathless. 'I didn't hear the church bell toll,' she said, then stopped, surprised. 'You both—then who?'

'Nobody,' Pedro Saldanha said.

'Nobody's died?'

'Nobody.'

'But—'

'Nobody's dead.'

'Is anybody sick?'

'No!'

'Then why?'

'I'm preparing for your funeral,' he said, exasperated, and Josephine Aunty fled, hysterical, the gate clanking repeatedly after her as it swung on its hinges.

He closed the shutters against the fading daylight. 'I'm getting in,' he said. 'There are candles wrapped in that paper. Light them and place them all around.'

'I won't do it,' she said. 'You've never been quite like this.' And she asked again, leaning into his face: 'Have you gone stark raving mad?'

'You may have to do it for me someday,' he said. 'Might as well practice now.'

The candles lit, she left the room.

'Geraldine!'

She reappeared in the doorway.

'It's no good. I can't see myself, not like this. Hand me a mirror.'

She stood by as he watched himself intently for

long minutes.

'It's no good,' he said. 'It's not the same. Holding the mirror, looking at myself, it's not the same.'

He climbed out.

'Are we done then? Can this thing go back?'

He was looking at her with eyes of fire. Frightened, she backed away.

'Get in there,' he ordered. But when, trembling, she finally tried to climb in, he shouted: 'No! No! Not like that! Put these on!' and began to strip.

'God forgive me!' she wept, covering her eyes.

'What's the matter, woman? Have you never seen a naked man before? Wear this!'

And he tossed her his clothes, standing there near-naked. As she lay in the coffin, clothed in black, he handed her a crucifix. 'Clasp your hands!'

He paced about the room, muttering to himself. Time and again he turned to look down at her, peering at her ashen face, but not seeing her trembling lips, nor the spasmodic shiver that shook her frame, not the tears that rolled from her eyes, tears she did not dare unclasp her hands to wipe away. 'Not a word!' he admonished her, again and again, rapping on the side of the coffin. 'Not a sound out of you! Not a peep! Not even a peep!'

Around midnight, when the candles had burnt low and he had fallen asleep exhausted, she climbed out of the coffin and carefully led him to his bed.

As she turned to leave he suddenly sat upright.

'We must build a chapel on the hill,' he said, and fell back on his pillow.

She shut the bedroom door and went out into the coolness of the garden.

Moneyman

Peter Nazareth

Mr Manna Leitao had joined the civil service at a time when no Goans owned cars. In those days, it was quite normal for him to be seen walking all over the place, holding his umbrella like a walking-stick. But now, decades later, when Goans had passed through the bicycle age and were affluent enough to own cars, it was strange to see him drifting doggedly along the footpaths and bylanes. He seemed to creep along the edge of one's consciousness, until one suddenly wondered, 'Who is this odd-looking fellow?'

Odd-looking indeed he was. He had a large mouldy face. The hair on his head looked like one of those ferns you see at a swamp—pokers sticking out at the edge and disappearing into a disc at the centre. His ears italicized his head, hairs standing out of them like mini-television antennae. His lips looked sensual, lending credence to the story that he was secretly a satyr, although he had never married. The Goans thought that he had remained single because looking after a wife and children would have cost too much.

He often boasted that he was the richest man in the little town of Apana. Incredible, for how could a lowly civil servant who never played the stock market get rich? Well, in two ways. The first was the straightforward one of usury. There were always other lowly civil servants in Apana, particularly Africans, who were dead broke around the third week of the month. The bankers never lent money to those who really needed it, so this was where The Man stepped in. He would lend money for a maximum period of two weeks at about forty per cent interest. Not per annum but per two weeks.

This is why Manna Leitao came to be known as Money Leitao and, finally, Moneyman.

Then there was the second way he made money. He did not spend any.

Late one evening, Mrs Carmen Dias heard a groaning outside her house. She told her husband and son to investigate. They found Moneyman lying in a gutter in their compound, holding his leg in agony. The story went round later that Moneyman was chasing a spry young African miss across the lawns when he fell into the gutter and broke his leg. Yes, he broke his leg, as the Diases discovered eventually. They would have discovered it sooner had they taken him to the Grade A hospital but, despite his pain, he insisted that they take him to Grade B, where the poor were treated free of charge. His leg was put in plaster, and he was put to bed.

The Diases wrote about Moneyman's plight to his only traceable relatives, who lived in a neighbouring country. They arrived post-haste. Moneyman refused to see them. 'They have come here hoping I will die,' he said. 'They only want to get my money. Well, I won't, and they won't. Off with them!' Despite all efforts, the relatives had to give up and return home in disgust.

So, Moneyman had to be looked after by the Diases. They felt that he was their responsibility as they had found him on their doorstep, so to speak. Who would look after this stubborn old man if they refused? They even cooked his meals because he said he could not eat African food. Father and son had to take turns at cooking the meals because Mrs Dias had already made plans to go to Goa to visit her parents, and Moneyman's leg took a long time to heal. Needless to say, Moneyman did not pay the Diases anything, taking advantage of traditional Goan hospitality. What is more, after he realized that he was assured of regular meals, he started telling father and son what sort of meals to cook!

Moneyman's brush with death must have made him realize what a lonely man a single man is. At any rate, not long after he left the hospital, he gave up his lonely house and moved in with a family, the Fernandeses. The Fernandeses consisted of mother, father and three sons. It was surprising that they should have taken him in at all. Mother was a hard-headed, tough-hearted woman. Her husband, who owned a printing shop, was an inveterate drunkard, and the eldest son was a playboy. The second son was taciturn and determined. Nobody knew what he was determined about, but it looked as though he had secret ambitions. The youngest son was kind-hearted, but he was painfully shy and it was difficult to imagine him breaking out of his shell and making contact with anybody.

Gradually, it was noticed in Apana that Mrs Fernandes was running the printing shop. Mr Fernandes could be seen hanging around, cast aside like an empty bottle of liquor. The creditors had been about to foreclose when Mrs Fernandes stepped in. She paid off some of the debts and promised to pay the others in due course. The creditors agreed to wait provided she undertook to run the business herself. She accepted, even though she did not know anything about printing.

One day, Moneyman turned up at the house of Mr Pobras D'Mello, one of the elders of the Apana Goan community. Mr D'Mello was puzzled to see him because Moneyman was not a social man, let alone a sociable one. After the formality of informal talk and drinks, Moneyman said, 'I would like your advice, Mr D'Mello.'

Surprised at this request, and secretly a little pleased, Mr D'Mello replied, 'Of course.'

'Please read this letter,' said Moneyman, handing over a sheet of paper.

'Mrs Fernandes,' read Mr D'Mello, 'you have abused my sympathy and my kindly nature . . .' and a few rude words followed. 'When you borrowed four thousand shillings from me in June, you promised to repay it, plus a small lending charge, within three months. But you have not paid anything, and I demand it all back immediately, you . . .' and a few obscenities followed.

'Well?' said Moneyman.

'Well?' said Mr D'Mello.

'Don't you think it is a good letter?' said Moneyman.

Mr D'Mello was known for his tact, so instead of answering directly he said, 'Tell me a little more about this matter.'

'Mrs Fernandes was in trouble because of her husband's debts. She begged me to do her a favour and lend her four thousand shillings to pay off the debts. Feeling sorry, I lent her the money. Besides, I had already stood guarantee for her son's purchase of petrol, and the other day I had to pay a bill of nine hundred shillings . . .'

'You mention a service charge in your letter,' said Mr D'Mello. 'What is this?'

'Well, you know,' said Moneyman, 'I lost interest by drawing my money from my savings account at the bank, so it is but fair that I should be compensated . . .'

'How much?' said Mr D'Mello.

'I . . . er . . . er,' said Moneyman.

'How much?' said Mr D'Mello, a little sharply. 'How much is the service charge?'

'Er . . . one . . . two thousand shillings . . .'

'Per annum?' asked Mr D'Mello, amazed.

'No, to be paid as soon as the money was due.'

'Well, do you want to know what I think?' said Mr D'Mello. 'I think you are a mean, miserable skinflint. However, you have asked for my advice in respect of this . . . this letter, and I shall give it. The letter is extremely rude and offensive and, if you send it, Mrs Fernandes can use it to take legal action against you. Besides, from what you say, I don't think you have it in writing that you gave her the loan.'

'I already gave her the letter this morning,' said Moneyman.

'Then I will ask you to kindly leave my house,' said Mr D'Mello.

Moneyman got back home in time for dinner. He

sat at the dinner table, where the atmosphere was decidedly frosty. Finally, he said in Konkani, '*Udoi coddi,*' which should mean 'pass the curry', but if translated literally means 'throw the curry'. And the second son did just that. He picked up the dish of curry and threw it at Moneyman.

'You bastard!' he yelled at him. 'You have been staying with us, no? Do the few shillings you have lent us make up for the inconvenience? But you have the cheek to write an insulting letter to my mother! I'll teach you!' And he began beating up the old man.

The eldest and the youngest sons pulled the second son back, but not before Moneyman had had his other leg broken. The eldest son had to take him to the Grade B hospital. After all, the car contained Moneyman's petrol.

Moneyman was abandoned at Grade B. He sent word to the Diases, who found this time that they could leave a stubborn old man to his distress without any qualms of conscience. When Moneyman was finally discharged, he did not press charges. He had nothing in writing, while the Fernandeses had. Besides, the lawyer would have cost too much.

But Manna Leitao has benefited from his experience; he has learnt his lesson. He does not trust people any more; people are not as dependable as money. He can still be seen walking around Apana, shabbily dressed and with his ubiquitous umbrella; and whenever he passes the thriving Fernandes Press, he mutters to himself and tightens his grip on his umbrella, as though it is a bankroll from which he does not wish to be parted.

The Confessor

Peter Nazareth

H ave another drink,' said Ramos Pacheco. I tried
to protest. The doctor had told me to cut down
on beer because I was developing a paunch. Besides, I
wanted to go home early from the Goan Institute. A
few pints of East African beer down Ramos's gullet
acted as an 'Open Sesame', and once the storyteller got
out, I would not be able to leave. That was why, after
the Walt Disney cartoons and comics, we called him
Uncle Ramos.

'Barman, another drink for Felix here!' he said.
Before I could move, the beer was before me. I sighed.
There is nothing so oppressive as Goan hospitality.

'Cheers!'

'Cheers!'

'It feels good to down holy water,' said Ramos,
licking his lips. His body was draped like the third
letter of the alphabet from the barstool to the counter.

'Yes,' I said, 'the spirit in you likes to contact the
spirit in the bottle.'

Ramos threw back his head and laughed, looking

with his beard and moustache like a thin Fidel Castro.

'No wonder so many fellows like to become priests!' he said. 'They can be men of spirit with the blessing of God.' His eyes glazed, looking at the darkening window, he said, 'Did you know, Felix, when I was studying in secondary school in Goa, I nearly became a priest?'

I didn't. He had told me the last time that he was studying to be a doctor but had to give up and come back to East Africa because his father couldn't afford it.

'But before I could do that, I decided to come back to Africa for a holiday, a last look around. Once here, old memories of childhood came back and made me change my mind. Like other Goans, I joined the civil service. We were trained by Portuguese rule in Goa to be obedient.'

He was waiting expectantly, so I asked the question: 'What really made you change your mind?'

'Look,' he said, leaning towards me confidentially, 'like you, like all Goans in East Africa, I am a Catholic. Just an accident of fate. If Goa did not have a natural harbour the Portuguese wanted, I might have been a Hindu. Or had the Arabs held on longer, a Muslim.'

How much like a Hollywood Arab he would look, wearing a tarboosh like our night-watchman! According to legend, one subcaste of Goans is descended from shipwrecked Arabs looking for spices, before the Portuguese.

'Still, no religion contains—what did the judge say?—The Truth, the Whole Truth, and nothing but the Truth. So I might as well be Catholic.' He took a long gulp from his mug. 'The snag is—' he burped, 'Confession! Those Latin Portuguese brought us their feudal religion, so rigid, so like that of the Arabs who had ruled them. But worse, with a visible hierarchy. Even when little, I found it hard entering a sentry-box to talk to a dim priest. I doubted he had a hotline to the Almighty. Besides, was everything I had to confess a sin? Could a thing like, say, beating up my brother during a game of hockey be a sin? After all, he used to cheat!'

Ramos shook his head. 'According to our priests, to show we were really sorry, we had to confess at least one mortal sin. If we hadn't committed a mortal sin since the last confession—' he raised his mug, drew deep, and turned it upside down, pretending to squeeze it—'why, we had to dredge up a sin from the past. 'I was a good boy and committed only one mortal sin.'

'Mr Barman,' I said, 'give Uncle here some more fuel.' The mug was refilled. Ramos took a sip, sighed with satisfaction, and said, 'There is nothing like East African beer, except Goan fenim.'

'You were saying?'

'Ah, yes. In those good old days of British rule, we lived in the barracks. Structures by the colonial government for its faithful Goans, civil servants. A row of compartments concertinaed together.

'One day, our neighbour returned from Goa with a new wife. Boy, was she luscious! Marilyn Monroe had nothing on her. And that's what I wanted. Like a normal boy of eight or nine, I had a burning desire to see her in the nude.'

I lit a cigarette and took a puff.

'I thought of breaking into the house through the window and hiding behind a box of something. But these wild ideas couldn't work. The best bet was to see her while she was taking a bath. But how? All our bathrooms had frosted glass windowpanes.'

I offered Ramos a cigarette and lit it for him.

'One day, I came across the solution in a Do-It-Yourself manual: make frosted glass transparent by sticking transparent sticky tape onto it. One night, returning from hockey, I crept up to the window of the neighbour's bathroom and stuck a piece of Sellotape on it. Guess what happened?'

I shrugged.

'Nothing! The glass remained opaque! I tore up the Do-It-Yourself manual.' He rubbed his finger along the rim of the beer mug. 'But the following night, coming back from cricket practice, after dusk, I saw the bathroom light on and heard splashing. I was drawn to the window. Heaven be praised! The strip had created a peephole for me! How did it happen? Who cares? Maybe dew penetrated the tape. Trembling with joy and anticipation, I put my eyes to the window.'

Ramos swung the mug up and took a gulp. I ordered another beer for both of us.

'There was my heart's desire,' said Ramos, putting his mug down and wiping his mouth with his sleeve. 'With nothing on! Those breasts—like ripening avocado pears! Those curves, the two luscious halves, like . . . like a sliced watermelon. And the most delicious portion—the dark fruit between her soft, juicy thighs, protected, hidden. As I watched, she obligingly parted her legs. Man, it was tempting, like a ripe, red, slit guava!'

I stubbed out my cigarette.

'I began to think about the enormity of the sin. But I kept watching till she had gone through the whole ritual of drying herself, patting the peach, putting cups over those pears, covering the whole dish . . . When the room was empty, I tore off the strip of Hello—er, Sellotape, took it to the kitchen, and threw it into the old firewood stove. The tiny flame magnified, consuming me for all eternity.

'After a sleepless night, I went for confession.'

I asked the barman for a packet of potato chips, poured them into a plate, and sprinkled hot Tabasco sauce liberally. Ramos took a couple of chips and bit into them.

'The confessor was Father King, the crusty old fellow, near senility, convinced he was serving God's mission, trying to save us poor heathens. He was very absent-minded but given to bouts of severity when he woke up.

' "Bless me father, for I have sinned",' Ramos quavered, crunching another chip. ' "It has been so many weeks since my last confession." I started to recount all the small sins I had committed, such as stealing a classmate's sweets, hitting somebody's knee while playing hockey, and so on. And I slipped in the sin about having seen a nude woman taking a bath. I raced on to some more venial sins and was just telling old King that I had lied once to my father, when "WHAT? WHAT DID YOU SAY BOY?" '

Everybody in the bar looked up. This was the time when someone usually took out his office frustrations on somebody.

' "I lied to my father once," I said. "NO!" he roared. "Earlier. About a woman." Trembling, I whispered out my crime.

' "A Woman?" he bellowed. "A WOMAN—NAKED??"

'I shrank into my compartment and would have crawled away if he hadn't impaled me with his voice. "Terrible Boy! Already a pawn of the Devil!" He gave me a dressing down, punctuated by my Yes Fathers. I didn't register a word, except that I had a penance of ten rosaries to recite. I promised never to look at naked women again, I think. Creeping out of the confessional, I saw the whole line of penitents looking at me accusingly. Afraid that now that I had woken up the King, they would catch hell.'

My cigarette had burned out. I lit another. I offered Ramos one. He lit it, puffed, and blew a ring at one of the sports trophies kept against the wall.

'You know, I was basically a good boy and did not commit any mortal sins after that. So I had to confess the sin of the Nude Woman whenever I went for confession. After regurgitating the Woman several times, I suddenly felt that the whole thing was absurd. I mean, what the hell? How could that be a sin? Several religious people I knew used to visit women to do more than just look at their nude bodies. Maybe not Father King: for him, a hole was something you fell into if you weren't careful. So one day, when I went for confession, I confessed hardly anything.

'Was old King pleased that he did not have much spiritual baggage to carry off my back? No. A fellow like me, by definition, could not have committed so few sins. He had to probe the things that bothered him. Was I not troubled by thoughts of sensuality? No, I told him, I was not. To tell you the truth, Felix,' Ramos said, digging me in the ribs and guffawing, 'instead of being troubled, I rather enjoyed such thoughts! But old King wouldn't give up. I admitted that I had sensual thoughts, but pointed out that such thoughts were natural. Therefore they were not sins. King got mad. We people were carrying the mark of Cain, so how could we be free of sin? "It is possible to deceive oneself," he said. "If a man kills another in the heat of a quarrel, is it not a sin? Even if it were natural?" '

'Daddy!' we heard a little voice saying. A boy of six had come into the bar. It was Neil, Ramos's son. 'Daddy, Mummy says to come. She wants to go home.' Ramos's wife Melba was in the hall playing cards with the other ladies.

'In a moment,' said Ramos, buying Neil a packet of chips. Neil left the bar happily.

'I stayed away from King and confession for a while. But it is murder to escape the hold of the Church after four hundred odd years in Goa and a few more here. The priests had drummed into us that we had to go for confession at least once a year. As the end of my year approached, I got scared. I couldn't put it off. So I went, my heart in the soles of my tennis shoes. One more for the road, Mr Barman! Give Happy here a beer. I'll switch to a double-scotch on the rocks.'

'Scotch for me too,' I called out. 'With ginger ale.'

' "Bless me Father, for I have sinned," I began. There was a pause. "Father," I said desperately. "Father, do you remember that murder case around here some time ago? The European?"

' "You mean Mr Rex Carr?" said King. "Mr Carr who was found dead in his house about six months ago? That wasn't murder. The police said it was suicide. An overdose."

' "It wasn't suicide. I killed him."

'I swear the priest fell off his stool!' said Ramos,

digging me in the ribs. 'He exclaimed, "Why? How?"
"I was visiting him because he owed my father a lot of
money," I said. "He was my father's boss. You know
how these single European colonizers chase after local
women. He was living beyond his means. My father
had saved most of his money to support his family
here and in Goa. But my father couldn't say no to his
boss. He gave Carr the money. But when my father
wanted the money back—my grandmother was very
ill and we had to pay for medical treatment—Carr
refused to give it back.

' "I decided to go on my own to Carr's house one
evening to ask for the money. When I did, he just
laughed in my face. He said I had no proof we had lent
him money. Did I have any signed receipt? I got mad.
I wanted to teach him a lesson. Make him pay for all
that the White Man had taken from us."

' "But how?" gasped the priest, white. "The police
said it was suicide—"

' "He was drinking when I arrived at his house," I
said. "While talking to him, there was a noise at the
back. The servant had arrived but the back door was
shut. Carr went to open the door, leaving his drink on
the table. The servant was drunk and insisted on
receiving his wages immediately. While they were
quarreling, Carr shouted, in Swahili, 'One of these
days, you will drink yourself to death!' That gave me
an idea. I had a bottle of sleeping pills in my pocket,
which I had bought for my father—he was having
trouble sleeping. I poured the entire contents of the
bottle into Carr's drink, stirring it with my scout's
knife until it dissolved. Carr was so angry when he
returned that he gulped the drink down without

noticing a thing.

' "I left immediately. Carr died in his sleep that night. Suicide, an overdose of sleeping pills, the police said." '

Ramos took his glass and thumped it on the bar counter. 'King was really in a mess!' he said, throwing back his head and roaring with laughter.

People looked up. I'm sure they thought a fight was starting up.

'King could only ask me if I was truly sorry. I said I was. And whether I would ever commit the same sin again. I said I would not.'

'Daddy, Mummy says to come!' Neil was back in the bar with an empty packet. 'It's late. If we don't go, the servant will go off. He won't warm the food.'

'Coming,' said Ramos, sliding his shanks off the barstool as his son tugged his hand. Taking a last gulp from his glass, Ramos said: 'Just before receiving Absolution, I said, "Oh, Father, I forgot. I have one more sin to confess. I have told one lie since my last confession." '

The Sacristan and
the Miser

Lambert Mascarenhas

The banging on the door was so loud and protracted that it fell on the ears of the village miser like the clap of doom. Who could this maldicoado be at this unearthly hour, he wondered. Striking a match he looked at his ancient pocket watch lying on the bedside table. It was just past three a.m. Blast it! To wake up a man, a sick man besides, at this time of the night was the height of inconsideration and cruelty. He laid his hand on his chest and noticed that his heart was pounding louder than the wooden clatter of the rattle on Good Friday. A shock like this and it would be the end of him! It is true that the doctor had told him that there was nothing wrong with his heart, but after all, the doctor was his cousin, who, of course, wanted him to die so that he might inherit his property and his money. He would trust none of his relations, oh no, not his kin, all of whom were just waiting like hawks to pounce on his fortune the moment his eyes were closed.

The knocking sounded again, urgent and portentous, and the old miser sat up, shivering. 'Wait, wait, I'm coming,' he bawled out, and lighting the oil-lamp, began to put on his trousers. Despite the December cold, he would sleep in the nude, as he had discovered that the clothes wore off quickly when in friction with the bed. He was also reluctant to sit on a chair or pew for fear of wearing out the seat of his pants. Despite his age he remained standing in the church even during long sermons, on the pious plea that he felt nervous of sitting down in front of the Almighty. And the women of the village who did not suspect his true reasons cited him as 'the humble and God-fearing Torcat baab' when remonstrating with their errant children who were the first ones to run for the few benches in the church.

'Wait, wait, I'm coming,' snarled the miser again, as the pounding outside mounted. 'You will break my poor door, just wait, please, I'm coming, just wait!' Then he set upon lifting the barrier, for barrier indeed it was. First he rolled away the massive grinding stone· leaning against the bottom of the door, then he tackled the two strong wooden beams placed across from wall to wall, and finally unlocked the three padlocks, each of them as big as the sizable liver of a cow.

During the elaborate process of opening the door, which took a good five minutes, the miser asked from inside: 'Who the devil are you at this hour of the night? Who are you?' In reply he only heard sounds which resembled the gurgling of a porker when the butcher's knife is thrust in its throat. The miser was puzzled and frightened. But when at long last the door was opened, there he saw under the faint light of his oil-lamp the pale face of the sacristan, bedewed with perspiration, muttering unintelligibly.

'Why, why, it's you Bostiao, why . . .' And before the miser could complete the sentence, the sacristan rushed to him and embraced him and began to drag him into the interior of the house as though he were afraid of staying outside any longer. He trembled like a chicken drenched in the rain, breathing fast and making gurgling sounds in an effort to talk.

'Why, man! You act as if you have seen a ghost!' said the miser, perplexed. 'You'll kill me, you will, with that expression on your face. You nearly did it with that pounding on the door, do you know? Come out of it, what in the name of Heaven is the matter with you?'

The sacristan, having slumped in the chair, did not reply, but signalled with his hands to get him a drink. The miser at once fetched a glass of water, but the sacristan would have none of that worthless, impotent liquid. He looked disdainfully at the miser, and between his teeth muttered 'fenim', the first intelligible word he had uttered during this interlude. A glass of country liquor having been handed over to him, the sacristan drained it with an artistic movement of the hand, quick as lightning, and then slumped over the dining table. His cleft chin rested on the boards, his arms were outstretched at an angle of thirty-eight degrees. Anyone seeing this posture would have believed that the sacristan was demonstrating a new pose of crucifixion.

'Wake up, man, wake up, are you out to kill me?' exclaimed the miser in extreme distress. 'If you must die, please do your dying in your own home. I'll have none of that nonsense here. I am a poor and sick man, and don't want to get involved in other people's misadventures. Come on, come now . . .'

But the sacristan remained unmoved. The miser grew panicky and moving towards him, felt his pulse. The man was not dead, thank God! He had liked this man. Of all the people in the village, the sacristan seemed to have understood the miser, had always spoken to him with such deference as shown not merely by a poor man to a rich one, but by one who seemed to respect the miser's concept that there was no such thing as a worthy cause, that poverty was a Godsent tribulation no man had a right to mitigate, that giving away money, either in charity or as a loan, was the bane of our civilization, that money dropped in various boxes in the church only tended to turn the priest lazier. Such was the sacristan's sympathy with the miser that he had discreetly avoided him when he descended on the congregation with the collection box during Sunday Mass. The miser was grateful to Sebastiao for saving him from a great embarrassment, as even peasants, fools that they were, would drop a pice into the box. And this, above everything else, had weighed with Senhor Torcato, the miser, in alloting the sacristan full marks for common sense, honesty, integrity and perspicacity.

As he regarded him now, lying there in a state of coma, there arose in the miser a strange desire to examine the other man's pockets. Slowly he approached him and began the search. In the left-hand pocket of the sacristan's jacket he found a five-rupee note and some small change, which at once set the miser wondering why people were so thoughtless and foolish as to carry so much money on them for no rhyme or reason, and that too at night. The right-hand pocket contained a rosary and a pouch of tobacco, but when the miser tried to put his hand in the inside pocket, the sacristan winced, as if tickled, thus putting a stop to the miser's explorations. .

'Aam-Aam, there, there, you're coming to, thank God!' the miser simulated relief, at the same time hoping that the sacristan was unaware of his unchristian exploits. 'Wake up, man, wake up, and don't give me the frights.' But seeing that the man on the chair made no further claim on life he shook him vigorously. This having proved ineffective too, he brought a jug of water and poured it on the head of the lying man.

'Aoiss!' jumped the sacristan, and lifting his head, regarded the miser with a look of stupefaction. Then he slowly withdrew his arms from the table and leaned against the back of the chair, as though completely exhausted.

'What's happened to you?' asked the miser, solicitously. 'You act as if you have seen a ghost. What's the matter?'

The sacristan opened his eyes wide and then with a shudder hid his face in his hands.

'What?' asked the miser again, impatiently. 'What's the matter?'

Slowly, the sacristan turned his face towards him and after staring vacantly into the other's face nodded his head: 'Ghost, indeed, I have seen,' he replied faintly. 'Your wife! She was sitting there on the wall of the cemetery, crying and gnashing her teeth.'

'Ma . . . my wife, wi-wi-fe!' The miser was stunned and the words came out of his mouth as if it cost him money to utter them.

'Yes, your wife. I saw her with my own eyes, God forbid such a sight again!'

'That's impossible! You must be making a mistake! Not my wife, please—not my wife? . . .'

'Yes, it was your wife, I spoke to her,' assured the sacristan.

'My God! You spoke to her?' exclaimed the miser, his face a mask of horror. Then he said, as if to himself: 'Poor thing! And I loved her so much!'

The sacristan who had now shifted his position on the chair passed his fingers through his hair before replying: 'You didn't, Torcat baab. Torcat baab, you starved her to death.'

'What confounded nonsense!' spluttered the miser. 'How dare you say such a thing!'

'I don't say it Torcat baab,' said the sacristan humbly. 'It was your wife, sitting there on the wall, who told me so. If it didn't come from her, I wouldn't have believed it, knowing how good a man you are. She also told me that she was neither in Hell nor in Purgatory but in another place where it is terribly cold, and that if it weren't for her empty stomach she would bear the cold better.'

'Saiba, what blasphemy are you uttering, man?' said the miser, shocked. 'What cold place are you referring to? There's no such place in the Hereafter!'

'That's what your wife told me, and I am only repeating what she said.'

'What was she wearing, Bostiao, what was my wife wearing, if it is really she who appeared to you?'

The sacristan made a wry face, closed his eyes and clenched and unclenched the fingers of both his hands as if he were about to fall prey to an epileptic fit. Softly he muttered: 'No . . . nothing.' He dragged out the first syllable. 'She told me that the dress you put on her back was of such inferior quality that it fell to bits on the passage to . . . She showed me, oh, how dreadful!— she showed me her stomach . . . her ribs, and they protruded from her back. How could you do such a mean thing, Torcat baab?'

The miser's face underwent a complete transformation. He turned pale, his eyes popped out of their sockets, as he felt his thumping heart. 'My God! My God!' was all he said, as if he himself had seen the unpleasant apparition.

'She told me that they laughed at her when she arrived there in that cold place wearing only a sleeve,' continued the sacristan, mournfully. 'They sit there, she told me, huddled together, telling stories, the fat people being in great demand on account of the heat they generate. But your poor wife, being only a bundle of bones, is shunned—nobody wants her near. Pity! Poor thing!'

The miser began to shiver as though he himself was in the place described by his spouse to the sacristan. He went to the shelf and, pouring a stiff drink, gulped it down quickly, albeit with less artistry than displayed earlier by the sacristan. 'What—what is it that she wants of me?' he asked half-angry and half-frightened. 'What is it that she wants? Please tell me.'

'She wants you to offer forty masses for her, ten high and the rest low.'

This information at once dispelled the miser's shivering. He now felt hot. 'Forty masses!' he exploded, not believing his ears. 'Has she gone crazy? Why . . . that will cost a fortune!' He at once calculated that were she to be still alive, things would have been much cheaper. 'Are you sure she said forty and not fourteen?' he asked hopefully.

'Forty, Torcat baab,' replied the sacristan nodding his head. 'In fact, I asked her the same question, and to make herself clear she wrote with the bit of coal she was carrying in her hand the number forty on the sole of her foot. She also told me that once in a way bits of coal come flying from Hell into their enclosure and that the inmates use them for painting landscapes and . . .'

The miser, who was not interested in the cultural and artistic activities of souls in the next world, cut the sacristan short. 'Won't she be satisfied with a few masses now, some the next year and the rest in the following year? How can I spend so much money all at once? It is really hard on me. With expenses mounting every day, with prices shooting up, how can I shell out such a large sum?'

The sacristan allowed the miser to plead his case fully, and then spoke meekly and softly. 'I cannot answer those questions, baab. I am only repeating to you what your wife told me. She said that you being a miser—those are her exact words—will not heed her request and as such I should go to the neighbours and repeat the story and request them to raise a subscription or something and offer the masses.' The sacristan paused, and wiping his face on the sleeve of his jacket, made an effort to rise. 'I thought it proper, however, to come to you first, lest you hold me responsible for maligning you. You know how our people talk! But now, since you are not prepared to comply with your poor wife's wishes, I have no other alternative than to go and inform the villagers and ask them to do the needful.'

'Wait, wait, sit down, don't be a fool!' spluttered the miser. 'Did I say that I don't want to offer the masses? Did I, did I? Thank God you came to me first. What a shame if the people come to know of this! My wife haunting the place, begging for help! They will think that I killed her! No, no, they mustn't know about it. No, I'll do her bidding even if I have to sacrifice milk for a whole year. Yes, I'll stop cutting my hair . . . buying meat, and what else . . . but I shall hold the masses for her.'

He fumed and ranted on like a mad man, grimacing and pulling his hair. 'Terrible . . . this is really terrible . . . just wait, please, for daylight and we shall both go together to the vicar and I will eke out the money even if that means the death of me.'

The sacristan, who by now was fairly composed, held the miser by his hand and asked him to relax. He took his right foot from his slipper and placed it on the edge of the seat of the chair and began to stroke it. 'It was not a pretty sight, what I saw, I can assure you, Torcat baab. I thought I would not live to reach here and tell you the story. It was pretty ghastly . . . ohhh-ohhh,' he shivered and closed his eyes. 'But I haven't told you all that your wife has told me.'

'What! Does she want something more, too?' asked the miser jumping up from his chair.

'No, no, she doesn't want anything more, but she told me that you haven't given her a single mass since her death a year ago. You had promised to spend a part of her dowry on masses, hadn't you?'

'Fotteo, lies, nonsense!' The miser denied this insinuation. 'I made no such promise, damn you! And, besides, what is left of her dowry? Hadn't she been eating and dressing all the past thirty-five years she was with me? And didn't I give her a mass on the seventh day of her death? You know that, Bostiao, don't you?'

'Yes, I know that, Torcat baab,' agreed the sacristan, hopefully. 'Indeed, I corrected your wife on that score, but she told me that not a single puff of warm air has come her way since she arrived in that cold place. She asked me to tell you not to pray for her, that is, if you are praying for her soul at all, as according to information reaching them from reliable sources in Heaven, prayers from persons like you are not entertained.'

'Damn her, what does she mean? What bloody nonsense is this?'

'That's what she told me, Torcat baab,' said the sacristan, shrugging his shoulders. 'She said that on the seventh day, she shivered the most. She also said that most of the inmates of that cold place are complaining about the non-receipt of masses, and that they fear that some of the priests down here are pocketing the money without fulfilling their obligations.'

The miser looked goggle-eyed, his mouth distorted with anger.

'Blast it!' he exclaimed. 'Can it be possible that these . . .'

'That's what your wife told me,' continued the sacristan, phlegmatically. 'She also said that Ana Preciosa, wife of Antonio Jose, from near the chapel, is with her in that cold place. She can't believe that her dear husband who loved her so much was capable of forgetting her.'

'But her husband has been dedicating masses at regular intervals, Bostiao, you know that! Why, he gave a mass only the other day, didn't he?'

'Yes, I know, I know, Torcat baab, but what am I to say? I am only repeating what your wife told me. And what can a poor gravedigger sacristan say about some of the priests?'

The sacristan wiped his face and crinkled his brow as if he were trying to remember something. Then he snapped out of his reverie and turning to the miser, said: 'Oh, by the way, she also told me that she saw your cousin, the Regedor of Dovelim, passing her enclosure on his way down to Hell. She said that her teeth were chattering with the cold so much that she could not even say hello to him.'

The miser seemed sorely distressed. 'Poor Elesbao, poor Elesbao!' he remarked mournfully. 'He has gone to Hell, did she say? Why, he was such a good man, always went to church, was a good friend of the Portuguese, never ate meat on Fridays, promptly reported the criminal activities of those bloody nationalists, poor fellow . . . Did she really say he has gone to Hell?'

Then the miser stood up and began to pace the floor. 'What am I to do now? If the masses don't reach them, then what is to be done? The situation is most unbearable.'

'It is not,' replied the sacristan, shaking his head. 'Your wife told me what to do. She . . .'

'Did she?' interrupted the miser. Then he lost his

temper. 'Why in hell did she not appear to me instead of sending messages through you, damn it! You are driving me crazy, telling me bits here, bits there! Tell me everything and be done with it! You're killing me, Bostiao, do you know . . . Why didn't she show up to me and tell me . . .'

'That's exactly what I asked her myself, Torcat baab . . . why she did not go to you instead of frightening a poor man like me. But do you know what she said to that? She told me that she hates the very sight of you. She called you a murderer, a thief . . . that you had won that demanda after . . .'

'Stop it, stop it! I don't want to listen any more!' yelled the miser, plugging his ears with his fingers. 'I am going to hold the masses, am I not? Haven't I told you so? Then why are you harassing me? Tell me, tell me only what is to the point. I have no time, I am a sick man, I haven't slept a wink . . .'

The sacristan passed his tongue over his upper lip. The miser, panting as though he had been running, passed his fingers through his hair. Outside, dawn was breaking.

'She told me,' began the sacristan softly, 'that there is a pious and holy priest in Rachol Seminary who should he entrusted with the masses. His name . . .'

'Rachol!' exploded the miser, banging his hand on the table. 'Has she gone out of her mind! Does she expect an old and sick man like me to go all the way to Rachol? That is impossible. The only place I shall go to is to my grave, and that seems to be pretty soon. Rachol! How can I go there, Bostiao, how can I?'

The sacristan did not reply at once. He scratched

his head, stroked his chin and began to ruminate. Then after a minute or so, he said: 'I have a lot of work in the field after my church chores. Still, I am prepared to go to Rachol if you so desire.'

'Will you, my friend, will you?'

'I think it is my duty to help a soul in distress. Poor woman! She thought it fit to appear to me and nobody else, didn't she? Yes, she has placed her faith in me and I must not disappoint her. As a good Christian, I must not fail her. I will go, Torcat baab, I will.'

The miser seemed relieved. He sat forward, placing his hands on his knees. He looked into the eyes of the sacristan and then said to him coaxingly: 'Will you go to Rachol, my friend, on foot, without any added expenses? Will you, Bostiao?'

'Yes, on foot I shall go—that is, if you don't wish to give me the busfare.' The sacristan paused, thought for a moment, and then continued: 'Yes, I shall go on foot and dedicate the hardships of the journey to her soul. Poor thing! I hope she rests in peace after this!'

The miser, touched by the sacristan's noble gesture, went into the bedroom. A few minutes ticked by, but when he appeared again he had a bundle of one-rupee notes in his hands. He counted them again and again, and reluctantly handed them to the sacristan.

'Count them, please, Bostiao,' he said sorrowfully. 'There's hundred and twenty rupees, I think, but you had better count them. I might have made a mistake and given you more.'

As the sacristan counted, the miser's eyes fell on the oil lamp burning on the table and immediately blew it off. 'Blast it,' he said angrily. 'It has been daylight for the past half-hour or more and this ponti has been consuming oil. I can't afford any wastage now, can I?'

Then, turning to the sacristan, he asked, hoping that the other might return to him a rupee or two, 'Is the sum correct? Won't the priest reduce the price of the church services in view of the wholesale aspect of the thing? No? Anyway, please ask him . . . what name did you say? Padre Francisco de Souza? Please ask him for a rebate. All right, please hurry up and go there with God, as soon as you have finished with the church. And take good care of my money, understand, put it in the inside pocket of your coat . . .'

The December morning hid behind a veil of dew. There was an invigorating nip in the air and a spring in the sacristan's stride. Placing the money in the inner pocket, next to his heart, be began to walk towards his home. When he reached the bend in the road, he looked back, and noticing that he was beyond the view of the miser, descended into the field and began a shortcut to the neighbouring village to buy with the miser's money the calf he had arranged for the previous day.

And as he walked he whistled softly a popular hymn in praise of the Holy Ghost.

At the Shrine of Mary of the Angels

Hubert Ribeiro

There stood in Westlands, Nairobi, a mansion, gloomy with dark passages and shuttered rooms, every one of which looked like an untidy antique shop. The hall itself was so stuffed with artistic flotsam and souvenirs of travel that one had the impression its contents were awaiting an auctioneer's hammer. There were Shiraz carpets, Chinese porcelain, water-buffalo skulls, Egyptian alabaster, polished turtle shells, Portuguese silver, African rawhide drums, hand-carved Kashmiri furniture, a jade Buddha, a bishop's throne and a Steinway piano. Whatever could not be displayed was crammed into tall narrow cupboards which stood against the walls like mummies' coffins. This was the residence of Mrs Maria dos Anjos de Silva-Santa Rosa, Lofric's maternal grandmother.

Once a week the cluster in the hall was added to by her relatives and their children, who gathered there on Saturday evenings to pay homage to the wealthy widow. The emaciated old lady held court seated on the bishop's throne, with her withered feet propped up on an embroidered footstool. She looked like a faded velvet cushion lost in the crimson upholstery of the throne. Only her voice retained some of the volume and authority which had prompted some of her more irreverent servants to nickname her 'Memsahib Kilele' behind her back. In her heyday such insolence would have invited a kick in the ribs; but now in her eightieth year, she was as brittle and creaky as some of her own furniture. Her remaining energy was used up in her yearning for Heaven, where she could be with her God and her husband.

On her right sat Uncle Exodus, her first-born, and on her left Uncle Miracle, her only other son. Round her feet sat her three daughters, and interspersed among the relics in the room was a multitude of grandchildren. Lofric sat as far from the tide of cousins as he could, but made sure that the food and drink were accessible. This consisted of high drifts of potato crisps, pyramids of samosas, wines, spirits and mineral waters. The samosas had been bought in River Road because they were twenty cents cheaper than elsewhere, and their fillings compelled respect from all but the children, and the gluttonous.

Brahmins who were not of the highest sub-caste Mrs Santa Rosa could never tolerate. And though she understood English perfectly, she would not condescend to speak it, for she considered it a barbarous tongue, lacking in the Latinate refinements which pleased her delicate ear. Therefore at these weekly gatherings, while her children—who were not linguistic purists—spoke mainly in English, the old lady proudly confined herself to Portuguese.

'Have you thought of coming back to the Church, Exodus?' she inquired of her older son. 'You were once a Prefect of the Sodality,' she reminded him sadly.

'We all make mistakes!' chuckled Uncle Exodus.

He would have made a merry little monk: a short, portly man with a bald head ringed with a narrow fringe of hair. He had spent a decade at Oxford, studying medicine and struggling to survive on the monthly allowance of £ 30 which his father sent him. England for those who had never visited it was considered a land of unimaginable splendours, a sort of European Xanadu, since it was the home of the Anglo Saxon world conqueror, and it seemed impossible that any but the rich could afford to live there. Old Doctor Santa Rosa had often written to his son to ask if his allowance was sufficient to maintain him in the costly thirties, but Exodus, mindful of the needs of the other four in the family, had bravely refused any increase and managed to make ends meet on what was sent to him. He had his medical books bound in vellum, spent his holidays on the French Riviera, and was the first student in Oxford to own two motor cars.

At his first encounter with free thought Exodus had abandoned the Faith, but was careful to keep the information to himself until his return to Kenya, for as he had rightly surmised, he was immediately disinherited. He was, however, still expected to attend at Parklands on Saturday evenings. He was now the State Pathologist in Kenya, and his duties extended beyond the practice of forensic medicine to include the inspection of prisons and attendance at executions.

'Your father died of a broken heart,' his mother

continued. 'He could not bear to think of the disgrace you had brought on the family by becoming an atheist, instead of following his good example. You were cursed in England.'

'His good example!' exclaimed Uncle Exodus. 'He did his rounds mounted on a zebra, fed human blood to his grapevine, and stuck uvulas to the walls of his surgery with Sellotape. Is that the example you want me to follow? How do you think it would look if I rode to my post-mortems on a zebra?'

'Your father was a great man,' admonished the old lady. 'Have you forgotten his antimalarial pills, or how he stopped an epidemic of bubonic plague, or that he was the Portuguese consul? It was not for nothing that he was decorated by two governments.' Her voice rose with pride and her eyes brightened within the gloom of the throne.

'He could have been as tinselled as a Christmas tree for all I care,' Uncle Exodus said with contempt. 'How long do you think his name will be remembered in Kenya? Do you think the stump of his grapevine will become a national shrine, or that his zebra will be stuffed and exhibited in the Coryndon Museum? There will be much shuffling with names after Independence; there will be whitewashing and denigration, and I rather think our sunburnt friends will prefer to immortalize their own *Kamau Kipongoro* before Doctor Santa Rosa.'

'There's a long time still before Independence,' said tiny Aunt Annunciation. 'Just now, Africans haven't even got shoes!'

'They're never grateful for anything,' added Aunt Ethelvinha. 'And they stink, my! Europeans also. It's their perspiration.'

'Is there some correlation between gratitude and BO?' asked Uncle Exodus interestedly. 'You should go into the deodorant business, and then one day, for contributing to racial harmony, you too may be decorated, like papa.'

'Don't make fun of papa,' said Uncle Miracle vehemently. 'You're not fit to be his son. Look at all the money wasted on you. What have you got to show for it? Nothing! Look at your clothes. You're not only ungrateful, you're a sadist, and you're mad!' Uncle Exodus was somewhat taken aback by this onslaught. He looked thoughtfully from his yellow waistcoat to his shimmering Turkish slippers, with their pointed, turned-up toes.

'I think it only fitting for an artist to affect flamboyant dress,' he said.

'You're an artist?' cried his brother incredulously.

'My dear fellow, *hanging* is an art,' explained Uncle Exodus. 'Used to be a sport as well, before the British killed it with their scruples. Nowadays you have to dope the prisoner—I never dope him!—strap and hood him. There's no more spectacle. The only thing that amuses me now is the pattern on the wall when the rope swings across the light. And I can't even watch that for long because I have to run down and make sure the fellow's dead. And that bloody fool, the priest, is always getting in my way with his oils and his mumbo jumbo, muttering—*Nomini domini!* I shove him aside and say—Leave him alone, he's finished. If your religion's so marvellous, why don't you bring him back to life? If you can't, then step aside and let a scientist get on with his work.'

'Don't talk nonsense about priests!' cried Mrs Santana indignantly.

Uncle Exodus ignored her. He looked at his brother and said with a touch of anxiety in his voice, 'What makes you think I'm a sadist?'

'Because when you were small you hung up cats and shot them with your airgun, and you pushed broom straws up dragonflies' behinds!' shouted Uncle Miracle.

'Is that all?' Uncle Exodus looked relieved.

'What's your definition of a sadist?' demanded Uncle Miracle.

Uncle Exodus lifted a hand laden with rings. 'My dear fellow, a civilized man never defines anything.'

'You think you're too clever,' accused Uncle Miracle.

'It doesn't take much to be cleverer than a cretin,' Uncle Exodus said charitably. 'I should have committed suicide if I had been endowed with your stupefying intellect.'

'Suicide is a mortal sin,' broke in Aunt Ethelvinha, whose husband had killed himself. 'Only cowards do it. It's such a shame for the family. When Osorio died I was so angry I just couldn't forgive him. He died like a dog, so I left him like a dog—on the floor—until it was time for his funeral. And what bribes we had to give the priests to bury him properly so that no one would know! I hope he's frying his guts out in Hell!' Her mouth twitched grimly, and her sunken eyes flickered with passion.

'That's what comes of marrying beneath your station,' said old Mrs Santa Rosa, with an edge of satisfaction to her voice. 'Osorio was an ordinary Brahmin. His father was a Johnny Nobody who sold books in Marmagoa. I've never been able to get over the humiliation of having a bookseller's son in the family. But it was worth it to teach you a lesson. And now we'll see what sort of a match your daughter makes for herself.' The daughter referred to was thirty-five years old, with a hooked nose, popping eyes, and acne. She glared at her grandmother but said nothing.

'Beggars can't be choosers!' chortled Uncle Exodus. 'She'll have to take what she gets. She's no spring chicken.'

'It's only old bulls who like tender grass!' cried the maiden angrily. 'Until I find the right husband for me, I'll manage very well.'

'By masturbating like hell!' shrieked Uncle Exodus, his belly wobbling with laughter.

'*Exodus!*' came his mother's horrified voice from the bowels of the bishop's throne. 'Such immorality happens only in Europe, not here. And please remember there are children in the room.'

'How could I forget,' said Uncle Exodus, 'when I can hardly hear myself for the sound of the little shmoos stuffing themselves.' He looked at his youngest sister and shook his head disapprovingly. 'What a farrow you have, Annunciation,' he said.

'At least I'm a good Catholic mother,' retorted the diminutive lady. 'Not afraid of obeying God's command: *Increase and multiply*.' She looked for support to her potato-nosed husband standing knee-deep in progeny. But he was busy drinking.

'I know someone my daughter fancies,' interrupted Aunt Ethelvinha slyly. 'But he's dark. Doesn't look so bad in the light, though. Neck is fairer. Face also isn't bad. But the children are bound to be dark. Not worth it.'

'What rubbish!' screeched her daughter, her acne flaming. 'I haven't got anyone! I would die before I let a dark man touch me.'

'You'd die if any man touched you,' interjected Uncle Exodus.

'Dark people are very ugly,' stated old Mrs Santa Rosa, and her voice quavered. 'I told Annunciation how ugly her children would be if she married Natividade; but she insisted, and talked some nonsense about being in love with him! Fair people can't love dark people: it's unheard of! But that's what happens when girls are educated—they think they're too clever to listen to their elders. Now she has to suffer for it.'

And the old lady swept a glance of vindication over the lake of hirsute, mud-coloured children around Uncle Natividade.

The offended gentleman made a feeble attempt to wade through his children and confront his mother-in-law, but diverted the effort into the opening of a fresh bottle of brandy.

'I love my children!' his wife wailed, clutching the youngest of the yahoos to her bosom.

'Pass us the Scotch, Miracle,' said Uncle Exodus, eyeing the very generous measure his brother had poured for himself.

'Don't look at mine!' said Uncle Miracle peevishly, swinging his glass away from Uncle Exodus's critical eye.

'Why?' asked Uncle Exodus, reaching across his mother for the bottle, 'Is it any different from anyone else's?'

The telephone rang.

'It's for you,' someone said to Uncle Exodus.

He had always to keep the CID informed of his whereabouts, so that he could be reached without delay in an emergency.

He got up and took the receiver. There was an excited police officer on the line. 'Doctor Santa Rosa? You'll have to come over immediate: A man's been murdered.'

'What's the hurry?' asked Uncle Exodus, calmly reaching for a greasy samosa. 'If he's been murdered, he can wait.'

'But he's dead!' came the officer's frantic voice.

'It's not uncommon for murdered men to be dead,' Uncle Exodus informed him. 'I'll be along in good time.'

He put down the receiver and sat down contentedly.

'Where's your sense of duty!' his brother scolded him. 'It's a wonder they tolerate your cheek. Your work is really cushy.'

'Try working yourself sometimes,' suggested Uncle Exodus. 'It'll be a traumatic experience.'

'What! The son of Doctor Santa Rosa work? You're mad!'

'Eccentric,' allowed Uncle Exodus. 'All clever people are eccentric. At this very moment the tune The Hands of a Criminal is running in my head, while Mama's samosas are playing havoc with my stomach.'

Uncle Miracle's pale aquiline face distorted in a sneer. He was crippled with resentment against his brother. His father had forbidden him an overseas education for fear that he would follow in Uncle Exodus's heretical footsteps, and he believed that he had been denied a fair chance in life. The fact that his brother's disinheritance had left him sole heir to the family fortune did not compensate Uncle Miracle for much, for on the expectation of that inheritance he had, by fatuous extravagances, owed it all before coming into it. He was now waiting impatiently for his mother to go to her reward so that he could briefly come into his, settle his debts, and emigrate to Brazil.

But the old lady would not oblige. She lingered on, insisting all the while that she suffered from at least a dozen fatal diseases. She gave a lavish banquet on her birthday, because she was convinced that it would be her last, and after twenty years and twenty banquets Uncle Miracle began to have the terrible suspicion that he would die before she did, a possibility which day by day grew less remote as his frustration fretted his body to decay.

'Wait till God puts his finger on you,' he said bitterly to Uncle Exodus. 'You'll be kicked out of your job, and you'll die in the gutter like you deserve. Then we'll see how eccentric you are. We'll see how cocksure you are in Hell.'

This tangle of dire prophecies left Uncle Exodus unperturbed. 'I won't get the sack because I'm indispensable,' he said modestly. 'My job calls for a special kind of dedication—a vocation if you like—and it'll be decades before the post can be Africanized.'

'I don't know what's going to happen after Independence,' said Aunt Annunciation in the despairing tones of one who anticipates a nameless doom.

'I'll tell you what's going to happen,' said Uncle Exodus, his manner suddenly intense. 'This country will be in the hands of its rightful owners, and if we're kicked out, it will serve us right. We've lived on the fat of the land long enough, and if we're not prepared to share the swag we've collected, we may as well get out. We're as alien here as the British are, and if we want to stay, we'll have to accept the natives as equals, in spite of all the tales we've been told about them.' He cast a significant look at the bishop's throne, and continued: 'The only sort of integration which the Africans will recognize will be a total one, involving intermarriage. So stop looking for your fair Brahmins, because they're as rare as three-legged chamberpots. If our children want to be Kenyans, they will have to live and marry among the first Kenyans: the Negroes. And if they don't want to contaminate their precious blood, they'd better get out while they have the chance.'

There was a short furious silence.

'You'll look lovely with a *Giriama* bride!' jeered Aunt Annunciation. 'Just imagine marrying a native! Putting up with his stink!' cried the outraged Aunt Ethelvinha.

'Africans are the descendants of Cain,' said old Mrs Santa Rosa. 'That's why God made them black, the same colour as their souls.'

'Only constipated people are the descendants of Cain, because they aren't able!' said Uncle Exodus.

His flippancy was not well received.

'I don't know where you get your ideas from,' Uncle Miracle said irritably. 'The British will never leave here. They're having too good a time.'

'They'll be packing their bags soon enough,' said Uncle Exodus, serious again. 'And the Goans had better do the same because when they have the opportunity, the Africans will prove themselves as good as the best of us.'

'They'll prove potatoes,' said Aunt Ethelvinha contemptuously. Uncle Exodus's eyes were hard. 'You're so blind and stupid that you can't begin to conceive of self-government here,' he said to his sister. 'All you think the Africans capable of is a kakistocracy.'

The term meant nothing to anyone else in the room. 'A cacastocracy,' said Aunt Ethelvinha, and looked around her for her clever pun to be applauded. She was not disappointed; everyone laughed appreciatively. Everyone but Uncle Exodus.

The children had locusted the drifts of potato crisps and the pyramids of samosas. They had drained every available bottle of Pepsi Cola, and gravitated to their parents, huge-eyed and hungry. Uncle Exodus bounced to his feet.

'Duty calls,' he said, bowing comically to his mother and the assembly. 'Good night, Mama.'

'Good night until next Saturday, if God wills it,' said his mother.

Uncle Exodus's departure killed all conversation, and brought the evening to an end. He was the inadvertent nucleus which made the family cohere.

'We'd better go also,' said Aunt Annunciation.'The children have to get up early to go for mass.'

She and Uncle Natividade made for the door, with their children oozing after them like lava. Uncle Miracle stood up and offered his *Boa noite*.

'Come on, Lofric,' said Mrs Santana to her son, who had been curled up in a corner, trying hard to keep pace with the intellectual gymnastics of the grown-ups.

Mrs Santana and Aunt Ethelvinha scattered away from their mother's feet as if by magnetic repulsion.

The old lady creaked to her feet and swore before God and her dead husband that she humbly accepted the fate of being abandoned by her children and left to die like a rat, alone in her mansion. She crossed herself piously and moved slowly away into the gloom, hunched and wrinkled like a marabou stork.

The house would be silent for a week.

Antonio's Homecoming

E.R.A. da Cunha

My uncle, Antonio Xavier Menezes, sat on one of those reclining chairs so popular in the old Goa houses, legs resting on the extended armrests. This was his favourite position. His face was at a lower level than his toes, so anyone who passed by the front of the balcony could see his feet, which were none too clean. But should my uncle spot the passerby, he would invariably call out to him: 'You seen Calcutta, no?'

For my uncle was born and bred in Calcutta and his favourite topic of conversation was bread. He had made his dough, quite simply, from dough. And whether the passerby had been to Calcutta or not, my uncle would start on his favourite theme: 'You should have seen Calcutta in the British days, man! Best shopping in New Market—all foreign goods. Posh hotels, Grand and Great Eastern, Goan bands. Only Europeans allowed, babus not admitted. Fast trains taking you to Botanical Gardens. What Goa is man? Nothing, man, nothing, I say.

'And what bread man! Goa bread nothing! I started

life as semi-humble assistant baker in De Souza Bakery at Chowringhee. And what people came to buy bread at the shop! All British army officers, ICS officers, British company directors. Very few babus—and if they came we served them from the back door. Our customers say our bread better than even Firpo's bread.

'But my boss De Souza is too much drinking like, drinking from morning to night and when he can't get sleep he drinks during night and all. Beating his wife and children and all. My boss says I best in kneading and baking dough. So he promotes me as humble assistant baker. But when he drink he laughs like and say you no humble assistant baker, you proud assistant baker. Hee, hee, hee!

'And one day boss De Souza with two empty bottles in his pockets tells me he is broke like and please to lend him rupees hundred. I tell him I give, not lend him, rupees five thousand, but shop is mine. He says "OK", takes rupees hundred advance and staggers to Stephen's Bar round the corner. Now I not humble assistant baker but proud owner of shop. I change name to Menezes Bakery. I run the shop for ten years and then Independence comes. Now what dal chapati babus know about bread? I sell shop for rupees fifty thousand and settle down in this ancestral house in Aldona.'

That was his fond and inevitable narration.

My uncle was a tall man as one would notice if patient enough to wait till he stood up. He seldom did so because he suffered from acute gout. 'Jose, get me some brandy, boy!' he would shout to me and then proceed to rub the brandy into his knees, sipping every measure as if to make sure it wasn't poisoned. He said it made him feel better, but I suspect that the feeling of moderate intoxication made him forget the gout.

My uncle was also a man of letters—he had four from his son in Kuwait and three from his daughter in Bombay unanswered. He would tell his wife Anna Rita to answer them and the poor woman would oblige despite her numerous chores like cooking, washing and massaging her husband's knees.

It was a Saturday morning in May. The sun high up in the sky streamed through the holes in my uncle's vest and underpants. He had refused to discard these vestments because he said the heat was good for his gout. Like brandy and much cheaper! He called out to me, 'Jose, my boy, go to church and ask Padre Vigario what time last mass tomorrow and high or low.'

I found the vicar at his lunch. I seldom found him in any place other than at the dining table. A popular joke in the village was that the doctor had advised him to take eight tablets of Daonil daily, one after each meal. The priest prayed little and ate much. He loved to preach, especially on Sundays—next to food, he was in love with his own fluency in Konkani. Now, he had a huge plate of rice and fish curry before him. He ate heartily despite his doctor's advice to cut down on carbohydrates because of his acute diabetes. It was obvious that if he suffered from a lack of insulin, he didn't suffer from a lack of money. 'Must eat well,' he said, 'to have enough strength to resist illness!' and he helped himself to more salt fish. As I went down the stairs I heard him call: 'Maria, bring the pudding, my girl.'

Next morning at a quarter to nine my uncle was

ready for Sunday high mass in a black suit, black tie, black socks and black shoes, all apparel old enough to vote. The suit was stitched during the Second World War and my uncle would proudly display the label 'Rankins, Calcutta' on the waistcoat. 'Best tailor in Calcutta,' he would brag. 'Customers only Europeans but they stitch for me because I supply good bread to master cutter.' My uncle then walked to church as fast as his gout would allow him, accompanied by Anna Rita in a black dress and a black veil.

They invariably occupied the front pew in the church. My uncle would nod during the long sermon and Anna Rita would strike his knee sharply with her fan whenever she heard him snore. Later, invigorated by the short nap, he would stride up to the communion rail and be the first to receive holy communion.

At times he would go to his bank where he had had his account transferred from Calcutta. He would sit in the manager's cabin and recount stories of his days in Calcutta which the manager had heard many times before. It was no surprise therefore that he always got his money in a jiffy, while he was not even half-way through his first story. Disappointed, he would peruse his passbook to make sure nobody had embezzled his money (he had read so much about bank frauds in *O Heraldo*) and then slowly leave the bank.

Some evenings he would go to Carvalho's Bar which was frequented by friends he had known in Calcutta. They would sit at a table and talk nostalgically of the good old days in Calcutta, the Saturday evening dances at the Railway Institute, the Sunday morning jam sessions, the picnics in the Botanical Gardens, the quaint rickshaws, the tram rides. They were all old men who, becoming maudlin under the effects of too much feni, would step joyfully back into their boyhood. On occasion my uncle had to be helped back to his house and when Anna Rita chided him he would say he had had only one tot of feni.

But one day while sitting in his favourite chair he felt a cold sensation in his stomach. At first he thought it was because his underpants had slipped down. But when the cold feeling was followed by a hot sensation in his head, he called out in panic to his wife and me. He blabbered that he was dying and we should call the priest and the doctor right away. We carried him to bed and I went to the church. Padre Vigario took some time to come because he was in the midst of his favourite meal, breakfast. The doctor followed a little later. Telegrams were sent to the son in Kuwait, the daughter in Bombay, and his priest brother in Margao. They arrived in the course of the week.

For a fortnight Antonio lay between life and death. But sometimes he was better and then he would tell his wife, 'Anna Rita, I am dying. Promise me that you will arrange for our daughter Isaura to get married. She is earning rupees two thousand per month as a secretary in Bombay and I am leaving a dowry of twenty thousand for her. Also find a nice girl for our son Cosme. Not a flighty modern girl who don't know to sew or cook and only wants to dress and go disco dancing. Get a girl like you. You always good wife to me. In Calcutta you helped in bakery and now you work in kitchen.' After that Antonio would drop off into a deep slumber.

But one morning he woke up looking brighter. His cheeks were rosier. He said he had dreamt that he was in his bakery and the Governor of Bengal had stepped in and said he had tasted his bread. He had liked it so much that he was appointing him as the supplier of bread to Government House. The next day Antonio had proudly displayed a sign at the entrance:

Menezes Bakery
By Appointment to H.E. the Governor of Bengal

Whether the dream was true or not, Antonio's health improved marvellously thereafter. Within a week his appetite returned, insatiable and insistent as before. A fortnight later he was sitting in his favourite chair in the balcony. A stranger passing by would hear a voice floating over feet which were none too clean: 'You seen Calcutta, no?'

Uncle Peregrine

Leslie de Noronha

If Uncle Peregrine lacked the positive qualities to go down in posterity as an unforgettable character, he more than compensated by creating a legend: his search for a profession.

An only child, he was born seventy years ago to great wealth and considerable promise. As a child he was a definite success. Proficient in his studies and music, he won credit for deportment in dancing class, always reciting, with mime, at innumerable tea parties to the pride of his doting parents and the joy of numerous maternal maiden aunts and bachelor uncles. The married ones hated him.

In religious matters he was considered a joy, turning a saintly smile on all who crossed him, the same smile with which he had borne with exemplary piety such rough misadventures of childhood as being pushed into muddy puddles.

The burning question now arose of what—having been considered bright at the Lyceum—he should do for a living. Business and the professions were out, so going to Portugal was not to be thought of. Mama and the maiden aunts were of the opinion that his health was delicate, so priesthood and the diplomatic service were out. ('You never know where they might send him.') Papa, however, always practical, suggested a trifle testily that, as the youth Peregrine would one day inherit a sizable fortune and property, a man of affairs would be ideal.

Joyfully, Mama, the maiden aunts and bachelor uncles agreed. The youthful Peregrine was dispatched forthwith on an extended tour abroad to cultivate such unspecified knowledge as would equip him for his chosen profession, and was given a princely monthly income to boot.

Peregrine was in his teens at this time, and the next ten years were chronicled in weekly letters home to an anxious Mama, Papa, maiden aunts and bachelor uncles.

The tour, after visiting relatives in Lorenzo Marques, began with a prolonged stay in Italy. He spent much time studying at close quarters the murals of Florence; Naples, Genoa, Sienna, Milan, Verona and Padua were scrutinized at length. He then proceeded to France, Austria, Hungary (he fell in love with Budapest), Germany and Holland. London was a failure as the fog brought on his asthma, so silent communion with Tudor ghosts in the Tower of London had to be abandoned. He returned, via Vienna, to Paris where he rebelled suddenly and decided to live according to his natural talents.

Music was one. After a comprehensive course in appreciation which necessitated numerous overnight trips to the Scala in Milan, he studied briefly in Brussels where he lost his heart to its medieval beauty. History claimed him, then art. But art, studied at the Sorbonne, was abandoned too, although he had persevered in a fairly expensive Parisian apartment—an attic on the Left Bank, though colourful, proving hard on his asthma.

Remembering suddenly, after a delicately reproving letter from Papa, his chosen profession (the rebellion had been abandoned) he staked his claim in history as a man of affairs by buying a lovely but rather dilapidated villa on the Italian Riviera. There were some beautiful statues in the sunken garden, true, and a superb mosaic adorned the terrace, but the villa was riddled with white ants, the sanitation was hopeless and the place had to be sold for one-twentieth the price he had paid, which was its real worth all the time.

A slight cough necessitated, at the age of twenty-eight, a further sojourn in the Mediterranean area. Italy exhausted, he turned his attention to Spain, and for the only time in his life came near something worthwhile. It turned out, while shopping in Barcelona, that he actually had a flair for objets d'art, especially religious ones. But although as a dilettante he acquired some priceless pieces of religious art, including a huge marble Christ on the cross, all of which were carefully shipped home, the idea that trade was reprehensible was so deeply inbred in him that he blithely turned his back on what was his truly God-given talent. He let business that would have brought him a fortune slip through his fingers and, after a year of visiting with relatives and friends in Lisbon, proceeded to Egypt, Palestine and Greece.

Greek history fascinated him and the beauty of the

male statuary held him enthralled. The sadness lifted when he was at the Acropolis. But when he examined the athletic figures or read the tales of Theseus, he felt a deep nostalgic hunger for the richness of the Greek Empire.

All this was sublimated on his return to Rome, via Corsica and Majorca, in a six-page poem he composed— 'Musings in the Sistine Chapel'. Then he was stuck on page six for a word to rhyme with 'purgatorio'.

The dilemma was solved unexpectedly. A telegram arrived. Papa had died of a heart attack. Mama, prostrate with grief, had taken to bed.

He flew—not literally, as planes were unsafe in those days—to her bedside and there he remained for the next fifteen years. If there were yearnings to travel, to see the Taj by moonlight, the cherry blossoms in Japan, he bravely suppressed them. Not for him, now that Mama needed him, the adventurous life of the hardy traveller.

The Old House in Panjim had many rooms, richly furnished with useless bric-a-brac and some priceless objets d'art—which acted more as dust traps than decoration. A few valuable paintings hung on the walls, but Mama, as a finnicky dona de casa, preferred that space be given more to faded sepias and daguerreotypes of ancestors. There was also the hall chandelier that could take five hundred candles, a set of carved rosewood chairs, camphor chests from Macao, Chinese wall-plates with the willow pattern, Ming vases dating back to Abbe Faria's time, and a lovely wide curving staircase, a thing of sheer grace and beauty that made one think instinctively of crinolines and magnolias and Scarlett O'Hara . . .

Life in the Old House depended greatly on Mama's Days.

On her Good Days, Roderigue, his manservant, bathed and shaved Peregrine, dusted him liberally with talc, arranged him carefully in an immaculately pressed white linen suit, showered him with lavender water and tucked a fine cambric handkerchief into his breast pocket. Then Mama and he would stroll round the park, Mama resting lightly on his gallant right arm. Or they would ride, as Mama tired easily, up and down the Avenida da Republica in an open landau, Peregrine always doffing his cream-coloured Panama straw to the ladies driving by in open carriages.

On Mama's Fair Days they would spend a cosy evening in the drawing room playing bezique. Or he would entertain her with Debussy on the harpsichord. Or read her sonnets. Or expound on the music scores of operas. Mama would sit painting pastel flowers on eggshell porcelain or spread her embroidery out on her tabouret and the two would hold long earnest discussions on the exact shade of pink silk for a rose petal.

On Mama's Bad Days he would sit by her bedside, while she lay well wrapped up in a fluffy woollen shawl on a wide Louis XV sofa, feeding her teaspoons of hot chocolate, or tenderly bathing her forehead with eau de cologne in the gloaming.

Sometimes they gave intimate little dinner parties, the food exquisitely cooked, the sauces prepared by Peregrine himself. After dinner the guests would examine the objets d'art, exclaiming politely while the ladies obliged the company with lilting mandos.

One thing emerged from the pursuit of such

turbulent activity. Peregrine had found his chosen profession. He was a Gentleman. And Mama, content, called upon heaven, visitors and friends to witness that her son Peregrine was indeed a blessing.

Then tragedy struck brutally. One of the breasts, the same that had suckled Peregrine, developed an ulcerating nodule. Mama was a lady. She never groaned or moaned. Ironically, though this he did not know, these next three months were the only months in her entire life she had been really sick. Mama died, leaving Peregrine the house, a fortune and some property in Anjuna, Loutulim and Margao.

Roderigue and his wife Marianna now took possession of Peregrine. Roderigue waxed his moustache, laid out his pyjamas, dressed and undressed him; Marianna took over the housekeeping. Her chicken caldo was perfect for Peregrine's digestion which required coddling. She had a way with an egg and a teaspoon of sherry that positively caressed his stomach. She was absolutely invaluable where colds in the chest were concerned, rubbing him down with embrocation. Nothing came of this—not very surprising as nothing could come of that chest over which the skin stretched like parchment and the two nipples lay like pale desiccated rosebuds.

Then Peregrine developed dissolute habits. Every evening he had, before dinner, a tablespoon of wine diluted with six of water. At Christmas this was increased to two tablespoons by that old devil Roderigue, as Peregrine roguishly called him, which was remarkable as Peregrine never used any bad words, partly from prudery and partly because he never knew any.

Social life was abandoned because there was no lady in the house to chaperone. Otherwise life fell into a fixed pattern for the next twenty years. After a light breakfast Peregrine took a stroll in the park, dressed as usual in his crisply ironed white linen suit, carefully removing his cream-coloured straw hat every time he passed a lady.

In the evenings he sat in the library—the rest of the house was shut up, opened twice a year for cleaning—in a quilted dressing gown and a smoking cap with a tassel, reading poetry, following the yellow-leaved musical scores of operas, or working on 'Musings in the Sistine Chapel' which had now reached page fifteen and which he was seriously thinking of publishing.

There he sat, evening after evening, month after month, year after year. His voice was never raised above a genteel whisper. When the tassel on his smoking cap wore out, Marianna stitched on another; she got the tassels from the curtain cords in the closed rooms. Then Roderigue would come in and help him slowly up the lovely, lovely staircase, and so to bed.

Every morning Uncle Peregrine went for a walk in the park. Roderigue had to go with him, but the trouble was that Roderigue was so old that more often than not Uncle Peregrine had to help Roderigue along. So the two of them, master and servant, would totter feebly around the park. When they met a lady, she would stop and wait. Slowly Uncle Peregrine would transfer his weight to his Malacca walking stick. Then, painfully, because of his arthritis, he would raise his arm, trying in vain to reach his cream-coloured Panama straw hat. He would smile ruefully, apologize, lower his arm slowly. Then he would bow jerkily from the waist, extend a hand like a pressed leaf, on which the veins traced an exquisite filigree, till he took the lady's fingertips and brushed them with lips that were like dried butterfly wings.

Notes on Contributors

UDAY BHEMBRE is a lawyer by profession and editor of the
Konkani daily *Sunaparant*. He was a Member of the Legislative
Assembly between 1985-89. He has published a collection of
articles, *Brahmastra*, in Marathi.

SUBHASH BHENDE has taught Economics in colleges in Goa. He
has published several collections of short fiction, humour
and satire. Three of his novels have been serialized for
television. He lives in Mumbai where he retired as principal
of a suburban college.

ORLANDO DA COSTA won the Ricardo Malhieros Award in
Portugal in 1961 for his novel *O Signo da Ira* (The Sign of Ire).
He has published plays and volumes of verse. He lives in
Lisbon, Portugal.

E.R.A. DA CUNHA has worked as a bank manager in Sri Lanka
and Pakistan. He retired as the General Manager of a bank
in Bhopal. He lives in the village of Salvador-do-Mundo in
Bardez, North Goa.

LESLIE DE NORONHA published two novels, *The Mango and the
Tamarind Tree* and *The Dewdrop Inn*, and a collection of short
stories. He worked as a pathologist in hospitals in UK and
USA. He died in Mumbai in 1997.

VIMALA DEVI is the pseudonym of Teresinha de Almeida. She has published several short stories and a book of poems, and co-authored a history of Indo-Portuguese literature with her husband Manuel de Seabra. She lives in Barcelona, Spain.

MEENA KAKODKAR has published two collections of stories. She won the Sahitya Akademi Award in 1991.

NARESH KAVADI taught in a college in Margao for several years. He has published a collection of short stories, *Six Cans of Beer*, in Marathi, among many other publications. He is a well-known critic of Marathi literature. He has won the Sahitya Akademi Award for his translations.

RAGHUNANDAN V. KELKAR is among the prominent young Marathi writers in Goa. A school teacher, he has published several short stories.

CHANDRAKANT KENI is a prolific Konkani writer. He has published five novels, eight collections of short stories, and two books of essays. He won the Sahitya Akademi Award in 1988. He is the editor of the Marathi daily, *Rashtramat*.

LAMBERT MASCARENHAS worked as a journalist in Mumbai for several years. He was editor of *The Navhind Times* in Goa. He has published a novel, *Sorrowing Lies My Land*. A collection of his short stories, *In the Womb of Saudade*, appeared in 1996.

DAMODAR MAUZO has published three collections of short stories, two novels and three books for children. He won the Sahitya Akademi Award in 1983. He lives in the seaside village of Majorda in South Goa.

PUNDALIK NAIK is a playwright, short story writer, novelist and a leading figure in contemporary Konkani literature. He won the Sahitya Akademi Award in 1984 for his collection of one-act plays. He has published three volumes of short stories and a novel.

PETER NAZARETH is head of the African-American Studies Programme at The University of Iowa, USA. He has published two novels, and his 'Elvis as Anthology' class has been very popular in the US and elsewhere. His most recent book is *In the Trickster Tradition—the Novels of Andrew Salkay, Francis Ebejer and Ishmael Reed*.

EPITACIO PAES, a schoolteacher, has published a book of short stories and has had his plays broadcast over the radio.

VICTOR RANGEL-RIBEIRO has recently published *Tivolem*, a novel. He lives in New York where he taught writing and communication at schools in minority education programmes. He has covered classical music concerts for the *New York Times* and is the author of two volumes on Western classical music.

MAHABLESHWAR SAIL won the Sahitya Akademi Award in 1993. He has published three novels and two volumes of short stories. He is the postmaster of Canacona in South Goa.

LAXMANRAO SARDESSAI (1905-1986) was a prominent literary figure of Goa. He published over fifteen volumes of short fiction in Marathi, besides a novel. Linguistically adept, he also published stories in Konkani and poems in Portuguese. He taught Portuguese and French for several years at the Colegio Almeida in Ponda. He won the Sahitya Akademi Award in 1982.

VASANT BHAGWANT SAWANT is a state government employee and has published a collection of short stories. He has also written plays.

READ MORE IN PENGUIN

In every corner of the world, on every subject under the sun, Penguin represents quality and variety—the very best in publishing today.

For complete information about books available from Penguin—including Puffins, Penguin Classics and Arkana—and how to order them, write to us at the appropriate address below. Please note that for copyright reasons the selection of books varies from country to country.

In India: Please write to *Penguin Books India Pvt. Ltd. 11, Community Centre, Panchsheel Park, New Delhi, 110017*

In the United Kingdom: Please write to *Dept JC, Penguin Books Ltd. Bath Road, Harmondsworth, West Drayton, Middlesex, UB7 ODA. UK*

In the United States: Please write to *Penguin USA Inc., 375 Hudson Street, New York, NY 10014*

In Canada: Please write to *Penguin Books Canada Ltd. 10 Alcorn Avenue, Suite 300, Toronto, Ontario M4V 3B2*

In Australia: Please write to *Penguin Books Australia Ltd. 487, Maroondah Highway, Ring Wood, Victoria 3134*

In New Zealand: Please write to *Penguin Books (NZ) Ltd. Private Bag, Takapuna, Auckland 9*

In the Netherlands: Please write to *Penguin Books Netherlands B.V., Keizersgracht 231 NL-1016 DV Amsterdom*

In Germany : Please write to *Penguin Books Deutschland GmbH, Metzlerstrasse 26, 60595 Frankfurt am Main, Germany*

In Spain: Please write to *Penguin Books S.A., Bravo Murillo, 19-1'B, E-28015 Madrid, Spain*

In Italy: Please write to *Penguin Italia s.r.l., Via Felice Casati 20, I-20104 Milano*

In France: Please write to *Penguin France S.A., 17 rue Lejeune, F-31000 Toulouse*

In Japan: Please write to *Penguin Books Japan. Ishikiribashi Building, 2-5-4, Suido, Tokyo 112*

In Greece: Please write to *Penguin Hellas Ltd, dimocritou 3, GR-106 71 Athens*

In South Africa: Please write to *Longman Penguin Books Southern Africa (Pty) Ltd, Private Bag X08, Bertsham 2013*